Waltham Forest Libraries

Please return this item by the last date stamped. The loan may be renewed unless required by another customer.

18/6/21	0 8 MAY 2019	
	2 8 JUL 2019	
	2 0 SEP 2019	
	2 2 NOV 2019	
	2 7 NOV 2019	

Need to renew your books?
http://www.walthamforest.gov.uk/libraries or
Dial 0333 370 4700 for Callpoint – our 24/7 automated telephone renewal
line. You will need your libra   not
know your PIN, contact you

D1346374

WALTHAM FOREST LIBRARIES

904 000 00483650

Away to the Woods

Away to the Woods

LENA KENNEDY

LITTLE, BROWN AND COMPANY

A *Little, Brown* Book

First published in Great Britain in 1995
by Little, Brown and Company

Copyright © The Estate of Lena Kennedy 1995

All rights reserved.
No part of this publication may be reproduced,
stored in a retrieval system, or transmitted, in any
form or by any means, without the prior
permission in writing of the publisher, nor be
otherwise circulated in any form of binding or
cover other than that in which it is published and
without a similar condition including this
condition being imposed on the subsequent purchaser.

A CIP catalogue record for this book
is available from the British Library.

ISBN 0 316 91110 0

Typeset by Hewer Text Composition Services, Edinburgh
Printed and bound in Great Britain by
Mackays of Chatham Plc, Chatham, Kent

Little, Brown and Company (UK)
Brettenham House
Lancaster Place
London WC2E 7EN

THIS BOOK IS DEDICATED TO
MY LOYAL AND CLEVER SON
FREDERICK KEITH SMITH

I thank my Auntie Molly, who had 'a heart of gold', for helping me to translate my mother's diaries. She died in 1991 – Lena's only sister.

Angela Kennedy Smith

Contents

Spring

Mollie World

Sometimes I look at the world and
It makes me sad,
Then I think of God and I feel glad,
For we can depend on him
To send us beautiful spring.
The trees are blooming and
The birds singing merrily in the trees;
The lovely spring flowers spring up everywhere,
The little frogs on the green,
The little fishes swimming in the stream;
For God in his Heaven so made us a lovely world,
If only we open our eyes
At all these beautiful things.

Mrs Mary Clark (Auntie Mary)

Preface

I gaze dreamily out of the tiny window of my little shack in the woods, with its rustic frame of roses and honeysuckle which ramble wildly up the timber walls. I am looking out on to a pleasant green lawn dominated by an immense oak tree and dotted here and there by rose trees that I have planted so haphazardly through the years. I can see Christmas trees of various sizes that were put into the moist earth each year after they had done their duty at the Christmas celebrations. Brought down from London to take root – which most of them bravely did – they flourished in the wet clay of Kent and now spread their sweet-smelling branches towards the sky. I look at each one in turn and think, now that was a good Christmas, or that was a sad one.

It is not really so hard for me to recall the last thirty years. I have spent many springs and summers here in this shady woodland – it has become a second home to me and is very close to my heart. I always dreamed that one day I would leave London's smoky town behind and build a cosy bungalow here. However, even though I am now an established author, I still reside in town. I am old and filled with nostalgia for the past, so I sit and dream of what might have been, and savour the lovely memories of youth.

I am the last of the shackdwellers. Around me are posh houses and bungalows, and outside the front gate cars and lorries go tearing past on a concrete stretch of road, but still my lovely garden and my wooden shack stand firm and I still spend my happiest moments here. So now I would like to recall for posterity how it all began.

Book I

The Last of the
Shackdwellers

Chapter One

Buying a Plot of Land

Caring for my dear old dad in the last days of his life had affected me. I was no longer the happy-go-lucky person Fred had married and sometimes we got a little frustrated with each other. So we decided that summer to go on a camping holiday, which would be cheap. We had an old Austin Seven car which we loaded up with the kids and the dog – and almost everything but the kitchen sink – then chugged off to find the sea.

We started out very nicely, but Shooters Hill defeated us. 'Told you not to bring so much luggage,' grunted Fred. 'Carrying too much weight – won't get up this hill.'

I sat with fingers crossed, strongly determined not to go home. The kids jumped up and down, playing merry hell in the back seat. They were sitting high up on top of the tent and what-not, while Peter, the dog, who was always a swine, was barking at everything that moved.

Heroically, Fred almost pushed that old banger up the hill – and at the top we got a flat tyre.

After a lot of hard work and slaps all round for the kids, Fred repaired the tyre and we went on our way, but twenty miles further on we got another puncture and the light was fading fast.

'You've got a choice,' said Fred in his quiet yet firm manner. 'Go back, or spend the night on the roadside – because you'll never get down to the coast tonight.'

'Oh well, it would have been nice,' I commented as I made a cup of tea on the little primus stove at the side of the road – a cup of tea always cheered Fred up.

'Might as well go back,' said Fred. 'It's no joke driving this old banger with you lot yelling your heads off.' He was always inclined to moods but got over them quickly.

There is something in me that cannot bear defeat. I sat there turning over in my mind a solution to our problem when along the road came two little girls dressed in the uniform of the Girl Guides. Right! if anyone knows about camping they do, I decided.

They stared suspiciously at me as I approached them. I've never been a beauty: I'm short and plump and was then well past thirty and not looking so good, having had a very harassing day. My blouse was grubby, my slacks crumpled and my hair very windblown – I probably looked like a gypsy, and I suppose their mothers had warned them not to talk to gypsies.

'Excuse me, dears,' I confronted them, 'can you tell me if there's a camping site near here, preferably near the sea?'

'Oh yes,' one said. 'Allhallows – it has its own sea front, and lots of people camp there.'

She pointed the way, about ten miles across country towards the river.

Fred was definitely against it. 'What if we break down in one of those lanes? It'll be dangerous late at night and some of them are so narrow two cars can't pass each other.'

Having little knowledge of driving, I wasn't impressed by this, so we argued until I got my own way and then we bumped along in the dark through those long, winding lanes of Kent, towards the banks of the Thames where it flowed to meet its mother, the sea.

It was a long, hazardous journey but I have never regretted it. One headlight went out, and yet another tyre began to go down, and the engine was hot and snorting like some old horse – and to add to all that, it was raining cats and dogs. Yet we did eventually arrive at our destination, a little camp site by the sea. There was only one other tent on the field and we had to rouse some old fella out of bed to let us in – he was exceedingly irritable.

By this time the children had tired themselves out with their squabbling and had gone to sleep, so we left them in the car with the dog and we put up our small tent on the damp field, in the dark, with a fierce wind blowing over the marshes. If any of my readers have ever attempted this sort of thing, I know I will at least have their sympathy.

Afterwards we lay in our sleeping bags, tired, cold and weary, swearing that this was the last time – tomorrow we would go home to the comfort of a warm bed and a nice coal fire.

Early in the morning I was awakened by the barking of Peter, who was obviously anxious to get out, having no doubt spotted the green grass all around him.

For fear that he would awaken the children, I stumbled stiffly from my sleeping bag and let him out of the car. He tore off, tail in the air, in the direction of the sea, while I stood and looked at that beautiful scene, a scene that to this day I still love: a little stony beach with gentle waves rolling happily to the shore. The sky was blue but still tinged with red and gold, the sun shone with early morning glory and a swift, salty breeze clung to my nostrils and cleared the cobwebs from my brain. I breathed deeply of the wonderful ozone and felt on top of the world, in spite of the previous day's disasters.

I climbed down to the stony beach and walked along it with old Peter, who trotted happily, tail proudly in the air, pausing every now and then to cock his leg on bits of seaweed. He occasionally looked back and seemed to smile at me as if to say, 'This is a nice change'. I soon realised this was an estuary, because I could see the opposite shore, far away in the mist, as the Thames emerged from fresh water to salt water and flowed out into the English Channel.

What impressed me most was the amount of space, with piles of golden sand here and there, and only I to share the early morning peace with my old dog. I had spent the best part of my life in London, and the odd day trip to the coast was the limit of my travelling experience, so to get up in the morning and be confronted by this amazing scenery really did me good and filled my heart with joy. I looked out to the horizon and could see the deep-water line with a convoy of big ships going out with the strong morning tide.

On the way back I stretched out my arms, then began to run. I just felt a sudden impulse that it was something I had to do. Peter thought it a great joke, leaping up at me and chasing round me in ever widening circles.

We arrived back at the camp very breathless but strangely elated. Fred was awake and already making himself a cup of tea, for if his day does not start with a cup of strong tea it's a terrible catastrophe for him.

'It's great here,' I cried, really feeling full of beans.

'It's bleedin' draughty,' said Fred, hugging his pullover tight about him.

'I've been to the beach – it's wonderful for the kids to play on and we can watch them from up here.'

'Be thousands of bloody kids here by midday; we're right on top of a town,' complained Fred. 'Better get moving if you *are* going to the coast.'

'No!' I said firmly. 'We'll stay here – it won't be so far to get home from.'

I got my way as usual and we stayed. Later, as the sun came out, other campers arrived and put up their tents. As Fred had predicted, lots of kids ran all over the place, but I was fascinated by this little shore and had no intention of going any further.

Strange to relate, we stayed the rest of our holiday in that one place and had a really super time. It was also quite inexpensive, which really pleased Fred, for there was very little for the children to spend money on. There were a few swings and roundabouts, but most of all there were lots of children to play with and a safe beach for them all to play on – what more could we ask?

We made friends with other campers who were mostly younger but, like ourselves, not too well off, and our own little community developed. We went back to our camp site every weekend that year, and I began to feel very fit. My hair seemed softer, my eyes brighter and I lost that fear that most women get when past thirty that I was getting old and becoming unattractive. Fred took up a new hobby – fishing – and the children got a lovely suntan.

We went back again the next year, and this time we brought a large ridge tent, which we kept on site permanently erected all season so that the ground stayed dry underneath it. We furnished it with chairs, a table and the old double bed which we brought from home. It was a funny sight that day: Fred came chugging along the track to the camp with the bed tied on top of the old Austin, and all the other campers lined up to cheer us.

There were not many amenities at the camp site, and the toilets were a very primitive affair – when they were emptied in the evenings it stank to high heaven. A very fat lady called Liz used to sit by the toilets and had the audacity to take a penny off anybody who wanted to use them. She owned a café up by the station, and in the evenings with cheeks painted red and a scarf under her chin, she ran a club there with Pilki, her gypsy lover. She was a pleasant enough person, but she was always chewing something – I often wondered what it was, but I never found out.

The people that camped at Allhallows were mostly working class. They came from the big industrial towns, looking for a cheap holiday and a chance to give their children a breath of sea air. They were happy-go-lucky and, in spite of the sordidness of the place, the kids had a whale of a time.

That second summer things began to change a little, because they had begun to build a big oil refinery out on the Isle of Grain. Workers came from all over the country, but the majority of the men were Irish. They camped out on the Isle of Grain and came down to our local on Saturday nights and punched the hell out of each other. There were also families that had come from other oil towns looking for work and trying to find a home. They put up little tents and lived in them, while their men went off to the Isle of Grain to work and Allhallows began to take the look of a shanty town.

I started to come down to Allhallows in the week, while Fred stayed in London to work. I made friends with a woman called Frances, who lived in one of the permanent caravans. She had a little girl, also a redhead, who became very friendly with my children. Frances was very extrovert and had a beautiful voice. She used to do one-night appearances at the village pubs, where she would sing Irish ballads and popular numbers that went down well with the Irish community.

I also saw a lot of my friend Madge, the mother of Angela's schoolfriend Pat. Madge was tall with auburn hair and shrewd, deep-set eyes that always seemed to be smiling. She was lively and talkative, and adored children. She came backwards and forwards during the summer holidays with Pat and several other kids. We had an arrangement with Frances where one of us stopped in and minded the kids and the other two went out on the spree.

I often went to hear Frances at her impromptu concerts. When she reached her final number she would suddenly yell over the microphone, 'start running!' and this was the signal for me to start running for the 9.55 bus and hold it till she had finished. If we missed the bus we had six miles of long, lonely country lanes to walk, which could be very dangerous. In spite of the hazards of the situation, we had lots of laughs.

Fred would come down on Fridays and bring his wages, but I would often run out during the week, so we would volunteer to do spud bashing up at the café, for five shillings a morning, as we peeled the spuds, the kids would hang around the door, waiting for ice cream and sweets and spending our money before we had earned it.

It is always in my mind that amid all this happy-go-lucky atmosphere there was extreme poverty, and the permanent caravan dwellers often lived hand-to-mouth. The women worked out on the fields and the men worked on the Isle of Grain – money was easily come by but easily spent. By midweek their cupboards would be empty and the kids would be sent out to scrump the fields for apples, cabbages, and potatoes, and the menu would be bubble 'n' squeak and apple pie.

In spite of the hardship, we were a happy community, but, as so often happens, a dark cloud suddenly came down over our nice camp. It was the year when a great polio epidemic started and became prevalent all over England. At that time there was no such thing as inoculation – that great discovery was yet to come. Small children became ill and if they survived, it was probably as a cripple. It was all terrifying to me, as my kids were my whole life. There were all sorts of rumours – some said it came from the water, so swimming was taboo. The kids down at Allhallows often played around the community water tap and this worried me too. Finally, when several of the children at the camp contracted the disease, I said, 'No more. I'll stay at home and keep my children out of harm's way, even if it means we have to do without our weekends by the sea.'

We took down our tent that hot August and decided not to erect it again until that terrible illness was gone from the area and it would be safe once more to go back. So we stayed at home, and decorated the house, but we both felt edgy, and we knew we needed that hard-won freedom.

To cut a long story short, we began to look for a private spot in the country to make another camp and that was how, on a hot afternoon in late August, we found ourselves driving through the shady lanes of Kent, looking for a more secluded place to put up our weekend tent. After we had driven around for hours, the kids were hot and extremely disagreeable, but even though we bumped along under bad conditions, I still loved to see the long miles of orchards and the fruit hanging in abundance from the trees and all those lovely cottage gardens full of the late-blooming roses which seem to do so well in Kent.

Fred said, 'We'll make for a place I know – it's called Cliffe at Hoo and right off the beaten track. I used to stay there on the Country Holiday Scheme when I was a boy.'

For the uninformed, the Country Holiday Scheme was for poor kids from London to take a country holiday: each paid a few shillings, and charity gave the rest. In our youth that was the only kind of holiday the majority of us could afford.

We turned off the main roads and went through very narrow lanes past quarries and chalk pits. Fred talked about when he was a boy and he and his brother used to hunt lizards in these gloomy-looking quarries. The kids were very interested, but I had no intention of camping in a deserted quarry full of creepy things. 'Let's stop for a drink,' I suggested.

We pulled up at a very rural-looking inn with tall chimneys called the Merry Boys, which lay back from the road. A cricket match was in progress in a meadow alongside the inn, and old folk and children sat watching play. Chickens ran across our feet as we entered the inn's cool interior.

'It's so rustic,' I said, 'as if nothing has changed for centuries.'

All Fred wanted was a cool glass of ale – he was not too impressed with his surroundings. The children charged off to watch the cricket and we sat on long wooden benches to drink the cool beer. Behind the bar it was like a grocery shop – all sorts of commodities were displayed and there were lots of sweets for the children, which they soon discovered.

We were in a hamlet consisting of just a few cottages and that ancient inn which seemed to cater for all needs. I really liked it and asked the dark, rather chatty landlady if the inn was very old.

'Been in the family for three hundred years,' she said. 'Someone else had it before then, but don't ask me who.'

'Any chance of renting a plot of land?' I ventured.

'Now that's dodgy,' she said, 'because there are a few very posh farmers about here and they don't like strangers, but anyway, why don't you ask Alfie? He knows most of what goes on around here – he's just coming in now.'

A chap came in, small in stature, wearing a cloth cap, and a colourful choker knotted around his neck. He was fair, alert and smiling. 'How do,' he greeted us. His look told us that he knew we were strangers and no doubt was wondering what we were doing in the district.

'Folks are looking for land, Alfie,' said the landlord as he poured his pint of ale.

I nudged Fred to get up and pay for Alfie's drink, and

this was a gesture that Alfie really appreciated. He joined us on the narrow bench and we had a very instructive session as he told us the history of this hamlet and the Cliffe Woods that adjoined it.

'Don't see many strangers about here,' he said, appreciatively sipping his ale. 'We hides off the road here.'

'Yes, it is very nice and peaceful,' I told him. 'Any chance of renting a spot to put up a weekend camp?'

That Alfie was a womaniser, I was quite sure, so if any cooperation was to be got from him it certainly looked as if it might have to be won by me. I watched him as he craftily looked at my full bosom, of which I am very self-conscious. 'Is there no chance at all, Alfie?' I queried, staring him full in the eyes.

'Well,' he said thoughtfully, 'trouble is, in this place they is afraid of gypos – can't get the buggers off the land once they gets on it.'

I laughed outright. 'We're not gypos, Alfie.'

Well, this broke the ice and Fred got up to get some more beers and Alfie looked at me with that sly grin he had. 'Tell you what your best bet is – buy a plot in Cliffe Woods.'

'Where is that?'

'Just along the lane there. It's got lots of plots with little shacks on them and people come in from the towns to spend weekends there.'

'Well, that does sound interesting,' said Fred as he came back with the drinks. 'Tell us more about it, Alfie.'

'I'll do better than that,' said Alfie, clutching his second pint, 'I'll take you to a bloke that wants to sell a plot of land.'

'Great!' said Fred. 'Drink up and we'll go with you.'

'Leave yer car here,' said Alfie, 'because this top end of the lane is bad, very muddy, but it improves down near the road.'

We collected the children, put old Peter on a lead

and walked with Alfie through a copse. We progressed along a very muddy lane through beautiful woodlands, then followed a path that led uphill. When we came to a clearing, Alfie said, 'Look down there.'

It was a spectacular sight. We could see for miles: farmlands stretched out like a colourful patchwork blanket of different shades of greens with the occasional streak of blue water that went right out to the river. We saw the graceful bend of the river as it wound out to sea, and small sailing ships cruising by the strand.

'They call this "the view" – grand, isn't it?' said Alfie. 'Look over there – that's Gravesend Reach; then over there, that's Southend Pier.'

We stood spellbound, recognising the landmarks as Alfie pointed them out to us.

'Now down there in the woods, see all them shacks?'

Along the winding lane ahead of us were lots of tiny matchbox buildings, each in its square of garden.

'They reckon there's more than fifty plots down there,' said Alfie. 'It's unadopted, so the council don't maintain it – no water or light – but the people seem to like it and come here most weekends, and there's some old boys lives here all the year.'

'Let's go down,' I said eagerly.

We went along the shady lane, hedged by great elm trees. It was so peaceful – only the birds' singing broke the silence.

'That's the place what's for sale,' said Alfie, pointing to an over-shadowed spot with a rickety gate. 'Bloke what owns it lives in that place next door. I'll scarper, 'cause we ain't what you calls friendly, so don't say I put you onto it. See you up at the Merry Boys.' He gave me that sly grin once more and with a last 'Good luck!' he disappeared back into the woods.

We stood there for a short while. 'It's very nice here,' said Fred, 'but can we afford to buy a place? In fact, I very much doubt if we can.'

'Well, let's look at it anyway,' I suggested.

I stood in the shady lane watching the children playing with the dog, and in spite of the racket they were making, a kind of peaceful stillness suffused the air and I had the strangest feeling that I, after a long time, had come home. Overhead the tall elms kissed the sturdy oaks on the other side, forming a kind of luxuriant green arch with only little beams of sunlight splashing through the branches. It was cool and a little bit creepy. I looked at the rickety gate and wanted to go into that overgrown jungle.

Fred came back with a key and unlocked the rusty padlock on the gate and we went inside.

'Crikey!' I cried. 'It looks as if no one has been in here for years and years.'

We fought our way through the nettles and wild brambles to a small clearing with a tremendous oak tree in the middle. Wild flowers grew in profusion: pink wild English roses climbed everywhere and tall mauve fluffy plants made a kind of background for the variety of grasses that grew waist-high; and the bird songs were glorious. It was like entering another world.

'Oh, it's lovely,' I cried, 'like going into an old church.'

'I dunno about that,' said Fred. 'A lot of work would have to be done to make it habitable.'

'How much does he want for it?' I asked.

'It's out of our reach, I'm afraid, dear – it's seventy-five pounds.'

It seemed a terrible lot of money. 'Never mind, let's explore it.'

We pushed our way right down to the end of the plot and found a little old deserted shed standing there with ivy trails clinging over it. On entering we found a primus stove, and an old mug with the tea leaves still in it.

'Strange,' I remarked, 'it looks as if the last occupant left in a hurry and didn't come back.'

'Something like that,' replied Fred. 'He used to come down from Gravesend every weekend for a bit of bird-watching. He used to ride a bike all the way, but he dropped dead going home one Sunday night, according to the chap who's selling it on behalf of the widow.'

'Oh, how sad, poor little man.'

There were only the little home-made bird baths dotted all around the overgrown garden and this desolate caravan to prove that the man had existed.

'Still,' said Fred with optimism, 'it's an ill wind that blows everyone harm – it's a good piece of land for the price.'

'Can we buy it?' I queried.

'I'm not sure. We're got about twenty-five quid holiday money; might be able to borrow some . . . Anyway, the man said to give him a deposit and he'll give me a bit more time to raise the rest. He wants to get this lot off his hands.'

We rode back to London feeling very pleased with ourselves.

'It will need a lot of clearing but at least the kids will have plenty of freedom to run around.' Fred had become almost as keen as I was on the idea of buying this land.

'Why don't we borrow the children's savings?' I suggested. In those days they still issued war bonds and stopped the money from the men's wages to give them the incentive to save, and Fred had saved £25 for each of our children, having paid a small sum each week since they were born. 'We'll tell them that this land belongs to them, half each, if that will ease your conscience,' I told him.

He argued, but in the end we made up our minds that this piece of rural England was to be ours and, several

weekends later, in September, off we went with the
rest of the money. On the journey we discussed
all sorts of plans; even Fred was getting excited.
'Could put up a lovely place there,' he said. 'I'd
build it myself, the way I'd like it to look and in
my own time.'

When we arrived, the autumn mists were in the air
but still there was the same hush, that holy silence
which had impressed me before. Two young squirrels
were dashing about under the oak tree, gathering
acorns for their winter store. They sat up in shocked
surprise when we approached, then scampered off.
We went down to the little glade and set out the
lunch. The kids began to run and jump about with
the sheer delight of freedom and space. A little watery
sun cast rainbow colours through the trees and flocks
of starlings swooped around the treetops. As we
picnicked Fred said, 'I'll go in and settle up with
the chap next door when we've had our lunch and
then this will really belong to us. Won't be time
to do a lot this year but next spring I'll really get
cracking.'

'Fred, if I can have this lovely spot to spend our leisure
time, I know I'll be so happy.'

Then from the shadow of the trees on the other
side came the face of gloom. It was our neighbour,
a certain Job's comforter, who looked very stern and
very uptight. 'Hallo!' he called. 'You ain't thinking of
buying this place, are you?'

'Well,' said Fred a little nervously, 'we had thought
about it.'

'Well lad, I tell you now, you'll be wasting your
hard-earned cash. They're going to put a compulsory
purchase order on all this land – I've heard it from the
best authority.'

Poor Fred looked very alarmed. 'Are you sure?'
he asked.

'I've been here twenty years, so I know what's going on,' the man informed Fred. 'You won't get tuppence a foot, let alone your money back.'

So they walked off together, the man talking all the time and Fred downcast, just listening.

I knelt on the grass, clearing up the remains of the lunch and looked forlornly up at those tall trees. 'Oh please, God,' I prayed, 'let no one take away this nice place from me,' and the tall trees swayed in the breeze and rustled as if they whispered to me, 'Don't despair, we are with you and always will be.'

The next move was that Fred flatly refused to part with his money. That grim-looking old fellow had apparently convinced him that he was going to be done out of his cash and Fred would never allow anything like that to happen, he was too careful.

I wept all the way home and we argued: 'I don't understand. How can the government take it away once it's ours and paid for?'

'Oh yes, they can. It's this new law that has been passed – they can compulsory purchase it and give you just what they like in compensation.'

But I would not be convinced. Later that night, as I shed real tears, Fred said, 'Why does it mean so much to you? We can look for somewhere else.'

'Oh, I'll be so disappointed,' I sobbed, 'and I've got a feeling that all that talk about compulsory purchase isn't true. I didn't like that man one bit; I'm sure he said all that nonsense to upset me.'

Fred cuddled me and said, 'Well, if that's how you feel I'll take the day off work and go down to the Council Offices and find out if it's the truth or not. They'll have official records down there.'

All the next day I was really depressed and went about my chores, after the kids had gone to school, in a very melancholy manner.

At three o'clock Fred returned, smiling very brightly.

'It's ours, dear. I went and paid the chap the rest of the money – here's the receipt.'

I threw my arms around his neck. 'Oh, thank you, darling!'

'It seems that old boy next door warns off everyone with the same story. He don't like kids and is very suspicious of strangers, according to the chap who sold me the plot. That's the pattern of life down there – those old boys are hanging on to their solitude.'

'I don't blame them,' I said, 'but it's ours now and while grass grows and water runs it will pass to our children when we have gone on.'

Chapter Two

Settling In

Now that lovely woodland spot really belonged to us, with just a few minor legal details to be settled, we took a few trips down on Sundays during that first late autumn. We picnicked under the trees and made great plans for the future. When I recall those halcyon days I feel a kind of sadness about the glory of late autumn as winter approached. I watched the trees each season turning back from green to brown, red-gold and bright yellow intermixed, making such a superb background that I wanted to paint it to keep it in my sight for ever. I think too of those grand autumn sunsets which cast their lacy patterns on the small patches of brown earth where the grass and the wild flowers struggled out towards the light, and the great orange sun which seemed to float on the sea as it sank out of sight. Such wonders as these I had never ever witnessed before. Oh yes, I had known they were there, but I had had no time to stand and stare. The bluetits and the blackbirds, who seemed at first to resent our intrusion into their territory, soon became quite tame and looked forward, I am sure, to the titbits they got on Sundays. The days got shorter and the evenings colder and hundreds of birds gathered in the trees as if this was a sort of staging post for their annual migration. I dug up a little patch of ground and put grass seeds in it.

Fred told me, 'You're wasting your time. It will have all grown back to undergrowth when we come back next spring.'

'Oh never mind,' I said, stamping the seeds into the moist earth which I so loved the smell of, and still do.

Soon a silver frost lay on the bare branches and it was time to stay at home in London, to build a fire and keep the kids nice and warm, having had their quota of fresh air to see them through the winter.

On our last visit of the year I stood under the great oak tree which held the centre spot like a sentinel and said, 'Goodbye, my dear. I'll see you in the spring.' I put my hand on the old, silver-grey, wrinkled bark and deep vibrations seemed to come from the earth, a kind of warmth, as if some large, gentle beast lay sleeping somewhere within. All that long winter amid the hustle and bustle of family life, the washing and the cooking, the taking and collecting of the kids to and from school, my mind would dwell on that silent woodland. I would think of the grand house I would have there one day, but that was only a dream which has slipped further and further away through the years. Fred, however, was more practical than I. 'I'll get the *Exchange & Mart* every week,' he said, 'and keep looking till I find a suitable kind of hut that we can put up on the plot – a kind of temporary dwelling. I can't see how anyone can object – there must be plenty of those little huts in the woods.'

So, with his cool determination, he did actually succeed in buying a wooden railway hut that could be dismantled and re-erected, for thirty pounds. Once the sale was agreed and the ten pounds deposit paid, Fred started to save, to pay off the rest of the money and also to get some extra to pay for the transport of the hut.

It gave us great comfort to talk and plan for our

'country estate' that long, cold, hard winter when the kids had colds and Fred and I were often exhausted. He worked long hours and I had taken a lunchtime job in a café round the corner to help buy the little extras we might need.

On the first bright day that spring we set off to visit our country estate. The day was fresh and bright, but still very cold, and the kids were wrapped up warm. Even our old dog Peter was excited. Once more into the Austin went the kettle and the primus stove, and when we arrived we made tea in that small, ramshackle old shed where the last owner had lived, then Fred rigged up a swing for the kids to amuse themselves. With stiff, cold fingers I cut sandwiches and made the tea, then, in that kind of holy silence which seemed to prevade this place, we ate our frugal lunch. Two baby squirrels ran from tree to tree and rabbits hopped about in the undergrowth, but there was still ice on the hedgerows and the ground was muddy and sloshy. The kids shouted and squealed, fell over in the mud and ruined their clothes. Fred, his nose red, rubbed his hands together and said, 'This is too much bloody fresh air, let's go home.'

We returned home, leaving very early, but I felt peaceful inside. I had seen my old friends the trees and they were still sleeping, but soon the sap would rise and they would awaken and I would have another glorious spring to look forward to.

As the weather improved we did eventually clear a spot big enough to erect the hut, but it was hard graft. The ground was wet, sticky and often flooded – not much of a place to park the kids when the rain teemed down. Often on Sunday, as we made our way home, we were tired and irritable, the kids were overexcited and the traffic was bad. This was way before they built a motorway system through the old tunnel, and it was very tricky. I used to sit there with my fingers crossed in case the old banger broke down in the tunnel, which it had done once before. That time a friendly lorry driver towed us out of the tunnel, but the claustrophobic atmosphere of the tunnel always made me nervous. I still sit in the car with my fingers crossed whenever we enter the tunnel, even though conditions are now vastly improved.

To amuse the children I would make up stories – even then I loved to make up tales. I told them that at one end of the tunnel lived a giant called Popeye, who lived upstairs in a castle high up over the traffic, and at the other end lived the woolly-haired giant. The two giants didn't like each other and very often gobbled up motor cars, but never Austin Sevens, which were too small to fill them up, even if there were dozens of them. The kids would squeal with delight as we passed under the castle, imaginary, of course.

'I can see Popeye,' they would cry, or, 'Woolly giant is looking out of the window.'

So in the heavy traffic jams I managed to keep them occupied so as not to distract Fred, for it was a tricky business getting through that busy, long, winding tunnel under the Thames on Sunday night, when we were all cold, tired and hungry.

Sometimes, when the kids were in bed, we would sit around the fire and Fred would say, 'Oh dear, I'm stiff all over. Let's hope, darling, that we haven't bitten off more than we can chew.'

'Oh, it will be all right when the weather improves and we get our hut put up,' I would console him, because never once did I feel that it was a waste of time. Something in me enjoyed a challenge. It was something to do with my pioneering background, I think – my Irish grandparents had walked behind a wagon across America all the way to San Francisco.

Just before Easter Fred found someone to help him put up the hut: 'My mate at work has offered to help

me. I think you'd better stay at home with the kids –
you'll only get in the way.'

I was disappointed but nevertheless agreed to stay
at home. I think that was the longest day of my life.
It rained heavily all day and I kept thinking of how
muddy it would be and how wet and cold they would
get, and I worried in case they had an accident. The
hut had seemed so big as I watched them go off on
the lorry with the heavy load of wooden frames, doors
and windows, the beginnings of my little house in the
woods.

Fred returned in the evening, wet, exhausted but very
jubilant, his white teeth shining in a cheery grin from a
very muddy face. 'We did it,' he announced, 'managed
to erect the hut in one day.'

On the following Sunday we went down to Kent to
inspect our new home. It looked a little forlorn standing
there amid the tall trees, but it was nice and looked very
substantial. It had four windows and a very good floor
and an arch-type roof.

Immediately I fell in love with it. 'Oh, it's great! What
shall we call it?'

At lunchtime we put out our camping table and chairs
and I cooked sausages and mash on the primus stove.
It was cosy in there and the windows looked out on
such a lovely view of the surrounding woodland. The
trees had begun to bud, and the dark green ivy climbed
the wrinkled bark, and those wild cherry trees were
covered in white blossom. I thought of a poem I had
heard somewhere: 'Cherry blossom like a bride dressed
in white for Eastertide.' Over lunch a debate was held
as to what name we should give our new house. Angela
had some very romantic ideas and Keith some modern
ones; I wanted something to do with trees, but it was
decided by Fred.

'What about White Oaks?' I said, remembering the
White Oaks Chronicles I had recently read.

'Well, the place where I bought the hut was called Seven Oaks,' he told us. 'I looked from the front gate and counted our oaks and there were five – the huge one just outside the door and two on either side between us and the front gate. I'm never going to part with those oaks, whatever you say, so we'll call it Five Oaks.'

'That's a nice, strong-sounding name, and when we build a big house that name will just suit it.'

We christened the hut with a cup of tea and then went back to work. I cleaned all the windows and Fred put the finishing touches to making it secure. We brought in the old bed from the Allhallows camping site and various items which were stored down in the old shed, and began to make the place look like a home.

'It's Easter next week, so I'll bring down bed linen and blankets and we can stay the entire holiday; like that I'll get some more land cleared,' decided Fred, who was extremely pleased with himself, having made us another little house to spend our leisure time in.

It was almost dark when we went home that night. We had lit the old hurricane lamp and given the kids hot drinks before we left. The sky was a great canopy of bright silver stars, and I stood looking up in amazement: 'How lovely the sky looks with almost a full moon and all those stars. Strange how one doesn't bother to look up at the sky in London.'

'Don't ever get the bloody time,' returned Fred with his typical dry humour.

But I was happy, fulfilled and in love with life. Something that had gone from my life was gradually returning.

That night in bed I snuggled close to my man, yearning to be loved, but a grunt and a deep snore was all I received as Fred lay sleeping heavily, very tired after the long drive home and all the work he had done that day.

It was all right with me. I was happy because, like the

trees in the woodland, I knew the sap was beginning to rise and I was in love with life again. For a long time I had felt my thirty-eight years, but now, suddenly, I was young again.

Chapter Three

First Easter

All that week I had been making preparations for our weekend in residence. I made pies that could easily be warmed up, lots of sausage rolls and cakes for the kids. Then I gathered together my odds and ends which I had collected through the winter. Curtains, a rug, bed linen, blankets, pots and pans, everything in fact but the kitchen sink was piled into the old Austin, along with the dog Peter with that perpetual grin on his face, sitting on top of the pile of blankets and barking at everything that moved as we wended our way down to Kent on that Good Friday. The weather was kind to us – nice and bright, with warm sunshine – and there was not a lot of traffic on the roads, so we arrived happy and relaxed and set about making a permanent abode.

I scrubbed the floor and put down the rug, made up camp beds for the kids and the big double bed for us – I was really surprised how much room there was in that hut. We had an old oil stove which I put the kettle on (the primus stove was for emergencies), and the hurricane lamp was our only means of light. We all went down the lane to find the water standpipe, which supplied the majority of shacks in the woods. There was as yet no sanitation, but that was the least of our cares. We had a lot of fun fetching two buckets

of water – Fred carried one and I the other, while the
kids marched ahead, chatting and reciting, 'Jack and Jill
went up the hill to fetch a pail of water.'

Fred and I drank tea, while the kids had hot soup.
We washed the kids in nice soft hot water, put them in
their pyjamas and then to bed, and after all the trials and
the tantrums they were soon asleep. We put two canvas
chairs out in the garden and sat around the bonfire that
Fred had lit earlier in the day, which was still a lovely
glowing red heap. The air was clear and fresh like wine,
with an aroma of burning wood, a smell that always
reminded me of Cliffe Woods. A huge silver moon
shone down on us, painting the trees a silvery hue
and casting soft shadows on the little patch of lawn,
which had grown since last year, despite Fred's gloomy
predictions. It was so peaceful and pleasant, relaxing in
that cool night air. All around was a complete blanket
of silence that made one want to whisper so as not to
break the stillness. There seemed no need to talk, and
we just sat enjoying our first night in the woods until
the fire died down completely, then we went to bed.

During the night it got very cold, and I got out of bed
several times to make sure the children were covered up.
Then came the dawn, with a rosy light and a chorus
of bird song. I got up and went out with Peter, who
tore off down the garden chasing a rabbit, while I held
my breath in case he caught it. We went on down the
winding, very narrow path to the bottom of the plot,
where the tall elms and ash trees formed a sort of arch.
As one entered it was like going into a cathedral. I
stood still for a moment and thought I should have
gone to church yesterday, Good Friday, but suddenly
I knew I did not need the church, for here was my
church. I felt that I was spiritually nearer to God in
this garden than I had ever been before. I stopped to
pick fresh purple violets and some golden primroses,
pressing the soft petals to my lips, then I went back

and put them in a small jar on the camping table and began to get breakfast ready.

For the first time on that Easter Saturday we went outside to explore our surroundings. We drove down to the nearest village, Cliffe, which was situated on the foreshore near the river. We rode around, looking at the ancient Norman church and the olde worlde cottages. Later, we found a real country baker shop which sold hot bread and buns, and an attractive shop called Harpers, with oak beams and an Elizabethan frontage, which appeared to sell everything you could think of: articles of every kind hung outside, all kinds of old pieces, tin baths, pots and pans of all sizes. The village was very old and I decided that when I had time I would rout out the history of it.

We also discovered a farm nearby that sold us fresh butter, milk and eggs. The air blew fresh and salty over the marshland and, as we looked out to sea, Fred said, 'When the weather settles we'll take the kids down to the shore and teach them to swim. I believe in children learning young.' I agreed – it all sounded wonderful.

By the afternoon it was back to the grindstone as together we mastered those huge patches of nettles and waded into the long, prickly blackberry canes, which grew so profusely. I discovered a mossy bank and patches of wild flowers I had never seen before, as well as blue periwinkles, and red wild strawberries growing in grand profusion under the long grass. We tackled everything with a will and a sharp scythe: slowly but surely another part of our garden was taking shape.

That night we all slept extremely well, even the kids, and the hut seemed warmer and a lot dryer. On Easter Sunday we all rose with the lark. The kids dashed out to play and I cooked the lovely large new-laid eggs which Fred had brought back from a farm near the village of Elmers. Fresh milk and newly baked bread completed the meal, and I don't think I ever enjoyed a breakfast so much.

When I remarked on this, Fred said, 'No, can't beat nice fresh farm food. Reminds me of when I was a boy. I used to come down to the country with my brother, and we'd stay in strange little cottages in the village. We had a great time catching lizards in the quarry.' He looked at the kids. 'I'll take you tomorrow if you behave yourselves today.'

The kids were thrilled, and I was surprised at Fred making such a long speech, for he was by nature rather taciturn. He never wasted lots of words when a few would suffice, and it was so pleasant to see him taking an interest in the children. He loved his family and was exceedingly good to them, but he had a bit of a Victorian outlook that children should be seen and not heard and was convinced when they played up that it was my fault. He used to tell me that I thoroughly spoiled them. It was true I gave them all the love, fussing and pushing them off to bed before he came home from work, knowing that he would be extremely tired and irritable. So to see him completely relaxed, laughing and chatting with them, was a real joy to me, and I began to feel more sure than ever that the discovery of this rural spot would change our lives for the better.

That afternoon Fred set about clearing some of the trees. I was upset to see those lovely proud trees lying there and, in my mind, gasping their last breath among their brothers and sisters after they had grown so tall and natural.

'They're rubbish, those tall ferny trees,' decided Fred. 'They have to go – must let some light and air into this place or no flowers or vegetables will ever grow.'

I knew he spoke sense, so I held back my tears. I just went right down to the other end of the plot and apologised to the larger trees who had spawned the ones that Fred was cutting down. 'Sorry, dear,' I said. 'They're your babies, I know.'

The kids, however, had a great time, as did Fred, who had a big chain attached to a rope to drag the trees out of the ground. They all hung on the rope, shouting 'timber', as they had seen in the lumberjack films. I hid myself in my little hut and cooked a nice lunch. It was warm inside and I looked out through the small windows as I worked, taking in the tall trees dressed in their ivy trails and wild honeysuckle and the little patches of blue berries everywhere. After lunch I sat on the step and watched the children play on their home-made swing, and threw crumbs to the little robin, who was so tame, and a shiny little brown bird who competed with him.

Meantime Fred, still bursting with energy, had progressed to another job: building a loo. Sweat poured from his brow as he sawed wood and hammered in nails. I began to think he was going to work too hard down here, and I felt I ought to help him a bit more, but I am inclined to be a little lazy. I like to sit and dream, and anyway, Fred would never let anyone help him once he started a project, having it all planned before he began.

Before sunset the wooden shed which was to house our primitive loo was erected, door on and bucket installed inside, then Fred called out, 'Who is to be my first customer? Lavatory's ready.'

I declined but the kids fought each other to get there first.

'But where's the chain?' cried Angela, who had won the battle.

'There isn't one,' said Fred, 'but don't worry about it – that will all do the garden good and make the vegetables grow.'

For the first time the rural life seemed a little distasteful to me, but I knew I must conquer my revulsion, because down here I had everything else that mattered and everything that I loved.

On Monday the weather had changed, and it was raining when Peter and I went out for our early morning run. I walked out of the gate right up to the top of the hill. Not a soul was in sight along the winding, rough road with little shacks on each side, and I counted the names on the gates: Woodlands, Dunroaming, Weekenda, Whitelodge and Copleigh. Through the tall trees which hemmed them in, I got a glimpse of little flower gardens and vegetable patches, chickens running around and, in one place, some large white geese. It all seemed silent and so very private, until a dog came racing down the path of one place and jumped up at the gate to let us know we were intruders, so I knew that someone must reside in those secret abodes. It all intrigued me, and I wondered what my neighbours were like and if they lived there all the time.

When I reached the top of the hill I looked down over the two rivers. A cool mist drifted over the hillside and the sun had just begun to struggle through the rain clouds. Suddenly a rainbow appeared, with a myriad of beautiful colours, its graceful arch seeming to span the whole world. I stood breathless with wonder, not coming back to reality until the frantic barking of old Peter brought me down to earth. He had trapped a poor old hedgehog and was going bonkers running around it in circles and barking like a maniac.

'Naughty boy,' I scolded him, putting on his lead and dragging him away. 'Poor old hedgehog – leave him alone.'

That evening we packed all our luggage into the old Austin and regretfully returned to London.

'Say goodbye, little house,' I told the children.

'Why?' they demanded in unison.

'Oh you must,' I told them. 'The fairies will take good care of it till we come back again.'

Sombrely they stood and together said, 'Goodbye, little house, see you next week,' as if repeating a little prayer.

To this day I still repeat the ceremony whenever we leave Cliffe to go back home to London.

Chapter Four

My Garden of Eden

As that first summer wore on Fred and I worked hard all the week, looking forward to Saturday mornings, when off we would go on our weekly trek to Five Oaks. We would put part of our wages away especially to spend on things we might need. At that time we were not too well off – wages in those days were very low, and the upkeep of our house in London and the supporting of a family took most of what we earned. But we indulged ourselves very little: we never went out to meals, did not drink, and most of our pocket money was spent on the children or on this special venture, our weekend home. My son Keith, then eight years old, made his own contribution: a small wooden plaque with 'Five Oaks' printed on it in big white letters, which was firmly attached to our gate. He was very proud of the finished result, for he had worked very hard to create it.

Angela, while playing in the garden, found a small brass pixie and dashed about asking, 'Does anyone want a special wish?' It was her idea that you must close your eyes and ask the pixie – lots of fun was had this way. Now, when I look up at him still sitting on a shelf, with his wizened face, I feel a tenderness towards him, as if he really did protect my little hut through the hazards of all the early years.

The spring had been extremely wet, and the ground was still muddy and sloshy, but the summer flowers grew nonetheless. First of all we bought six rose trees from Woolworths. They really thrived in that moist clay soil and by June they had buds on them. How excited I was to discover that first rosebud! I put packets of seeds in my little patch which I had dug over: marigolds, antirrhinums (better known to the children as bunny rabbits) and pretty little pansies. It made a bright spot amid all the greenery.

As I explored the wilderness, I made lovely discoveries in the uncleared parts of our woodland. I found a red may tree, a lovely willow and an old apple tree full of bloom, growing almost wild in the wood at the end of the plot. In the autumn it was weighed down with those large Kentish apples which make such lovely apple pies. Facing us opposite our gate was a great orchard, and the pale blossom in the spring wafted a lovely aroma over our little house, where I would sit on the step and savour the glorious perfume.

As the sunny days came, we spent most of our weekends scantily dressed, wading into the tall grass and getting covered with mosquito bites for our trouble. We uprooted six-foot high thistles and cleared more and more space, while the children ran about and got freckled faces and suntanned limbs. In the afternoons we would lie out on an old blanket under the trees and sleep – if the kids would let us. As the sap rose in the trees and the flowers poked their heads through the ground our love grew and matured. A kind of closeness that we had lost with the war years returned to us, and we would lie close together, holding hands and saying very little. The rural beauty all around us said it for us: that life was beautiful and really worth striving for. We struggled on, we sweated and toiled to conquer nature even though as fast as we cleared a spot the weeds grew back and the tall grass grew tougher. We were sure we would eventually win and encouraged each other when we thought it was becoming a hopeless task. This was my garden of Eden and I was determined no serpent would raise his head in it – and if he did, there was I with my sharp scythe to behead him.

Our friends and relations were perplexed. 'Where on earth do you disappear to every weekend?' asked my sister-in-law. 'Twice I have called on a Sunday and you've not been at home.'

'No,' I told her. 'I will not be home weekends now; I have a place in the country.'

'Not in this weather!' she cried, very shocked.

'Of course we go, whatever the weather is like,' I informed her.

'Goodness me, whatever do you do down there if the weather is bad?' she asked.

'We work,' I said, 'and we enjoy it.'

'Well! I don't call that much of a holiday,' she snorted.

I refused to be put off and, clad in my old woolly jumper and slacks and my wellingtons (also very odd socks), I continued my weekend work. It was strange how I always lost a sock during my travels back and forth, ending up with two odd ones, but still I plodded about in the wet mud, plotting my lovely garden of the future.

That year in July a long row of lettuces poked their heads through the soil, and some spring onions, and I spent a long day planting out fifty cabbage plants. My back ached and my nails were ruined, but the pleasure when I saw them grow was well worth it. Then in August we spent two whole weeks at our country estate, and we took the children to the shore, which was only about two miles away, as we had promised.

It was a wild lonely marshland that bordered the Thames and even now I still recall the swift, strong, salty breeze and the children laughing and romping on the little patch of sand. We put them in a shallow pool to teach them to swim. Keith took to it like a duck to water but Angela was nervous. That day we almost quarrelled for the first time in ages, simply because Fred tried to force Angela to stay in the water. She was very strong-willed, but I always dashed forward to protect her. Later on we combed the beach for shells and sat on the sea wall looking out to sea, watching the big ships going up to the London docks just out past the deep-water line.

Fred said, 'I would not give you a thank you for a smart crowded beach – this is what I like.' Even though the wind blew my hair into an untidy mess and my feet were cold from the sharp breeze, I was inclined to agree with Fred. This kind of solitude was not easy to find, and yet we were not so far from London.

We went on another outing during that first annual holiday, this time to the market at Maidstone, where we bought some fruit trees: three apple trees, a plum tree and a pear tree. We felt wildly extravagant. We planted the plum tree in front of the shack and the apple trees and pear tree at the back. Fred loved this kind of job. If he did anything, it must be done well and he must also do it himself.

Often that summer, friends and relatives popped in to visit us, the men in their best suits and the women with their silk stockings and high heels. They looked around our hut, at our makeshift cooking arrangements and our prehistoric loo, then made polite excuses and departed off to the south coast to the real seaside and a restful holiday. But I was not annoyed or embarrassed: this was my little bit of heaven, and I did not need them – though sometimes their reactions made me laugh. There was one incident when a very fat friend plonked heavily on to our loo and Fred's home-made shed collapsed, tipping her and the bucket sideways. Often the children who came would go into the loo and come out screaming hysterically because they had spotted a spider in there.

I had no patience with such things. I taught my children not to be afraid of small insects, explaining that they would not attack anyone; they were just part of the system of Mother Nature, who knew exactly why every creature was there. We got used to the wildlife – the stag beetles and May bugs whizzing about our heads in the evenings, the tiny fruit bats flying in and out of the trees, and the distant hoot of the owl.

During the school holiday I was visited by my friend Madge whom I'd met when Angela became friends with Madge's daughter Pat. Madge was quite a character – lively, talkative and she loved to gossip. We'd take the children on long walks and go strawberry and blackcurrant picking to earn extra money to treat them. This was great fun. Madgie and I would pick the fruit like mad and then the kids would come up to us with only half a basket. They would then snatch our baskets when they thought we weren't looking and declare them as theirs. It amused the children thoroughly and we got a little bit of pocket money out of it.

We also took the kids to the village jumble sales to get little bits of china and cushion covers. I had no false pride and if anybody offered me any little bits I took them. As long as I could make my little hut cosy, I was quite happy, and slowly I collected many things. One was a big Welsh dresser that Fred got from some job. Another time he picked up an old-fashioned gramophone and we had lots of fun with that. We put it on on Saturday nights and played the only two records we had: 'The Sheik of Araby' and 'Lily Marlane'. Eventually we did collect some more and Keith would wind up that gramophone until he almost fell asleep.

We also had lots of fun in the evenings at the local pub, the Merry Boys. We would walk there through the little back lanes, singing 'Davey Crockett'. It was very relaxed at the pub and the children were allowed in. This was the small inn where we'd first met Alf through whom we'd bought the land, and while we chatted with the locals and drank beer the kids played up merry hell. Then we'd all march home down the lanes, which were lit up by lines and lines of glow-worms, and the kids would sing loudly to frighten away the gremlins. They would put the glow-worms on their heads and dance along in front of us.

Madge was a lovely person and that was the beginning of a long friendship. The kids were very fond of her and now she's left this world, I think of her with great affection. I have planted a rose in my garden for her – a beautiful pink rose called Marjorie – and now her spirit will live in my garden forever.

By the end of our annual holiday, the kids looked fit and well. Angela had always been rather frail, but now she had filled out and lost that perpetual sniffle she used to have with all the colds that she seemed to contract.

We were sad to leave at the end of August, but we still had many pleasures to come with our weekend visits in the late summer. We lit bonfires, which covered us with smoke, but the wonderful smell of the wood burning and the baked spuds cooking in the hot ash compensated us. In early September we would all go down to the shore for a swim. The clean salt water not only cleaned us and freshened us up, but got rid of all our aches and pains.

We found a nice little pub called the Evening Star in the village and we would stop there on the way back for a couple of drinks while the children played outside. Then we made another discovery on our trips back from the sea: the meadows were full of mushrooms. We picked them, but unfortunately had nothing to put them in. I still had my swimming costume on and was carrying my knickers, so we tied the legs of the knickers and put the mushrooms in them. It caused great amusement in the bar when we offered the landlord some of our pickings. 'Great,' he said. 'I'll bet these will taste really good.'

Ah yes, those were good days, full of fun and adventure. They will never come again – that is why it is so necessary to record them. I remember the abundant orchards over the road where we collected the windfall apples, and the big treks we made deep into the woods in the autumn to collect blackberries. It was like no man's land in that great wood, with ferns growing to great heights, and partridges and pheasants running along the paths.

There was one spot that we named the fairy glen, where tall, purple, fluffy plants grew all around, enclosing a little glade. In the middle was a real fairy ring, where the circle of grass was very much greener than the rest. The first time I saw it, I cried suddenly, 'Let's dance around the fairy ring,' and the kids and I skipped and jumped around the green circle. I can see them now, the sun shining on Angela's golden hair and Keith's bunch of bright red curls. Fred sat at the side with his two buckets of blackberries. 'How bloody childish can you get?' he grumbled.

It made no difference, because I was feeling young at heart, as if I had been born again.

Sometimes we would walk through the woodlands to have a drink at the Merry Boys. All the locals would be there and slowly but surely we began to make ourselves known. They would chat to Fred about fishing, boating or gardening, and often someone would present me with a big marrow or a bag of plums. If you happened to buy one of these old chaps a beer he would always return the kindness in this way the next time he saw you. I would go to London sometimes with enough vegetables to last me a week.

By the end of that first glorious autumn, we had cleared a fair part of the land between the gate and the shack. The fruit trees were doing well and my salad patch had been very prolific. We had so many lettuces that I brought them back with me and gave them to my neighbours in London, announcing proudly, 'I grew them myself.'

The evenings were becoming misty and there was now a coolness in the air. Fred said, 'Not many week-ends left, love, better start thinking of the winter.' When he saw the sadness in my eyes at the thought of leaving my woodland, he added, 'Might try and get a nice wood-burning stove, then we could last out till October.'

He toured the scrapyards and one day came back with a rusty old kitchener tied on to the old Austin, which he soon installed and polished it till it looked like silver. He collected all the old bits of wood, and sawed them into logs. When the fire was lit that really made our shack look cosy. It threw out a great heat, and we made toast and boiled the kettle on it, and instead of going for walks on Saturday evenings we stayed in around our nice wood fire.

Soon a silver frost lay on the lawn and the snow clouds gathered in the sky, so we locked up our little shack and, saying a very reverent farewell to our Mr Pixie we went home to London till the spring.

My lovely trees had shed their leaves and were now sleeping; my roses had gone. I had collected flower seeds to plant next year, and the thought of another spring kept me going through that long, dull, cold winter in London.

Chapter Five

Country Affairs

That year back in London we often discussed the possibility of building a real house in the woods.

'We could sell this house and I would try to get a transfer from my firm down to Northfleet, because they have a place down there,' suggested Fred.

'It sounds like a good idea. How will you go about it?'

'I'll think on it,' returned Fred. 'I expect I'll have to apply for building permission, so don't get disappointed if we can't get it.'

I went about my chores that winter with my head in the clouds, thinking it would be so nice to live in Kent away from the smoke, fumes and noisy traffic of the metropolis.

Fred was bursting with economical ideas: 'If I get a van, I'll buy building material when I see it going cheap and store it down there, and we can live in the little shack all the summer while I get the house built.'

It all sounded very brave and, though I was a little uneasy as to his ability to build a house, I went along with him and mentally planned the house with its modern conveniences and the lovely garden surrounding it which I could work in all the year round. I had really got the bug to dig in the fresh moist earth and found that whatever my troubles I could still always lose myself digging in the clay soil of Kent. So all that long winter I mentally planned my garden for the spring: 'I'll put in runner beans this year – I'll plant them in boxes and take them down in the spring. Must get some seeds from those hollyhocks around the corner – they'll look lovely as a background for my flower patch.' Back and forth to school or to the market, my head was filled with these ideas.

Once someone said to me, 'You always look as if you're in another world. I often wonder about you – perhaps you should take something for your nerves.'

With my usual humour, I replied, 'My dear, my nerves are the least of my troubles. It's the cucumber and marrows that bother me.'

She stared strangely at me then changed the subject, convinced, I feel sure, that I was a 'little round the bend', but there is enough of the exhibitionist in me to enjoy being thought eccentric.

That year we said goodbye to our old Austin. We were sad to see it go, but it needed so much spent on it that it was like an albatross round our necks. A friend of Fred's bought it for ten pounds, then spent a year completely renovating it, and after thirty years that old vintage car is still on the road.

We bought a second-hand Morris van. It wasn't as comfortable as the Austin, but it suited Fred, who had begun to collect tools and various items to aid his work down at Five Oaks.

When we arrived at our weekend retreat at the end of February, I was amazed to see how my lawn had spread – the grass was fresh and green and about a foot high. Hazel catkins swung from the little nut trees and white hawthorn covered the hedges. There was a quiet, sad loneliness without the bird song – our wild birds had not returned from migration yet. The old shack smelt damp and was very chilly, but we soon got that big kitchener fire blazing and the kettle boiling and once more we were back in residence at Five Oaks.

A sleepy hedgehog wandered about, just out from hibernation, and the kids went scampering around to look for Jimmy the toad, who had visited us every Sunday last summer, sitting in the same spot on the path and, with an inscrutable stare, puffing and blowing his chest out. 'We can't find Jimmy,' they yelled, turning over stones and looking under the shack.

'No, dears, it's too early. He's still sleeping,' I told them.

The robins and the bluetits were still around and came down for their share of our lunch.

The children went down to get the water. They returned with half a bucketful, having spilled the rest as they squabbled while bringing it up the hill.

'I've met a nice girl down at the water tap,' announced Angela. 'She's got lovely long plaits, and she's going to ask her mother if she can come down to play with us. Is it all right with you, Mum?'

'Of course, darling,' I said. 'It will be nice for you to have a little girl to play with.'

So my first contact with the other inhabitants of the woods began that Sunday with the arrival of a very shy little girl, younger than Angela but a head taller. She had nut-brown hair which hung in two thick plaits to almost below her waist, and lovely green hazel eyes. She showed every sign of growing up to be a rare beauty, but she was shy and awkward and would not romp, shout and scream as my two kids did, but sat making little patterns of shells, arranging them very artistically. She told us her name was Henrique. I remarked that it was an unusual name.

'It's Polish,' she informed me. 'My mother and father come from Poland.'

I immediately wanted to find out their story, with my usual curiosity. It's a compulsive urge I have – I suppose that was the beginning of my getting this bug to write everything down.

I didn't even have to wait another day to satisfy my curiosity, because towards evening Henrique's mum came to collect her. She was a well-built woman, with skin that was rugged brown and weatherbeaten. She had shrewd little blue eyes, which twinkled with humour, and such a nice smile. She spoke very little English but while we had a cup of tea we slowly began to make each other understood, and this was the beginning of a long friendship, the first close one I had made in these woods.

The next weekend Keith found himself a pal whose name was Anthony, and I got to know his mother Rene. Her father and grandfather had been keepers of a big estate that had once belonged to Lord Cobham – the Cobham Estate went right back to the Elizabethan era. Rene still lived on the estate in the old keeper's cottage. She was nice but very excitable. Rene would laugh at nothing and sing and dance at nothing. She had one son – Anthony – who was just as wild. He used to arrive every Sunday dinner-time just as we served up the afters, for he loved peaches and cream. He was about nine, a little younger than Keith, and was another redhead. He would scoff his afters then rush out and pretend to be a train, dashing round the lawn shouting 'Hoot-hoot-hoot', sometimes nearly making me drop the pots I was carrying from surprise. My son would reassure me: 'It's OK,' he would say in his manly way, 'he just thinks he's a train.' And strangely enough, when Anthony grew up he became a train driver.

Anthony knew all about fishing and catching newts, and Keith would beg to go to the pond in the woods with him. I had let them go, but then spent most of my time walking back and forth to the pond to make sure they didn't fall in the water. Of course they got soaking wet and terribly muddy, but they were gloriously happy, and transported lots of weird little creatures back to the shack in jars. Fred promised them he would make a pool as soon as he had time.

It was nice to find the children so contented, as they had never got along particularly well together as brother and sister, and while they played with their friends it left Fred and me free to get on with clearing the land and growing vegetables.

That spring we went on lots of walks in the woods with the children – now four of them, because they wouldn't move without their pals. They would scamper along the leafy paths ahead of us because Anthony and Henna, as we called her, lived permanently in these woods and knew all the paths in all seasons. One day, they led us into the bluebell woods, a big open place along the slopes of the hill that was literally as blue as the sea, so thick were the bluebells. I sat on an old tree trunk at the top of the slope while the children played tag, then we gathered bluebells and went home to tea.

I made toast beside our wood-burning fire, then, when their friends had gone home, I gave my two a good wash in warm rainwater. By now, we had installed a big barrel that caught the rainwater, which we were able to use for washing and washing up, thus saving our fresh water for cooking. This meant fewer trips down to the community tap.

At bedtime, as the pretty coloured moths came in and buzzed around the oil lamp, I would tell the children stories about Mr Pixie, who lived with us, and all his relations, who still lived out in the woods. It was strange how even then I did not realise that I had the creative gift – I only knew that I loved inventing stories for the children and they loved hearing them.

In the mornings I always arose early, when the sky would still be glowing with the dawn and the air would be fresh and sweet. Often I would go down to the end of the plot and say my prayers and sometimes recite poetry.

A general favourite of mine was from Shakespeare's *A Midsummer Night's Dream*:

> I know a bank where the wild thyme blows,
> Where oxslips and the nodding violet grows,
> Quite over-canopied with luscious woodbine,
> With sweet musk-roses, and with eglantine.

The woods in Kent were my church and my steeple, and in the mass of tangled undergrowth lived my fairy people. As that spring passed on to a glorious summer and we spent more time in Kent, my pale face grew fuller, my skin looked fresher, and even my hair lightened with the clean air.

It had now become the custom for me, every Sunday morning, to go at about midday to visit Henna's mother, Ella, or Mrs Polish, as we called her. She had a small holding at the top of the hill, which had a grand view of the tiny village and the hamlets below, which looked like toys from this height, and the farmlands stretching like a patchwork quilt, with shades of greens, browns and yellows, to the sea beyond.

The reason for my weekly visit to Mrs Polish was to buy new-laid eggs and vegetables. She grew every vegetable you could imagine – marvellous potatoes, huge cabbages and marrows – and very cheaply she sold them too. I would stock up on a supply to take back to London.

She lived in a little wooden shack called White Lodge, which had a rustic seat outside where we would sit and chat. She would tell me the sad story of her life, and it went on episode after episode every Sunday morning: how the Germans had arrived at her father's farm in the Ukraine when she was only sixteen and taken her off in a lorry; and how she had been transported to Germany in one of those terrible railway wagons in which the Nazis packed all the refugees and all those poor Jews. Being young and very strong and healthy, she had been put to work on the land, but later on she had suffered the indignities and deprivations of those dreadful concentration camps. I was so intrigued and so sorry for her.

She was a sturdy and unattractive woman, with big hands and feet, and always seemed to wear, when working, man-sized boots with the toes cut out of them, which were usually covered in earth. I would often stare down, fascinated, at those large, wide toes, quite unable to believe my eyes. She was a sweet and simple person. Her English was halting, but seemed to improve each week.

One day she brought out two glasses and a bottle of home-made wine.

'This good,' she declared. 'I make from plums.'

Well, it certainly was potent. I found myself staggering a bit as I went back down the hill with a huge cabbage under my arm, and my cheeks were burning.

Fred said, when he saw me, 'Good God, where have you been? It's two o'clock and no dinner on.'

'Sorry, ducks,' I hiccuped. 'Been talking to Mrs Polish and drinking her home-made wine.'

After that I got the idea of making my own wine. I sent the kids scrumping in the plum orchards and began to experiment with brewing at home. Fred became interested too, so between us we got recipes, bottles and jars, and we had soon put down our first lot of home-made wine. Later that year we collected elderberries and dandelions, and in time our wine became varied and very potent and was later the basis of all the hot bowls of punch that we served when we gave parties.

The following year there was a heatwave and I took up Fred's suggestion of staying in Kent for the full six weeks of the school holidays. He came down at weekends and worked himself silly, cutting grass and taking down trees. Finally he hurt his knee and I got cross with him.

'What the hell use is this place going to be to me if you're going to kill yourself?' I complained.

He limped around, his face drawn and white with pain, so I nagged him into taking a holiday and allowing the garden to go for a while.

It was during this rest period of Fred's that we discovered an old cinema in the village, not far from the pub. It was just a sort of old tin hut and the films were as old as Adam, but we found it a godsend, because on Saturdays we could leave the kids and their friends there with huge bags of sweets, while we relaxed in the pub and felt much better for the change.

The Merry Boys was now our own local, and we enjoyed our walks there through the deep forest on warm evenings, and the company of the regulars at the little rural pub. Most of them had been born locally, and had never moved very far away from their village. The landlady told me that the pub had belonged to her family for hundreds of years. She had worked there all her life and never knew any other kind of existence. Her husband had died during the war, so she had been the sole proprietor now for thirty years, and did not wish for any other kind of life. In a way I envied her, living permanently in the midst of these green woods, keeping chickens, goats and many horses in her meadows.

Two of the most regular of her customers were Fanny and Reg. To one and all Reg was known as Shackles and was the local woodcutter, a tall, good-looking man with dark hair and lovely blue eyes. When I met Fanny she was past her prime like a lovely, dark-eyed pansy that had lost its bloom. Her teeth were discoloured and her skin sallow; she worked on the land and seldom looked clean except on Saturday nights when she was with her man in the local. They both drank beer by the gallon, and every time they had a drink it was entered down on the slate and paid for when they were in the money. Their attitude to each other was strange: they slanged each other continuously, and everyone in the bar enjoyed the descriptions of their sexual experiences, because they related them out loud to all and sundry.

Fred never cared much for Fanny – he was a little disgusted with her attitude and coarseness – but I found her very stimulating, especially when she had drunk enough beer to give us a song. This was usually 'April Showers', her favourite number, sung in a loud, untuneful voice.

She seemed to like me, and 'tacked' on to me. She would call in to see me on her way home from work, often bringing fruit or vegetables. We would have a cup of tea, but Fanny much preferred beer and would try to get me to go to the village with her. One day I gave in and accompanied her. We left the kids in the cinema and visited each pub in turn – and there were quite a few of them. We started at midday and finished at three o'clock. By this time my face was as red as beetroot and my knees were giving way under me. The donkeyman, who ran a donkey and cart, always took care of Fanny on her binges and would see that she got taken home after her boozy sprees. That day he had to take me. So, with the kids all piled into the donkey cart, we sang our way home, but the next day I felt extremely ashamed of myself.

The kids laughed and said, 'You was ever so funny, Mummy. We think you was drunk.'

'Don't tell Dad, will you, darlings?' I pleaded.

'No, we won't,' they said very earnestly, and they never did.

That was the last time I went anywhere with Fanny, although I knew her for many years. For me she is still part of the woodlands and the people who lived there.

Another regular at the Merry Boys was Ted Hazeldene. He was a dapper little man, dark haired, with a small moustache, and very neat – in fact, his tidiness stood out among the woodland population. You could usually find Ted in the little shed next door to the Merry Boys, where the kids could get their hair trimmed. He was a man of many parts: he shod horses, he ran a book for people who wanted to place bets, then at night he helped behind the bar and entertained us by playing the piano and singing in a very fine voice. It seemed there was no end to the accomplishments of our Ted, who also played the organ in the village church on Sundays. He was not a very popular man with the locals, as he had a dry, sarcastic manner, especially when he was drinking, but he was a wow with the ladies – except, perhaps, his rather pretty blonde wife, who was a teetotaller and was seldom seen in the Merry Boys. After many years and many hazards and lots of changes, Ted is still my friend. I see him walking his small dog through the village, often very drunk, with the dog guiding him home.

One of our woody folk, who will remain nameless, had some very odd ways. She would put a tea cosy on her head and dance around the lawn; once when there were some workmen working in the lane she served them tea topless, two shrivelled little breasts dangled on the tea tray. But these were the woody folk, people I miss very much.

Through the long years I have made and lost so many friends, but those woodland characters stay with me always.

Chapter Six

Historical Interests and New Friends

In those early years we seemed to have such long hot summers, beautiful days when the children played outside all day. I would do my chores and gardening in the mornings and spend the afternoons sunbathing in the open space in front of the hut, moving into the shade of the big oak when it got too hot in the afternoon. The cool leafy branches spread like a large umbrella over my head, protecting me from the sun's hot rays. A little brown bird would sit and sing, I felt only for me, and the bluetits would rustle about in the honeysuckle in their frantic search for insects. I would lie dreaming of the woods and imagining the days gone by, long before my time, thinking of the lovers of the past who must have come up from the village to make love under my lovely trees, and of the Knights Templar who rode through the woods on the way to their house in Rochester.

I had become deeply involved with the history of my woodland home and spent a lot of time at the local library in town, where I made some amazing discoveries. I found out that Henry IV and Falstaff had hunted in these woods. Falstaff we know as a fictional person in Shakespeare's plays, but he really existed as none other than the person of old Lord Cobham, who lived in the castle in the next village of Cooling. Such discoveries really thrilled me, so I dug deeper and deeper into the old books.

Fred was amazed at my preoccupation: 'What the hell are you diving into all those old books for?'

'It interests me. I love it, and I've never found the time in London.'

On our annual holiday that year we visited the old Norman castle at Cooling, which we discovered still had a big hole in the wall where James Wyatt shot a cannon ball through it. While the kids and Fred explored, I sat on the wall, recreating in my mind the traumatic scene: the wily rebel Wyatt outside the castle, and his fat uncle inside refusing to come out. It might seem a little crazy, but I felt inspired. I couldn't write it all down yet, but just kept it all in my mind.

I found out more about the history of the Cobham estates. They were given to the Lenox family when poor old Lord Cobham fell out of favour with King James. I went to visit the new hall at Cobham, but it didn't have the same appeal for me as the old ruined castle at Cooling, perhaps because they had turned it into a girls' school. The old Cobham estate finally disintegrated when the last Lord Darnley, just after the First World War, gave away a big tract of woodland to the soldiers who had returned from the war. They each paid £1 for a plot of land on condition that they cultivated it, and that was how the Cliffe Woods shanty town was born. My socialist friend Jim argued that Lord Darnley didn't give away his land out of generosity, but that the good lord was in trouble with the taxman. That may have been so, but these cynical views didn't impress me. I still like to think he was a generous lord.

It was a sense of the history surrounding me that egged me on to new discoveries. One of these was a very ancient priory dating back to the year 1100, called Lily Church. The prioress had been the sister of the King. It was now an old farm, with a big pond surrounded by willow trees, but I never passed by without seeing in my mind's eye the shadowy shapes of the ancient nuns going about their devotions.

The village was also a great source of adventure to me. While the kids played on the swings in the park, I would wander around the graveyard of the old Norman church, which stood at the edge of the marshland with a grand view out to sea. I would read the inscriptions on the old gravestones, wondering if I would recognise any of the names from my reading in the library. So very little had changed in this peaceful spot. The churchyard looked out over bright green meadowland, where hundreds and hundreds of woolly sheep grazed. I could see a huge black barn right out in the marsh and four stone cottages known as the coastguard cottages. These were scenes that pierced my brain and stayed there, as if I had been born before and knew all this so well.

It was in a later summer that I got to know some more of my neighbours. There was a small, neat dwelling, called Dunroaming, just two plots away, which I often passed while walking old Peter. I could hear children laughing and playing and looked with interest at this place that was almost cleared of trees, except for one huge oak in the middle of the plot and an elm, which held a rudely constructed tree-house. I used to see children scrambling like monkeys all over this tree-house, but so far no one had come down to the gate to acknowledge my 'Good mornings' – it was as if whoever was there didn't want to be seen.

One Saturday evening, a few weeks later, I took Peter for a walk up the lane. It was a bright, moonlit night, pleasantly cool after a hot summer's day. As I strolled along the lane, I was surprised to hear the sound of music. It was loud and modern, and such an unusual sound to be heard in our woods. When I returned from my walk, Angela came out to meet me – she had also heard the sound of pop music outside Dunroaming. As we reached the gate we saw a slim young woman standing there. 'Hallo,' she said. 'Would you like to come to a party?'

I could see the festivities going on – a band was playing like mad, with a drummer who was banging on the drums with terrific energy.

'Sixpence a ticket,' the young lady said, then, rather apologetically, 'it's in aid of the Communist Party, you know.'

Well, this was certainly a surprise in the middle of my lonely woods, but I didn't mind. 'Oh, I don't care who it's in aid of. A party is a party, especially on Saturday night. Give me four tickets, I'll go back and get the rest of the family.'

Fred put up a slight protest, but I lacquered my hair and powdered my nose, so he knew I was determined to go and he gave in reluctantly. 'Can't think of any worse time than spending the evening with a lot of boozy commies,' he grumbled. Yet I was never sorry that I attended that party, because it opened new doors for me and I got to know the rest of the residents, and Cliffe became a kind of social whirl.

The kids loved it. There was a big bonfire with lots of baked spuds, and someone presided over a hot-dog stand. A lemonade stall was also laid on, and out in front of the hut there was a bar with barrels of beer and bottles of various alcoholic beverages. The young man in charge of the bar was very drunk and gave double measures of whisky and gin, continually forgot to take the money, and often had to be reminded to give back change.

Fred handed me a glass full of whisky saying, 'That bloke must be crazy – that's more than a treble you've got there, and I only gave him ten bob and got two bob change back.'

In the centre of the lawn the population of Cliffe Woods danced to the loud band, whose sounds reverberated in the trees and out over the night air. We sat on the grass with our drinks, and then we joined in the dancing.

That was the first of many parties I have attended at Cliffe Woods. It was quite an experience. I found that to dance with abandonment out in the night air was a grand feeling.

I met our host and hostess later on: a very carefree young couple, called Maureen and Jim. They were from the East End of London, just like myself, and we hit it off right away. Jim worked at the new oil refinery near the village of Grain and in the summer Maureen moved from London to stay in the small bungalow 'Dunroaming' which he had bought cheaply from a mate who had gone to work abroad. The name of the bungalow sounded carefree and suited its inhabitants well.

When the party had quietened and all the kids were tired, Fred took our two home to put them to bed, but he didn't return. I guessed it was too hectic for him. But I loved dancing in the dark and afterwards we all sat drinking around the bonfire with our host until dawn. We talked and argued about politics, then sang Cockney songs.

The next day, in spite of a hangover, I felt completely stimulated, having let off steam after years of hard graft.

The first time I met Maureen after the party, she seemed a shy sort of woman, different to the one who had drunk whisky from a bottle and quoted Karl Marx. She came to visit me and we sat out under the trees and drank tea. She wore a lovely scarlet jumper, her hair was dark and her eyes were a soft blue. She seemed a little short-sighted, but she had a very warm smile. I liked her immediately, even though she was a little withdrawn at first, but once we started chatting she thawed out. We talked of the places we both knew in the East End of London.

'Jim would like me to move down here,' she confided.

'It would be nice,' I said. 'We're never going to get around to building a house here; at least, it seems most unlikely at the moment.'

Maureen twisted her hands in her lap very nervously. 'I don't think I could move.'

'Why ever not?' I asked.

'I'd hate to leave my landing,' she confessed. For a moment I was puzzled, then I realised that she was talking about the flats where she lived – blocks of box-like flats, each with a landing area where the tenants could congregate and chat. 'I've got so many friends in the flats, I'd hate to live with a lot of toffee-nosed strangers.'

I was a little surprised and couldn't understand this intense attachment to certain places or certain people, other than family, and it seemed to me that, given the choice of living in a smoky town or this lovely woodland, I knew just what my choice would be.

Yet, as time went on, I got to understand Maureen very well. She was essentially such a grass-roots kind of person that it was hard for her to associate herself with anything that was not of her own environment. We made a friendship that day which has lasted a lifetime.

Maureen and Jim had four children, all a little younger than mine – their twins were about three years old, Jimmy was eight and Denise was about nine. My children went off to play with them, and Jim would hire a pony from the riding school and let all the kids ride on it. He also rigged up a type of overhead railway, which the boys loved. Their plot of land was a sort of leisure playground, a forerunner of the present day playgroups as more children came to play.

Each weekend lots more children arrived. Most were cousins and their friends from London's East End, children who had seldom seen the country. They ran wild and a good time was had by all.

Maureen's two young boys were a lively pair. Whenever I tangled with Tom and Rob, the twins, I always lost out. They were about five, very sturdy, and very mischievous. I recall one day when I saw them coming up the lane, carrying between them a heavy bucket. I knew it belonged to the old mare who grazed in the orchard – this bucket was her sole means of getting a drink.

'Where are you going with that?' I demanded.

'We found it,' they replied, clutching the bucket and looking at me aggressively.

'It belongs to the poor old horse, now take it back, there's good boys,' I cajoled them.

'No, we bleedin' won't,' declared Tom.

'We found it, so it's ours,' cried Rob.

I tried to retrieve the bucket, but they hung on to it with both hands, shouting, 'We're going to tell our dad you're trying to pinch our bleedin' bucket.'

So I gave in and let them go, but I was furious and worried about the poor horse. In some ways these boys could be very nice, and later on they used to visit me, but I was always on edge, not knowing what they would do next.

We had some good times together and I recall one particularly amusing incident when a whole family of bluetits chose my letter-box to nest in. When Jim and his crowd called in for a drink one evening before going to a party, I told Jim, 'Mind my tits in the letter-box and don't disturb them.' This caused a great deal of laughter, with Jim yelling out, 'Mind Lena's tits as you come in!' We laughed over this all evening at the party.

After meeting Maureen and Jim, I began to get to know my other neighbours. Next door but one to us were an old couple, the Alywoods. Mrs Alywood was a very keen gardener and a very ladylike old lady. She would tell me the names of the different roses and the wild flowers, and the names of the birds. She was a lovely person – sweet, kind and gentle. She never had a hair out of place and always wore her gardening gloves when she pottered about the garden. She gave me various plants: a little blue flower called Mind Your Own Business, a nice michaelmas daisy that was called Peace and Plenty and a beautiful rose called Paul Scarlet that I planted in the front. The sweet-smelling honeysuckle that I planted in a bucket beside the hut, and which now completely covers it, was given to me by Mrs Alywood. She cultivated my interest in my garden – something I've never lost.

Eventually, the Alywoods decided they were too old to manage their shack, and they handed it over to their son, Bert, a happy-go-lucky little man. I called him the jolly cobbler, because he had a shop in town where he repaired shoes.

Bert's wife, Dot, was fastidious and hated to get dirty. She was plump and a little lazy, but loved a glass of wine and lively company, so we all got on very well together. She was also very fond of the kids and never made a fuss about all the noise they made.

Dot loved to sit by the garden gate sunning herself. I recall with humour how she came running over to me one day while I was cooking dinner. She looked very distressed and cried, 'Come quickly! An enormous great thing has just walked past my house.' I ran over quickly wondering what on earth it could be, only to discover it was just an oversized slug. I offered her some tea to calm her but she said, 'My dear, I won't drink out of a big mug. I like my tea in a dinky cup or not at all.'

On Sundays, when we were hot and dry from our

continuous battle with the land, they would come over with a couple of bottles of wine and biscuits, and we would stop work and sit around gossiping. They loved the woods – Bert had grown up there and had run around the woods during the school holidays, as my own kids did, and his ambition was to build a house there one day.

There was an empty plot between us and the Alywoods. Fred and I had already discussed the possibility of our purchasing this plot, which was going cheap. Old man Alywood had been very cagey – you could never find out anything from him – but his son was quite a different kettle of fish, and we would sit and discuss the possibility that one of us should try to buy the empty plot. 'If one of us doesn't buy, it could mean someone will get in between us,' suggested Bert. 'I can't afford to expand at the moment – the shop isn't doing too well – but I know who it belongs to if you're interested, Fred.'

Knowing my man, who could never resist a bargain, I realised straight away that we would soon own another plot. I started to get worried, knowing how hard we slogged to keep this present one going.

At the end of the season we became the owners of that other overgrown piece of land next door. It only cost £80, but it took all our spare cash. We consoled ourselves by saying, 'Oh well, it won't eat anything, and now there's a piece of land for each child.'

This idea the kids picked up on immediately and started to argue as to which piece of land was Angela's and which was Keith's, and then they staked their claims.

September came with all its autumnal glory. Apples grew on our trees, the hedgerows were full of black-berries and we dug up the last of the spuds and began once more to prepare for the coming winter.

Dot and Bert joined us on Saturday evenings around

our nice warm stove and often we would have a big bonfire. One night Dot had a family party. Her mother and father and sisters joined in and Bert dressed up in a pair of tight sailor's trousers. He actually leapt over the bonfire – I think it was the effect of our elderberry wine.

In October, as the leaves began to fall and the big oaks scattered the lawn with acorns, I said goodbye to my woods again. The squirrels collected the hazelnuts and the blackbirds who had decided to stay for the winter repaired their nests.

I went around the garden touching each faded rose. 'Go to sleep, darlings,' I whispered. 'I'll be back in the spring.' I looked across at the tangled jungle next door which was now ours, and wondered if we would ever get around to clearing it.

'Never mind,' said Fred. 'It's our bit of England we have bought with our own hard-earned money, and no one can take it away from us.'

That was a warm, comforting thought to take with me through the long winter months.

Chapter Seven

The Marshland and the Woody Folk

It was strange how attached I had become to the wild marshland which surrounded my little wooden shack. It was almost an island between two rivers, or maybe more like a peninsula as the land dwindled down to a narrow strip between the Thames and the Medway as they rushed out into the estuary, where they met the Saltings, a little tributary which ran across the marsh. So there were little grassy spots intermingled with the salt water that filled up at high tide then left the land as the tide receded, leaving behind bright little pools where the gulls gathered in small colonies and the wild geese flew down to rest.

Often we would ride out to the Isle of Grain on Sundays, but that was before they built the oil refinery and before the big tankers anchored there, spilling oil and destroying the wildlife which was then so abundant. In those early days Grain was just a windswept island where the last of the Thames barges battled their way out to sea. Huge, beautifully coloured dragonflies flew hither and thither and bullfrogs croaked a merry sound, while the blue flash of swift-flying kingfishers could often be seen. The beaches were often deserted and very pebbly, but it was a great place for a swim and a Sunday afternoon picnic. We spent many hot afternoons sunbathing on the beach and playing in the sea with the children. No French Riviera could have pleased me as did that breezy Thames shore.

Then there was our own shoreline nearer to Cliffe, where attempts had been made to drain the land and huge man-made dykes crossed the landscape. I loved this rich, green meadowland, with its hundreds of black and white cows grazing gently. I liked to sit on the sea wall and gaze over the estuary at the heavy swell as the river met the sea. At high tide you could see the big ships making their way to the London docks out on the deep-water line, a faint blue line where the deep water of sea met the river. We would play a game of guessing the names of the big ships and where they were likely to have come from. Fred eventually got a second-hand pair of binoculars and would tell us what the nationality the various ships were, but again, that was before the London docks became sad and empty.

It was strange, the magnetic attraction that the marsh-land had for me, a Cockney born within the sound of Bow Bells. I loved those clear little streams which glittered in the morning sunshine, the song of the lark high up in the air, the blaze of coloured ragworts, the vivid clumps of yellow and purple mallow growing out of the tall grass, the soft rich mud in the ditches, the tall-legged cranes standing on one leg in midstream – all things in sight delighted and excited me. Even at evening time, as the sunset left the sky as red as blood and black stormclouds were chased by the wind, I loved the silvery roll of the water and the shadowy shapes of ships going out to sea.

Later on, when I began to write, the wild marshland was to be my chief inspiration.

We now had a very convivial weekend community in the woods. We all took it in turns to entertain on Saturday nights and I got to know more and more of the woodland folk all around me. We would often go up to a shack called Blossoms, right at the top of the hill. This plot belonged to a very nice progressive young couple named Tricia and Pete, who had three lovely children, Kelly, Jimmy and baby Shaun. They resided permanently in the woods, having left the town to live in the clean fresh air and have plenty of space for the children to play.

Up at Blossoms there were lots of pets, including an old dog whose name was Dawg, a wonderful, intelligent old labrador who loved everyone except my poor old dog Peter – they fought tooth and claw every weekend. There were also lots of kittens and so many rabbits. I still recall the day when little Kelly came down the lane holding her favourite bunny. There were tears in her eyes as she said, 'I was going to take Timmy to get married, but I can't. She already got married to that rabbit down the road.'

Those outdoor parties at Blossoms were good fun. We would all stand at the top of the hill and watch the sun go down in a blaze of glory, then we would dance the night away until dawn and still be up there as the sun rose over the hill. When the younger children got tired they would all be put to sleep in a big room and old Dawg would look after them, while us grown-ups sat around the dying embers of the fire, listening to Pete strumming his guitar, and entertaining us with sea shanties.

Unfortunately Maureen and I always got a little tiddly. I remember one night when she kept taking me out to the shed at the back of the garden and insisting it was the toilet. I thought it was a strange sort of convenience but never argued, until Tricia asked, 'What are you doing in my coal-shed? The bathroom is inside the house.'

Another time I was going around with a bottle of sherry and missed my footing in the dark and fell down the rubbish hole, still clutching the bottle, and no one even missed me. It was a funny sensation, lying on my back looking up at the stars and finding it quite impossible to climb out of the hole. I sipped the sherry from the bottle and waited to be rescued – I was so happy I did not care either way. It might sound a bit ridiculous for a grown-up woman to act in this way, but that was the effect the woodlands had on me – I lost all my inhibitions and enjoyed living. I suppose I was some kind of drop-out, but only on Saturday nights.

Previously I had introduced my Polish friends to the woodland folk, so no party was complete without Henna and Ella. They would arrive dressed in their national costumes and dance a sort of Polish fling. That was fine out in the open air, but if the weather was bad and we had to go indoors, the weight of Ella and Henna was rather hard on the floorboards, because these little shacklike dwellings had no foundations. I would sit with my fingers crossed, feeling sure that the floor was about to give way and the shack would come down around us as Ella thundered by, waving her hands and stamping her feet.

Yet it was all good clean fun, this getting together of our small weekend community. Everyone always brought a bottle and someone would nip down to the village pub for some beer. We usually had a whip round for the food, with everyone putting their share of money in the pot, so the party would not be expensive. We all enjoyed the chance to let off steam, because it was always back to the grindstone on Sunday mornings – very often with a heavy hangover.

My circle of friends grew wider and my social activities were very hectic, but I had found peace and great happiness in my little shack in the woods. My children were growing sturdy and independent; they both had their own hobbies and chose their own friends – every weekend one or two more arrived, but I always managed to cater for them. Fred would announce dryly as I served Sunday lunch , 'All we need is miracle of five loaves and two fishes to feed that lot.'

But somehow I coped, mixing up huge batter puddings to eke out our Sunday joint, and making lots of fruit pies. All this I cooked on the big old range, which I had to keep feeding with logs of wood, while the sun shone and the children played out in the fresh air. I slaved over that red-hot oven, stifled by the incredible heat, so that the children could be well fed and happy.

Angela was getting a little difficult, as she was beginning, at thirteen and a half, to try her wings. She wanted to stay in London and go out with her friends to discos, but I wouldn't allow this, preferring that she brought her friends into the country with her. So a nice little gang of teenagers was formed from the country lads and the girls who came down from London at weekends. All of them would group about at the top of the hill, under a tremendous oak tree. They would either be up in the branches of this huge tree, or larking about around it, carving their initials in its ancient grey bark.

One particular boy was Angela's constant companion, a big, untidy lad of about fourteen called Nicky, who had a shock of uncut hair and always seemed to have a wide grin on his face. He would say, 'Oh you should see Angela climb a tree – she can climb trees better than boys.' He would boost her ego and give her confidence.

Nicky came from a rather distressed home, but he was a special pal. He reminded me of a Just William character, with his ragged trousers and tousled hair. He would wander the woods with the little gang not far behind him. As soon as it got dark I would begin to worry and go to look for them. They would all be hiding in battered old hulks of cars that had been dumped. I would keep calling out and hear the sound of suppressed giggles, and once they came I would run after them and wallop them all the way home.

I recall one particular day with some amusement. Angela had brought her girlfriend of the moment round to see us, a pretty little girl whom we called Wilma, because she reminded us of a Flintstone character on TV. She had the same, neat little figure, with good legs, and the same high cheekbones and merry dark blue eyes. She was a cute little thing and appeared to me to have the makings of a really sexy woman. Yet both girls were only thirteen edging on fourteen, so any ideas of that nature I put firmly from my mind. This was their last round up – time to have fun before they really grew into womanhood.

The day that Wilma came round, Angela told me: 'Mummy, Nick's going away to live in Australia.'

'Oh dear,' I said. 'I am sorry.'

'He's going to have a farewell party – can we go?'

'Yes, darling. I don't see why not.'

I brushed her golden hair till it shone and tied it with a blue ribbon to match her dress, then did the same for Wilma with a red ribbon. Off they went at about half past four to what I naturally thought was a tea party. However, at half past five I received an unpleasant shock. Angela came staggering along the lane, supported by two young boys, her face the colour of beetroot. Wandering along behind them, a little unsteady and very giggly, was her friend Wilma. I dashed to the gate crying out, 'Good God! Whatever happened to you?'

As I drew near to Angela I caught a reek of alcohol.

'Sorry, Mum,' she hiccuped. 'I think I've got drunk.'

I was furious. 'What the hell have you been up to?' I yelled as I whisked the two girls inside. The boys dashed away in terror.

'She drank seven port wines, just for a dare,' Wilma explained.

'Well I'll be jiggered,' I cried. 'Where on earth did you get all that drink? I thought it was going to be a tea party.'

'Well, Nicky's mum is always drunk,' said Wilma. 'So she said we could drink up all that was left because tomorrow she's going to Australia.'

I was astounded and thought, what goings-on for young people. I put Angela's head under the cold tap and slapped her legs very hard. She started to grizzle so I put her to bed and warned Wilma not to leave the grounds any more that day.

Later on that hot summer evening there was a disturbance down by the gate. I went to investigate and found a group of young boys absolutely drunk and acting in a most peculiar manner, falling off their bikes and fighting each other. They were dragging one little boy by the legs, who was unconscious and wore nothing but a pair of swimming briefs. His nose had been bleeding and he was smothered in blood. I was horrified to have this lot parked outside my house.

They stood by the gate and started chanting, 'We want Wilma, we want Angela!' and falling about in all directions. I shouted, 'Be off with you! Go away!' But they just roared and cheered, completely intoxicated. The half-naked boy got up and ran around in rings, looking ghastly and seeming completely mindless. I threw a pot of tea-leaves over him because he wouldn't stand still. It was indeed a shocking sight to be seen in this quiet country lane on a Sunday afternoon.

I ran to the rainwater butt and got a bucket of water. I threw it over the boys and some sank down on the grass, more or less subdued. 'Take him home,' I yelled. 'Go away, all of you.'

Suddenly it seemed that I had got through to them. They chased off down the lane except for one, a tall thin lad, who gave a gasp and sank down at my feet unconscious. I pushed him, kicked and thumped him, but could not move him.

My son, who had come with his pals to watch the fun, said, 'It's Jon, he lives at the back of us.'

'Well, go and fetch his mother,' I told him. 'Tell her to come and take him home.' Eventually she arrived with a haughty expression on her face, pushed her son into the car, then turned and gave me such a dreadful look, I felt sure that she was convinced I had got all these kids drunk: 'That dreadful Cockney woman!'

It took years for me to live that down, but later I became friends with Jon's mum and we had many laughs about it. She was called Beryl and lived in a bungalow named Janton, but she now resides in Spain and we are still good friends.

The next day, poor Nicky and his inebriate mum left the little shack for Australia. She sat for quite a while in the lane, having no desire to leave the wooden shack where her children had been born and her husband had died. She was still drunk when they carted her away to that unknown land. It was unfortunately often the case with the woodland people, that a lot of secret drinking went on. They came to the woods to escape the world they lived in, all with something to hide, and sometimes it was easier to get through the long, gloomy, lonely winter with a bottle beside them.

And so the saga of these woodland people went on as it had done for years, ever since the philanthropic Lord Darnley had divided up his hunting lands among the First World War ex-servicemen. That eighty acres contained many strange folk and every week I discovered more of them, nearly all of them with something to hide. They lived in their own small world without the necessities of modern life: no electricity, no mains water and just a bucket for a loo; still they built their shacks and lived off the produce of their own bit of land, digging into the moist soil, planting flowers, growing vegetables, tending their chickens and geese, all protected by the immense wood that surrounded them.

I remember one disagreeable old man, whose name was Bill Taylor. He would march down the lane with a sort of perpetual smile on his face, but actually it looked more like a snarl when he bared his teeth under his long moustache. I would watch him from a distance, wondering whatever had induced him to hide up here all alone. Then I discovered a romantic story in connection with him.

His family were wealthy farmers and still owned a lot of the farmland, but he had fled up here with his love, a village girl they did not approve of. Bill and his sweetheart lived in a home-made shelter built of brushwood until he managed to build them a shack. The gamekeeper of the family estate had been sent by the family to chase them out but Bill had retaliated and fought to defend his patch. His sweetheart had died young, but Bill still kept the little old shack he had built for her, and he still carried a gun. Someone told me that he had buried his love in a secret place, but there is no proof of that, and in all my wanderings in the woods I never found a marked grave.

One day I received a visit from Bill. He came with his gun over his shoulder and a very sombre expression on his face.

'I come to shoot your squirrels, missus,' he said.

'Do what?' I said.

'Yes,' he nodded. 'I get one pound for every tail and I'll split it with you.'

Well, if he'd pounded me in the face I couldn't have been more surprised and I just stared at him open-mouthed.

'You've got squirrels down there, I've seen them,' he continued.

'Yes,' I said firmly, 'and they're going to stay there.'

'It's the law of the land,' he said. 'Not allowed to harbour squirrels – they're pests. I've got a gun and I'll shoot them.'

'If anyone's a pest, you are,' I said, 'so go away and leave my squirrels alone.'

So old Bill went down the lane and never came near the shack again. But this incident inspired me to write a poem about a squirrel:

The Squirrel

I woke this morning and what did I see?
A little grey squirrel, looking through the window
    at me,
I crept out of bed silently, but he had fled,
He was by the birdbath stealing their bread.
The robin was furious and told the world so,
He twittered and chattered on a branch that swung to
    and fro.

Someone was watching; the squirrel looked round,
Waved his bushy tail daintily and hopped to the
    ground.
Sparrows and bluetits came in a throng;
They had waited anxiously till the squirrel had gone.

Go, little squirrel, up comes the sun,
The farmer will be here soon with a gun.
Don't let them get you, you're so very sweet;
They call you vermin and their food stores you eat.

He paused in the middle of the green lawn;
His bright eyes had spied a little acorn.
He held it gently in his tiny paw –
'No, I won't eat it, I'll put it in store.'
As swift as the wind he went to the treetop high.

Stay there, little squirrel, up near the sky
and no one will hurt you, certainly not I.

There was one very compact little shack called Woodlands, which was surrounded by a beautiful garden; in
fact, it was the best garden of them all, with many shrub
roses, lots of rhododendrons lining the driveway, and
lovely trellises of blood-red climbing roses, which used
to catch my eye when I passed on my walks. There
were also lots of coconut shells dangling from the trees
– I was most curious about these. One day I eventually
met the inhabitants of this wonderful garden, Dorothy
and Fred, who later explained to me that the upturned
shells were there to give food for the bluetits. Often after
that I would go to watch those pretty blue and yellow
little birds. Fred loved his garden and he would sit for
hours watching the birds. Dorothy, his wife, was a very
good-looking woman, very alert and gossipy, but I liked
her immediately. Fred had been involved in an accident
and had a brain injury which left him unable to go to
work, so Dorothy went breezily off to bring home the
wages and never complained.

I have never known such a devoted couple. I would
often see her light on quite late in the night when her
Fred was having a bad time, but she never grumbled.
She would just cover up her sadness, clinging to the
solitude that these great trees provided, a place to
hide from the world, deep in the natural atmosphere
among the bluetits, the roses and the virginia creeper
that covered the walls. Now her Fred has passed on and
she still keeps her shack and looks after his lovely garden,
for I know he is still there in spirit, and I often think of
him, living in peace and harmony in this mysterious
woodland.

Chapter Eight

Carnival Time

As I cast a nostalgic glance through the years I see the tall elms on the opposite side of the lane which threw leafy shadows across the lane. How grateful we were for those trees during the long, hot summer days when we lay out on the lawn. Now those trees have disappeared, the first lot when we had an epidemic of elm blight, and the rest when they were cut down to build the road.

There were some compensations for modern progress, however. I remember what a difference it made to our lives when we were connected to the main water system in the Sixties, and no longer had to struggle down to the water tap at the end of the road. The question of water rights had caused some friction with our neighbours in the past. Prior to our connection to the main supply, a few of the inhabitants had paid for a private pipeline and asked us to pay towards the cost if we wanted access. However, Fred decided to go to the Water Board to see why we couldn't be connected to the water mains. 'I don't want to pay out if I can get it for nothing,' he argued.

When the Water Board willingly connected us to the mains, some of the neighbours took umbrage and accused us of stealing their water, not realising that now there was a public supply.

It was great to have clear running water to hand, so we had a field day. Fred rigged up a kind of impromptu shower, which consisted of an old bucket and a big tin bath. A rope was attached to the bucket and it was levered down into the bath, which was full of water, then pulled up high to the branch of the tree overhead and given a quick jerk, and the whole bucketful of cold water descended on you. We had a lot of fun with it until the day when the kids let the bucket down on a little boy's head, and we ended up with a yelling, screaming casualty who had to be taken to the local hospital to have his head wound stitched. After that episode the shower was dismantled.

That was the year in which Fred decided to build a boat. I was a little concerned, because we had by now, after a lot of hard work, managed to make Five Oaks quite habitable. We had electricity, piped water, and quite a collection of old furniture that various friends had bequeathed to us. 'Oh, would you like this nice old chair? It will come in handy for your country cottage,' one person said. Strange to relate, I seldom refused. I like old-fashioned furniture and still use some of it to this day.

When Fred ceased to work in the garden and spent hours poring over blueprints of a do-it-yourself plan for a boat, I was none too pleased and obstinately kept on planting vegetables, picking fruit and cutting down tall weeds, for one thing I was certain of: unless I kept on working this land, it would revert to wild woodland in no time, and I wasn't going to allow that to happen. Still, there was no way that I could deter Fred once he had set his mind on something. Every night when we were back in London he would go down the garden to the shed and often remain there till well after midnight. One of the neighbours dryly remarked, 'Have you thrown him out? Does he sleep in the shed?' I just ignored these sort of remarks, and after a few weeks Fred emerged triumphant, with his plans all drawn up for the super boat he was going to build.

In August of that year we set out on our annual holiday with lots of wood tied on top of the roof of the old van, because it was too big to go inside. As soon as we arrived, Fred began on his new project, much to my dismay. First of all he rigged up a huge platform in the middle of the garden, which was then immediately taken over by Angela and her friends. They sang and tap-danced on it all the long summer days; they dressed up and put on their own form of plays; and soon the front lawn was alive with kids of all ages.

Our Saturday drinks were not forthcoming that year, as Fred busily built himself another shed and was locked inside it, mysteriously working on his boat and allowing the kids to play merry hell. I can see Angela now, with a cushion tied to her bottom and wearing an old straw hat over her long, golden hair, singing in her lovely voice, 'The Deadwood stage is coming along the trail – whip crack away, whip crack away', performing Calamity Jane to such perfection that Fred gave her the nickname of Calamity Jane, and it went with her into maturity.

The kids and I would go to visit Maureen and Jim, as we found their company stimulating and relaxing. We would talk about politics and about life in the East End of London, and Jim and I would swap stories of our poverty-stricken childhoods over a glass or two of whisky. We had lots of laughs, and I grew very fond of them. In the meantime, Fred struggled on with his boat.

Finally one day the boat was pushed slowly out of the shed and erected on the platform, which was now clear of performers. It stood like some prehistoric monster, a huge wooden frame in my rose garden. I then named the boat *Noah's Ark*, and all the neighbours naturally came to view it and make humorous comments about it.

Fred said very solemnly, 'I can take that, but when this

is finished it's me that will be laughing, because I'll be able to flog it for a couple of hundred pounds and so far it has cost me very little.'

Well, that was our Fred, and we left him to his labours.

There had been a few rumours of a compulsory purchase order on Cliffe Woods, but the matter seemed to have been dropped, and we all went our merry way. We still had lots of weekend parties, often up at Blossoms, high up on top of the hill. Tricia's pretty sister Sandra was often there. I called Sandra the nymph, for there were always lots of young blades around her, but it was obvious there was no harm in her — she just liked to lark about.

Both Sandra and Tricia liked dressing up and each year they entered in the local carnival, which was held in August. That particular year it was to be in aid of the local hospital. Angela had gone off with the school on a continental holiday, and Keith and his pals were off on their bikes on a fishing trip, so things had quietened down a little, leaving me free to get involved with the festivities, and it was a hilarious experience. First of all there were weeks of boozy discussions on what to wear, how to dress the kids up, and how to acquire a lorry from the farmer.

After all this had been sorted out, we spent hectic afternoons making the costumes. I made most of the hats, as I was rather good at that, then came the Friday rehearsal before the big day.

I had decided to go as Granny Clampett, an imitation of the old lady in the TV series *The Beverly Hill-billies*. I knotted my hair on top of my head and wore a dress with a wide skirt and big boots, and I carried a big jar of hooch (actually home-made wine). With everything as authentic as possible, I felt I looked the part.

Overnight we had decorated the lorry with lots of coloured streamers and greenery. In the morning the lorry arrived at my gate and the driver hooted on the horn. Off I dashed down the path, while Jim got ready with the camera. Unfortunately, as I scrambled on to the lorry, I overbalanced and went toppling upside down, legs up, with the funny old boots in the air and revealing all, including my old-fashioned split drawers. Jim, of course, got it all on film and that provided many future Saturday night entertainments.

The carnival was a great success and all the kids got prizes; in fact, I think we swept the board, much to the chagrin of the villagers, who still considered the woodland people as outsiders.

Tricia was attired as Robinson Crusoe, and Sandra, wearing just a few leaves and with her lovely body covered with boot polish, was Man Friday. I believe she was very popular with the boys. The children looked beautiful. Kelly, Denise, Jimmy and Shaun were all dressed up as Bo-Peep and her lost lambs, while Maureen and Jim were dressed as Arabs on a magic carpet. Ella and Henna, our Polish friends, were also there. Ella made a fine Bessie Bunter, and Henna was dressed in a voluminous nightie, to represent Sleeping Beauty.

We all travelled on the lorry, passing round a bottle of wine among the grown-ups and singing 'Yellow Submarine', a popular number at that time.

The twins Tom and Rob were dressed up as small angels, with gold wings and paper crowns, but I am afraid they did not act the part. They created havoc on the float, fighting each other to get at the coins thrown by the onlookers. Alas for them, their father, Jim, tipped them upside down to shake the money out of their pockets and made them put every penny into the collection boxes.

All in all, a good time was had by us woodland

folk, who finished up in the beer tent to end the day's celebrations.

Summer gave way to autumn, and Kent was awash with trees full of apples and pears all ripe and ready for picking, but it was the ones on the ground we gathered, or rather the kids did, as it was easy for them. The blackberries had begun to ripen, and the golden corn was being harvested. I loved the autumn, when the land gave forth its fruits, and the hard work of the spring produced results. I picked large, juicy runner beans and big cabbages, and dug up floury potatoes. I was thrilled, because I had actually grown them all myself. I gave them to neighbours in London, along with large lettuces and lots of onions.

The dahlias were in full flower, and there were lots of late roses. The honeysuckle had now grown right over the roof of my small hut, secluding it from the rest of the world, and around me those great oaks stood majestically, like soldiers protecting me and my family and my little home.

I pestered Fred to apply for building permission so we could settle here, but he seemed always to be evasive, as if he was not too keen to leave London. 'Might not get a job down here,' he would say. 'Anyway, in the country you get less wages. I have a job, so we'll manage as it is.'

As always, I respected his wisdom, but inside I was a little disgruntled and felt sure there must be a way to sell our house in Wellington Road and build here.

I should have realised that I would not be able to get Fred interested in a house when he was still so preoccupied by his boat. Right through that summer until September, he had worked on the clumsy-looking frame, and I became more and more convinced that it would never be seaworthy. I vowed to myself that there was no way he would get me or my kids into it.

I stared at the huge frame of carefully joined wooden struts very apprehensively. 'It's very big,' I remarked.

'Won't look like that when I've skinned it and built a cabin on it,' declared Fred, very proud of his efforts – but I was never convinced.

As winter approached, Fred covered the boat up with a huge tarpaulin. The acorns littered the lawn, and I had made many jars of blackberry and apple jam and cut back the rose bushes, so my garden began once more to settle down to sleep. The biting wind blew in from the sea and my fingers got very chilled while I pottered about the garden in the early morning. I kissed my favourite oak tree goodbye and we returned home for the winter. I felt very tired that winter. It had been a good year and an exciting one; there had been lots of booze-ups and lots of new friends; my mind was full of events to write about in my journal; but above all I needed to rest.

So when Fred said in his cool, inimitable manner, 'You know, dear, if you got a full-time job, now the kids are off your hands, you could help me to buy an engine for the boat.' I stared at him aghast. How selfish and foolish can a man get?

'Go to hell,' I said. 'I never wanted a bloody boat. If you do, you pay for it.' Things got a little cool between us, but it soon passed off.

Fred's Noah's Ark never was completed and sat under that tarpaulin sheet for many years, a constant reminder to me of my sins and Fred's shattered dreams. In fact, it is still there, practically covered up by the tall grasses and the wild blackberry trails that have grown over it. The squirrels hide their winter stores under it, and mice and voles hold midnight feasts in it.

Chapter Nine

The Serpent Rears its Head (1960)

Many summers had passed since our first camping holiday in Kent, and the children were growing up fast.

Keith, at twelve years old, was tall with fine shoulders, his hair a mop of red curls and his freckled features brimming with good health and good humour. He was full of his own ideas about fishing and camping and had very little interest in school.

Angela had become very extrovert, with an avid interest in the activities of her boyfriends and a taste for dressing in very way-out styles. Those were the days of hippy flower power and Beatle mania. She managed to combine all these interests and still do quite well at school. Her hair had grown long and was a lovely strawberry blonde; she was slimmer and not quite so hard to get on with.

I had an inner dread of my children growing up and fleeing the cosy nest I had provided for them. Well, let's face it, I was and still am a very possessive mother.

That winter in London, while Angela went to discos and Keith to Scouts, I got myself an evening job to put some cash back into our kitty, which our nice long summer had depleted somewhat. I went to work at Lesneys, the toy factory, every evening from five-thirty in the afternoon till ten o'clock at night. The wages were good and the work comparatively easy, but it was nevertheless still hard graft. We worked on a line of toys on a continuously moving track, and it was my task to put four little wheels on the cars. We had to keep up with the moving band, otherwise it snagged the work. I used to get extremely tired and irritable, but I pressed on nevertheless. A friend, Madge, worked with me and our daughters kept each other company.

In some ways I've always regretted taking this job, because it meant that I neglected Angela's music lessons, and she eventually had to give them up. I am sure that Miss License, her music teacher, was glad to see the back of her because she must have been driven mad by Keith's practical jokes, such as knobbling her bike and putting rude notes under the door while Angela was having her lesson.

Fred began to come round to my idea of moving down to Kent and building our cosy bungalow. He would sit making drawings of our dream house, and he began to collect newspaper articles on how to build your own house. Eventually we submitted plans to the Council, asking their permission to build. I was devastated when we got a letter back, refusing permission. My dreams had been shattered.

We returned to Five Oaks early next spring with a little apprehension, not quite sure what the authorities were going to do with our lovely woodland. As we drove down the lane it was so cool, calm and green, and a feeling of peace came upon me. We entered through our gates and bunches of golden primroses welcomed us and a young thrush sang a sweet song. There was our little shack amid the tangled mass of honeysuckle, waiting to welcome us.

Soon the fire was lit and the kettle on, while the kids dashed off to find their friends. Fred and I stood in the doorway, and he put his arm around my shoulders. It was unusual for him to show affection and I had a comforting feeling that he knew I could not bear the thought of any sort of change to this peaceful scene.

'Oh well, love, we still got our old shack for another summer, so let's not cross our bridges till we come to them,' he said.

We put on our old clothes and got out in our garden. Fred dug into the moist earth, while I cleared the weeds. We were back where we belonged.

The neighbours came visiting in the afternoon and were surprised to hear that we had been refused building permission, and we all began to discuss the fact that the Council must have something up their sleeve.

'Well, you know what these devils are like – they just can't bear the thought of a working-class man owning two properties,' said Jim.

Maureen agreed: 'Oh, the rotten bastards, I won't let them get away with it. I'll protest and get up a petition.'

Pete joined in, 'Well, if they do put a compulsory purchase order on this land they'll have to compensate us all and rehouse us. This is our home, after all.'

Bert was a little wiser. 'I shouldn't get too alarmed if I was you. There has been talk of developing these woods for years – my old man used to talk about it when I was a boy – but nothing ever comes of it. Some say this is such soft clay soil that it is not suitable to build on.'

'Well,' remarked Fred, 'Bert could be right.'

Dot simpered and showed her teeth, 'Oh, I would like to have a nice bungalow built here. I'm fed up with that poky shack.'

'You will, dear.' Bert, her husband, cuddled her and comforted her. He was so loving and kind; he treated her as if she were precious porcelain and Dot thrived on it. I used to be amazed when I saw him trotting carefully over the lawn every morning, carrying a tray with her morning tea. He would pick a fresh rose and put it in a glass of water on the tray, then take it to her in bed.

After a long discussion on the subject of compulsory purchase, the woodland folk decided to dismiss the whole idea of changes and get on with having a good time. This we did to everyone's great satisfaction.

It was not until a couple of weekends later that I realised I had not seen the Polish folk. I missed the little old man in his woolly hat, going down to the community tap with his two buckets suspended from a makeshift frame on his shoulders. I also missed the big shape of Ella, striding down to visit me with her apron tucked up and a bright scarf tied around her head.

'Where are the Polishers?' I asked the children.

'Dunno. Henna won't come out, she said her mother won't let her,' declared Angela, riding off madly on her bike, her legs thin and long under those tight shorts she wore.

I did eventually catch Henna coming nonchalantly down the lane with a small bucket, going to get fresh water.

'Hullo, darling,' I greeted her but she did not smile, and her pale face remained very solemn.

'Don't your Dad get the water?' I asked.

She just shook her head. 'Mummy and Daddy are going to be divorced,' she said slowly and coldly, dry-eyed and not a tear in sight.

I could not believe my ears. 'Going to be what?' I cried.

'They are parting – breaking up their marriage,' returned Henna very precisely.

'Oh no! I can't believe it, whatever for? Shall I come up and see her?'

'Mother does not wish to see anyone, she is too upset,' replied Henna, and went off in a stately manner down to the water tap.

When I told Fred, he said, 'Mind your own business and don't go up there.'

I continued to think of that heavenly place where the Polish folk lived – it was such a lovely spot, like the garden of Eden, with its fruit and flowers – and wondered what had gone wrong. I recalled how Ella had told me tales of her life in the concentration camp and how happy they had been to get to England. I had to know why they were breaking up; it nagged at the back of my mind. I walked past her gate several times and called her name, but no big, lively Ella came to greet me with her lovely wide smile. The fierce Alsatian dog they owned barked madly, but still no one came. I was very disappointed.

I walked on to Blossoms to visit Tricia. As I entered through the long archway, which was already full of early roses, I saw the children playing on a swing, and the cat installed in a basket under the porch with her latest batch of kittens. Tricia was making cakes in her very smart kitchen, which Pete had designed and built himself. When I asked her about the Polish folk, she said in her usual sunny way, 'Come to think of it, I haven't seen either of them. Still, I was never keen on them and it don't surprise me, because that little man and her fight tooth and nail.'

Well, I was very disillusioned, having built up such a romantic idea of these Polishers. Later on I discovered the reason for the divorce: Mrs Polish had found out that she was bigamously married, and she wanted her husband out of her home. Poor little Polish was ashamed, the poor old sod slept on the floor.

That summer there was murder going on at White Lodge. The battle between Ella and 'mine devil', as she called him, had reached a climax and Henna sided with her mother. Having decided to dispose of him, Henna and Ella proceeded to make his life as miserable as possible. Determined to find out what it was all about and get to the root of this problem, I went to visit. They came to greet me, Ella looking very overbearing.

'What's worrying you, Ella?' I asked.

'Come in,' she said. 'It's him, it's mine devil – I want get rid of him, I chuck him out, he not go, so I put old sacks on floor, he sleep like dog that he is.'

'Why do you want to get rid of him?' I asked.

'I good woman, I not have man ever, he has wife in Poland, she send for him, she find him, he not tell me. I have this child, he made her bastard.' I looked at Henna. She had a strange smile on her face and I suspected she was thoroughly enjoying the situation.

'What will you do, Ella?'

'Me – I find new man, I get new boyfriend, look you come see.' She produced a cardboard box full of letters and photographs.

'You see I wrote to newspaper to say I want new husband.'

I stared in amazement at the pile of photographs with stony-looking faces. Ella had evidently advertised in the paper for a new husband and was determined to get rid of mine devil.

This saga went on all the summer, and every weekend she would have a new incident to tell me about. She would sit outside the hut with her leg propped up on a stool telling me her troubles. I am easy-going and would sit and chat with her, but Fred would look very displeased, and would say, 'I hope they're not parked there for the night' and 'What about a bleeding cup of tea?'

After Mr Polish finally moved out, Ella still insisted on getting a new husband and, much to the amazement of the shackdwellers, every Sunday afternoon a new admirer would come visiting. The men would turn up in their best suits with boxes of chocolates or flowers, and would come tearing back down the hill again after ten minutes. The kids would give the signal

as the man came down the lane, and we'd have a good
giggle.

One Sunday I was going along the lane when Jim Burns
pulled up with a pal of his. They were on their way back
from the pub and asked me if I wanted a lift, which I
accepted. When we got to the Polishes' house I said,
'Come in and see this lovely place.' But when we got
inside the plot, Ella and mine devil were having a battle
over a pitchfork he claimed belonged to him. He swore in
Polish and she swore back in Polish. Jim's pal, known for
his short temper, was unable to stand the strain and said,
'Don't you want him to have that fork, lady?' 'Ni, ni,'
she yelled. So he stepped forward, caught mine devil by
the scruff of the neck, marched him to the gate and threw
him in the road. Mine devil went hopping and skipping
down the road and has never been seen since. Ella got her
pitchfork back thanks to 'that Teddy Boy from London',
as she called him.

The orchard opposite our land flourished and clouds of
pink apple blossom sent a wondrous fragrance drifting
out on to the air. The bluebells covered the glades with
a lovely azure carpet, and the children picked them then
left them lying around. This used to upset me and I spent
lots of time collecting the drooping flowers and putting
them into water in vases and jars, until my little hut was
overcrowded with refreshing blooms.

It was also a time for rescuing the young birds as they
haphazardly staggered over the lawn in their attempts
to fly. I always had a box or two of these little birds
recuperating in the hut from near misses with the cats,
and I got very upset if they died.

There was plenty to do, because we now had our own
soft fruits, blackcurrants and gooseberries. I began to try
my hand at making jam but was not always successful,
for that year we were overrun with wasps. I hated wasps
– beetles, spiders and even worms I did not mind – but I

loathed wasps. As I put my first lot of jam into a large pot, the wasps swooped down and I got nervous. I almost ran across the lawn with the pot of jam to escape them and fell down on to the path, breaking my nice potful of plum jam. The wasps descended on the spilt jam like dive-bombers, while I sat there crying and swearing loudly with sheer frustration.

Fred came over and lugged me to my feet, but then could not stop laughing at me. He did eventually conceive a way of trapping these wasps by putting down empty jam jars with just a smear of jam and water in the bottom outside the shack. Some weekends we had several jars full of wasps, but once the plum harvest was over the wasps abated.

I was beginning to learn the harsher side of nature – it was not all romance, but was often a little repulsive. That year the rabbits began to develop myxomatosis, and I would find the poor creatures as they lay dying with froth on their mouths and their eyes bulging almost out of their heads. Fred would remove them with a pitchfork and toss them on to the bonfire. 'Who wants roast rabbit?' he would jest, but I felt sick – I could not face this awful destruction of life.

Things had begun to go a little askew in our lovely woodland; the serpent had begun to rear its head.

Chapter Ten

The Big 'Ole

As we emerged into the Sixties I had an apprehensive feeling of change in the air. The children were now well into their teens and becoming harder to cope with each day, especially because of the constant fighting between them. When they were small and did not get on well together it was a different matter – I could slap their bottoms and put them to bed – but now I had two teenagers, whose vengeful battles devastated me. Fred was such a mild and kind father that I protected him and hid from him the various troubled days they gave me.

Angela had grown tall and very lovely, but she was wilful and had reached an age when she wanted to put on make-up and go out with boys. She had a circle of girlfriends with the same ideas.

Keith, however, was still a home-loving boy and liked his hobbies of fishing and dismantling bikes. His room was a mess, littered with old clocks and wireless sets, but he was a happy boy and no trouble – except when he squabbled with his sister.

That winter back in London I tried to cope. I got a part-time job at the toy factory and spent my earnings on the kids – pretty, smart clothes for Angela and various expensive things for Keith's hobbies. Yet still they fought tooth and nail, and often I was at my wits' end as to how to deal with them. My nerves seemed to be going to pot, so I was not sorry when the spring came and we began to prepare for our treks back to the woods at the weekends.

That spring Angela left school and got a very nice job in a West End office and immediately made a success of it – I was quite proud of her. But she also became a rebel, insisting that she would not go with us to 'those crummy woods at the weekends, to that boring place among all those young kids' as she expressed it.

I was anxious not to give in to her, and every Saturday there was a battle of wills, with me insisting that she came with us and Angela equally determined not to go. In the end I gave in and left her to stay at home with her friends, but I worried about her most of the time I was away from her. After all, she was only fifteen and not very mature. I got nightmares thinking of what might possibly happen to her.

Fred and Keith were quite impatient with me because of my worries and went on with their own things, Keith to his fishing with his friends, and Fred to uprooting my lovely trees. He insisted that there was not enough light coming into the garden and shack, and that nothing would grow properly. He declared that bad light forced the vegetables up, making them tall and spindly. I argued, but once more gave in and the lovely trees by the gate came crashing down and lay there, roots exposed and drying in the hot sun, and as I looked at them they seemed to me to be gasping for breath and water. I know I was becoming very emotional about it all, but I could not help myself. I would go to the other end of the plot amid the tangle of tall trees and the wild undergrowth which had as yet not been touched, and I would say a little prayer for the protection of my family and apologise to Mother Nature for the ill-treatment of her children, the tall, willowy trees which had been pulled down. This part of the garden became my own church, and still is. As I enter it by the winding little path where the trees meet overhead, a deep silence reigns and it is like entering a great cathedral. Voices seem to whisper to me, and I feel at peace with the world.

Fred did a lot of work that year. He dug a big hole, having cleared the row of trees, then he proceeded to dig out the remaining roots. One great old oak was so firmly entrenched in the ground that he dug and dug, sweat pouring from his brow, he was so determined not to be beaten. That particular hole got deeper and deeper; every spare moment Fred had was spent down there with his spade while I trotted back and forth with endless cups of tea, begging him to give up. Still he would not admit defeat.

'Where's Dad?' I asked Keith when I could not see Fred.

'Down 'ees 'ole,' came the cheery reply.

When visitors came by they asked, 'Where's your husband?' and got the same reply from me, 'Down 'ees 'ole.'

It was not long before I began to realise that this was Fred's escape hole. He would dive into this man-made crater as soon as a car drew up at the gate, indicating that we had Sunday afternoon visitors. At that time we had lots of relatives and friends dropping in on Sunday afternoons while they were having a drive out of town on fine days.

Fred loathed 'droppers-in' and would not even come up out of the hole to meet them. They would look down the hole and he would hold a gruff sort of conversation with them, until eventually they would go on their way.

'Oh dear, Fred,' I would remonstrate, 'why do you do that? It makes me feel awful.'

'I never invited them, did you?' he would ask dryly.

'No, but I was brought up to be hospitable. I can't help myself, I have to make them welcome.'

'That's up to you,' replied Fred, 'but I come down here to work, not to entertain, and I let them know it.'

'Oh well,' I would sigh, 'can't win all the time.'

My most constant 'poppers-in' were the Polishers. They came, big and ponderous, wearing their rather garish outfits that they made themselves from patterns taken from various magazines and newspapers. I must admit that they were both marvellous needlewomen, but they always wore the same style of dress. To see the slim, tall Henna in an ultra-modern designed dress was a treat, but to see her mother in an identical outfit was quite a shock, as she was a very wide and sturdy female and the stylish dresses looked decidedly out of place on her. I was fond of them and always made them welcome, but Fred would disappear down his hole at the sight of them bearing down on us.

Ella would plonk herself down in a chair all the afternoon, while Henna would sit beside her mother, not daring to move.

'Why don't you go and play, dear?' I'd ask her.

'No thank you,' she would say very precisely, and sit like a statue the whole afternoon.

They usually came on bright Sunday afternoons when I would have loved to be working in the garden, but still, these were my woodland friends and I could not desert them.

One day we received another afternoon visit, this time a rather unfortunate one.

I had made the acquaintance of a very nice smart woman and her husband in the village pub. They were Londoners and had settled down in Kent a good few years before. They had a nice cottage and two well-bred cream-coloured poodles.

Since I had been taken to view their nice cottage, I

thought I would return the compliment saying, 'Any time you are up near the woods, just drop in.'

On the afternoon in question they took me at my word and called on me. It was just after Sunday lunch, and I was untidy and harassed, having got Keith and his two pals a meal. They had been fishing all night at Dover pier, and now they sat out on the back steps, gutting about fifty mackerel they had caught overnight.

I looked with apprehension at all the fish scattered about, and more so at the buckets of fish guts. Keith and his pals were having the time of their lives.

'Oh my God! What are you going to do with all those fish?' I cried with alarm.

'Sell them,' they said, with all the confidence of youth. 'That's why we're gutting them – they'll be better for freezing when we get back to London.'

In spite of the horrible stench that clung around them, they had eaten a hearty meal. Now they were about to make off with the fish and leave the buckets of guts.

'Don't leave that stuff there,' I yelled. 'The bluebottles will come all over them; the smell is awful.'

'Go and bury it down at the back, there's good boys,' said Fred from behind the *News of the World*.

Off they disappeared with the smelly buckets.

At that moment, a posh car drew up outside the gate and a lady in a well-tailored white suit got out. I noted her grand hair-do as she emerged with her little poodles.

Fred, as usual, dashed for his bolt hole. I invited her in for a cup of tea, then had to apologise for the littered table and the fish scales all over the step.

The lady unleashed her poodles and off they dashed, but they were soon back. I never did get that tea poured out, because those little dogs had been rolling in the fish guts. Keith and his pals had just thrown the smelly guts on the ground and never even bothered to cover them up. The little dogs were covered from head to tail in the smelly mess, and now they tried to jump up on their mistress's lap – on her lovely, expensive white suit. Pandemonium broke out as I tried to catch the dogs as they dashed hither and thither about the shack. They jumped up and gambolled about, then finally ended up in an armchair.

That poor woman almost fainted with the shock and the smell of it all. We did eventually manage to call the dogs in and bathe them, and I loaned the lady a skirt while we washed her own. In spite of squirting the place and the dogs with air freshner, after we had washed them in a solution of Dettol, the stink was still horrible and lingered in the shack for weeks. That lady never did call again; in fact, that incident was a distinct blow to my social life, as all the village got to know about it.

While all this was going on Fred remained down his hole, and I expect he was grinning to himself.

The following year we decided to have a change and go somewhere else for our annual holiday.

'Let's have a change,' said Fred. 'Might look for another place – Cliffe Woods is getting too over-populated to suit me.'

I was a little forlorn at not going to my woods, but seeing that Keith was such an ardent fisherman, we went down to Westby in Dorset, leaving Angela to play merry hell in London.

I sat beside Fred and Keith on the harbour wall, watching as they fished, and dreaming all the time of my cool green woodlands and hearing in a dreamlike state the song of the thrush in the morning instead of the screech of those noisy gulls. I longed for a quiet spot to sit and write down my thoughts, but so far I had not had the time.

Chapter Eleven

Chasing Rainbows

I went out into the garden early this morning. It was green and moist from the overnight rain, and the hills rose up to the horizon, seeming to hold up the black stormclouds. A lovely rainbow arced over the sky, its deep curve full of glowing colours, and suddenly the sun shone through. I held my breath, absorbing the deep silence that one gets in the country away from the roar of the London traffic. My whole being was concentrated on searching for the mythical rainbow's end, and the rest of my life stretched out before me like an open field. In my youth I was always chasing rainbows and never did find the elusive pot of gold, yet here, in this piece of Kentish woodland, I had found a kind of peace and I wanted to end my life here.

In my mind's eye I visualised the lovely house I would have built and surrounded it with a beautiful garden for my children and my children's children, who would visit me, as I sat reclining in my rocking chair. This dream has gone with me through the years, but it has never been achieved. It seems constantly to fade further and further away, and I find myself recalling that time in the Sixties when I almost lost my lovely piece of woodland.

I remember the spring when we arrived to discover that the compulsory purchase order we had all feared had finally been served on eighty acres of our lovely woodland. The intention of the Council, it seemed, was to build small modern houses all the way over my lovely green hill – little boxes, no doubt, filled with town-dwellers who would desecrate our woods, ruin the lovely orchards and kill off our wildlife – it was too horrible even to think about.

That first Sunday morning I took a walk with old Peter, who was now getting on in years. His tongue lolled out as he scrambled into the thick undergrowth, then he seemed to get his second wind as he wildly chased the old striped badger who had always lurked about there. The bluebell glades were thick with flowers, and the air was like wine. The huge trees were just coming into bud and swayed in the breeze, whispering and rustling as if to warn me their time had come. I sat on a big fallen oak tree and racked my mind for a means to stop this terrifying thing that was about to overtake us all. A hymn came to mind as I watched a lonely gull flying high in the sky towards the sea: 'Fight the good fight with all thy might, raise up thine eyes and see the light.' I looked at that blue sky and out towards the river, a long silver strip in the hazy distance, and suddenly I knew I would stand and fight. I went home to cook breakfast, much lighter of heart.

Keith had stayed overnight with his pals and, after a hearty breakfast, they went off together fishing.

Fred dug over the vegetable patch, remarking in his gloomy way, 'Don't know why I'm bothering. The bloody Council is going to have this place as sure as eggs is eggs.'

'Oh, don't be such a bloody old misery,' I told him. 'We don't have to just sit down and accept it, we can fight if we get together.'

'Don't be so silly,' argued Fred. 'They're going to make a million pounds off this deal, that's why they wouldn't give me that building permission. They'll buy it cheap as green-belt land, then sell it again as building land and make a huge profit.'

This I did not dispute because I have no head for business, but the thought of my fine oaks and elms being devastated really brought the blood boiling in me. I felt almost murderous at the idea.

That Sunday all the woodland folk were in and out of my shack, Jim and Maureen, Pete and Tricia and the Polishers, all with the same tale of woe.

Where would they go? What would they do? How much money would they get? Would they get enough money to buy another house? The questions were asked repeatedly and we drank gallons of tea. I had my wood stove alight, and the big old enamel teapot was filled and emptied several times that day.

Jim was all for getting us all organised into one big fighting body.

Peter thought it would be better to get legal aid.

Mrs Polisher declared that no way would she be driven from her home – had not the Nazis persecuted her and driven her from her homeland? Never again would she allow anyone to push her out of her home.

So it went on all that nice spring. Fred wisely stayed out of the way, but all the time I was preparing a plan to go into battle. My first step would be to go and see the Council officer and find out exactly what their plans were for this part of our precious woodland, and how much land was involved. Mrs Polisher decided immediately that she would go with me but I was hoping she would not.

I had many hard words with Fred over this planned visit of mine to see the Council officer. He said, trying to put me off, 'You're wasting your time. Once a government body agrees to a compulsory order you can kiss that land goodbye – might get about enough out of it to buy a caravan, but that's all.'

But I would not be deterred and arranged an appointment with the planning officer. When the day came, I dressed myself up nicely for battle, then travelled by train to Strood, where I was met at the station by Ella, so big and flamboyant, and tall, languid Henna.

When we arrived at the Council building, we were conducted to a well-furnished office where we met two well-dressed men. All was going well and quite smoothly, until Mrs Polisher suddenly burst into a tirade in broken English about her rights and about how wrong it was for them to push her out of her home.

'Me poor woman, mine husband he go, me live on welfare, no place to go – me in big concentration camp.' She then burst into floods of tears, which flowed down her fat cheeks, and I knew by the looks of scorn on those well-bred faces that we were barking up the wrong tree.

Calmly they quietened Ella and then produced a map of the area, making us point out the parts we owned. I was interested to see that the man marked the map to indicate where we lived, and that we were the only ones so far shown there. I felt sure he knew very little about our woods and had no idea who lived there.

Then the rather nice man who had introduced himself as Mr Gardiner informed me, 'We're going to make a garden village of that area there,' pointing with his pen, 'with a through road plus shops and a school. It will be very nice when it's finished and you can all go back to live there.'

I was not convinced, ignoring Ella who still sat weeping a hail of tears. Mr Gardiner was a little nervous and lit one cigarette after another and continually mopped the sweat from his brow. 'You know, Mrs Smith,' he said, 'you're sitting on a gold mine with your piece of land.'

'Yes, but whose gold mine?' I asked. 'What price are we going to get for our land?'

'That is under discussion, but if you will co-operate with us we will certainly compensate you and all the others.'

So I was right: they had no idea what went on in our woodlands with their narrow, winding paths; the small shacks that had sprung up everywhere were all adding to their difficulty in completing their plans.

'You must understand that we must clearly prevent it from becoming a shanty town,' broke in the other man.

That was when I began to get angry. 'It is in no way becoming a shanty town,' I protested. 'There's a very nice close community up there. The shacks are well built and are taken good care of, and most of us spend only weekends and holidays there.'

'Yes, I agree, but some do live there permanently and rates are not being paid; people are squatting on land that does not belong to them.'

I knew he had a point there but decided not to make any comment. Instead, I continued, 'Why not let us build our own houses?'

'That is not possible – as you must know, most of the folk are old and could not afford to build their own houses.'

'I have a house in London, as many others do, which would cover the expense of building anything here.'

He looked concerned, not expecting so much opposition, so I added, 'I love those woods, and I have no intention of letting you destroy them. What about the wildlife and all those lovely old oak trees? I'll call in the conservation people; I'll find some way to stop you.'

They conversed with each other for a moment, then, 'May we have your London address?'

'If you want – certainly.'

While one of them wrote down the address, Ella went off into another tirade on how she had chucked out her no-good husband and was now forced to live on the state, and how her main livelihood was there in the woods.

At the end of this long tale of woe of Ella's we were discreetly ushered out of the office.

When I returned to London Fred said, 'Now that was a bloody waste of time – didn't I tell you it would be?' But somewhere in my mind was the satisfaction that I had made my point and had my say.

The next week the men at the Council asked me to call and see them once more. This time I got a lot of flannel – apparently poor old Mr Gardiner had had a bad time with the old boys in the woods when he prowled about trying to interview them. Of course, this pleased me very much.

I was given coffee and cigarettes and lots of cosy chat.

'Oh dear, Mrs Smith, I'm dreading that I'll be lynched in those woods one day – those old chaps are demons and they're determined to hang on to their bit of land.'

'Well, wouldn't you be?' I asked. 'Most of them came to live in the woods around 1919, at the end of the First World War. Lord Darnley bequeathed the land to wounded soldiers as long as they cultivated it, which is what they have done.'

'Hmm, I see you have been doing your history,' he replied, with a supercilious air.

'Well, why not? I'm very interested in this part of Kent.'

'Look here,' he softened his mood, 'to be quite frank with you, we haven't the faintest idea what is going on in these woods.

'We can see you're an intelligent woman and fairly comfortably off, the kind we'll be needing when we build our garden village. Incidentally, we have decided to keep its rural beauty,' he opened up a big map on the table, 'so perhaps you'll give me some idea if this map is correct, as it's only a rough guide to who does own land up there.' Casually I surveyed the map and there was our woodland all laid out before me with most of the little shacks marked out and ringed by a red line. 'Before we actually send it to the government department I would like to check it with you.'

I watched him trace a thin line with a pencil. 'This is the part we need. Those brick bungalows at the end of the lane by the main road will, of course, remain there. We intend to take a road through, so all this will have to go.'

I watched as he carefully traced a line which went right past my shack, not through it. 'It looks all right to me,' I said, trying not to grin to myself because he had left my place out, 'but you won't get away with it – they've all decided to fight you.'

He smiled. 'It won't do them any good once this compulsory purchase order goes through, but I must thank you for your cooperation, Mrs Smith.'

All that season there was chaos in our little woodland community. Some folk panicked and sold out right away. Most of them ended up in the old folk's home in the village – it was quite a blow to those grand old men who had tilled the ground for so long. Others formed a fighting band and appealed to the law, but most were then picked off one by one and got very little out of it.

I felt sorry for Pete and Tricia, who had three children and were very happy on the hill at Blossoms – the amount they were being offered would never buy them another house, and Pete had put such a lot of work into that place.

As time marched on everyone began to get very depressed, though Jim was still fighting fit, calling in the aid of the Communist Party to try to right the wrongs being done by our capitalist society. Maureen would get on her soapbox on Saturday nights and lay down the law about money-grabbing Councils not wanting working people to have a weekend place. 'They can 'ave their bleeding castles,' she would say, 'but if the working classes want two homes they quibble and are down on them like a ton of bricks.'

We had a public enquiry, which was a terrible farce. The old judge seemed to be half asleep and nobody was surprised at the outcome – I did not like it one bit.

I would sit brooding about it all. So far they had not made us an offer, but had I been right to think that we would be spared? Or had Mr Gardiner drawn the line in the wrong place? I crossed my fingers and hoped for the best.

Chapter Twelve

Compulsory Purchase (1963)

The winter of '63 in London brought the official letter which stated that the compulsory purchase order had gone through and that from a certain date eighty acres of woods at Cliffe Woods would belong to the government.

This made me feel so unhappy, I telephoned Maureen straight away. Her reply was, 'Well, I don't know what you're making a fuss about – you're well out of it, so are Mrs Roberts, Dot and Bert, but we have to go.'

I could not believe my ears. Had I been right about the wavy line I had seen on the map? Was it genuine? We went to Rochester town hall to find out the truth about this unhappy affair. Lo and behold, there was a map on the wall with all the boundaries marked clearly and a statement to the effect that the Compulsory Purchase Order of eighty acres of Cliffe Woods had been passed – but we were outside the boundary.

It was over the moon, but Fred was a little moody about it all: 'Might as well let them have it – don't want to spend my weekends on a bloody council estate.'

For the first time my lovely woodland world was badly disturbed. There was a big newspaper article about the terrible shanty town in the woods, where there were no proper toilets, no running water and old people lived in dire misery, which was of course all lies.

I wept for my woods being treated like a shy maiden, her garment torn away for all the world to see.

Fred looked around for another weekend place, while I stayed in London, not going to the woods at the weekends any more.

Angela suddenly got the travel bug and went off to work in a hotel in Switzerland. She was now seventeen. Keith made a new friend in London called Chris, who owned an old motorbike, and they would go off on their own, returning a few days later, broke, cold and hungry.

We once more returned to our woodlands and I was now free to stand and stare, and then to write – about the marshes, the windblown land and its wonderful bird life: the lovely moorhens who waded along the shoreline, and the black and white geese who migrated from another shore to greet the sun on our marshland. But it was a sad year for me: I missed Angela, and Fred got very moody, doing very little in the garden except to cut the grass and having very little to say.

Each week we would find that another little shack had gone up on the hill, bulldozed into rubble, but in spite of it all we kept up our Saturday night parties. The party to end all parties was with Maureen and Jim. They had at last found another place to live, at Herne Bay. The compensation for their home and piece of land had initially been very small, but Jim had fought hard and kept on fighting till he got a suitable amount, and he then bought a piece of land to put a caravan on prior to building a home.

We held the farewell party for them on our lawn, and several of the flat-dwellers in Bow came down from London to help Maureen and Jim on their way. I did my best to help, but it was chaos. All the food was laid out, buffet-style, in a ridge tent that I had hired for the occasion. There were too many of us to get into the hut and it rained cats and dogs, so all the adults went down to a pub called the Sarsaparilla and finished the merriment there. The old people at the pub had never seen such a rowdy crowd, but a good time was had by all and the country folk are still talking about it.

Pete and Tricia were the next ones to go, off to Australia. I was so sad to see them leave, but I still keep in touch with them.

Ella and Henna, my Polish friends, also went to Australia. One Sunday in June, I saw a taxi going up the lane, which was very unusual. Going down to the front gate I looked up the road and saw Ella and Henna, all dressed up, getting into a cab. The taxi stopped outside my gate and, to my amazement, they explained that they were off to Australia. I could not believe it. Poor old Ella looked very sad but Henna looked like she'd just found a pot of gold. She'd grown into a beautiful young lady and her green eyes were positively glowing as she told me they had said goodbye to the shacks forever. Well, with money, looks and lots of opportunity she would go a long way, but I worried for poor old Ella. I was glad that her years of hard work had now paid off, and I knew I would never forget my dear friend.

Later I walked up to see their place. It was heart-breaking to behold. They had smashed everything they couldn't take with them, and sawn down all the fruit trees and rose bushes. The earth was scorched with the remains of fires and it reminded me of the end of the world: desolate, empty, scorched earth.

So came the end of the woodland community. The last one to go was a Welsh woman, who clung to her family home where she lived with her grandchildren and lots of cats. She insisted that she would not leave, so they came and evicted her. I saw her going down the lane, head high and holding her grandchild's hand, with the rest of the family meandering slowly ahead of her. Just like Lot's wife, she looked back, and her little grandchild waved her hand, saying goodbye to Granny's shack.

We carried on with our visits till the end of the season, but I knew that next year would not be the same, as so many changes had taken place in our woods.

Chapter Thirteen

Summer's End

Another spring came round. It had been a long hard winter and I had not been my usual robust self.

Fred was a little disgruntled because we could not agree to sell Five Oaks. There was no way I would give in – I can be very obstinate when I choose – and though Fred will never go against me, he does get very grumbly.

'I've broken my back pulling out those big trees, spent the last year slaving away every weekend, and to what purpose? So that the bloody Council can come and pinch the land off us.'

'Look, dear, we're very lucky to be left out of the Compulsory Purchase. We might get building permission now, and then you can build me that modern bungalow.'

'Have it your own way,' he grumbled, 'but I'm looking for a holiday place in Devon next year.'

Angela had gone off on her travels once more, packing her little haversack and leaving with two friends for a hitchhiking holiday on the continent. The very idea of her hitchhiking in a strange country terrified me and gave me endless nightmares.

Keith, still the home-loving boy, had started work in a garage and still stuck to his old school chum Chris.

Fred and I, plus the old dog Peter, went down to Kent at Easter to see what devastation had been wrought in our woodland in our absence. At the top of the hill a huge oak lay dying, seeming to me to give out long gasps of despair at the cruelty being enacted. Everywhere we looked there were piles of rubble where there had once been a shack. It was indeed a heartbreaking sight.

There was no broad-hipped Ella standing grinning at the gate, and Blossoms – oh, the lovely Blossoms was gone, and the beautiful rose arch we had walked under to the warm, friendly little shack had disappeared. It was lonely and forlorn, half demolished and left open to the sky, with just one tall tree left to mark the spot. I shed bitter tears and went around picking up little scraps from the debris. Dunroaming was as silent as the grave. I found a tiny coffee jug which had been Ella's, and a little boxing glove which had belonged to one of the twins.

I got Fred, Keith and his pal to bring down the birdbath that Pete had made, and installed it in my garden. It is still there today, and when Pete and Tricia came visiting ten years later they were overjoyed to watch the robin, bluetits and little chaffinches coming to drink there – it brought back so many memories for them to take back to Australia.

Fred had lost heart, and would walk aimlessly around the garden, hands in pockets, but I went on pulling up little weeds persistently and making additions to my rockery. Wood violets, primroses and daffodils had sprung up all over the place, and I began to sow lots of seeds I had collected the year before. All the cherry trees were in bloom, and I read my favourite poem to cheer me up: 'To the woodlands I will go, to see the cherry hung with snow'.

One day Mr Gardiner came and offered me a price for my plot. 'It's lovely here, he said. 'I would like to build a place myself on this very spot.'

'Not on your nelly,' I told him a little abrasively. 'This

is the spot where I will live and die, and no one will get my land while I am living.'

Mr Gardiner finally managed to get a plot of land further up the hill, where he built a bungalow, but alas did not live long enough to enjoy it.

Next door Bert and Dot still came down at weekends. Bert loved his garden and Dorothy loved lying in the sun and being waited on. At lunch-time they would bring over a bottle of sherry and we would sit in the shade of the big oak and drink and laugh, remembering the happy parties and the funny woodland folk.

They also had plans for the future. 'We will now get building rights, I believe,' said Bert.

'My Bert is going to build me a nice big bungalow,' boasted Dorothy.

I was annoyed at this, thinking of how I had said to Fred, 'Why don't you apply for building permission again? We could move and live down here.' As usual he put up a barrage of excuses, but a little ray of hope glowed within me now that Bert was going to build, thinking that perhaps in the end Fred would follow suit. Sadly, he never did.

Summer slowly passed into autumn, and our woodland continued to flourish. Fred picked rosehips and blackberries, and started once more to make home-brewed wine, while I picked vegetables and enjoyed the solitude.

Yet there was change going on all around us. They had started to build the new estate and put in a road. Later on they widened the road, and this meant pulling up our front lawn. We stayed away for three weeks while this was going on, but eventually decided to go and inspect the damage.

I was disappointed on Saturday when it rained the proverbial cats and dogs. Fred didn't want to go to Cliffe because of the weather. He mumbled and grumbled and talked to the dogs instead of me ('Don't want to go, do you Sandy? Nasty and damp down there') but I ignored his comments and went on with the packing. For some reason he felt the damp woodlands would do him more harm than good, and complained that it wasn't the same at Cliffe since they started to build the new estate 'with all those council houses and any Tom, Dick or Harry can live there with his kids – it will be completely spoilt now'. Eventually for the sake of peace and quiet I ground to a halt. But on Sunday at 6 o'clock I peeped carefully out of the window – no rain – and I was out of bed like a rocket, with breakfast on the table and all packed and ready by eight, and Fred knew nothing would deter me.

As we made our way out of London I looked out at the pale, wintery sun shining silver in the sky, chased by blue rainclouds. I was feeling apprehensive, wondering what they had done to my woods in my absence. When we arrived we managed to get on to the new strip of road that they were still working on. It seemed to make my little hut look buried and desolate, but there was still our own little wood to protect it.

The wind was cold but still the golden brown leaves floated in the gentle breeze. It touched my heart to see the orchard opposite lined with tractors and lorries, and the old, gnarled trees stretching across the new road with the large Kent apples rotting at their side.

I went out in the garden to trim the hedge of wild rose and cut a bunch of rosehips, putting them in a jar in the kitchen, glowing red and warm orange and giving a promise of winter. Soon the snow would cover my roses, and the little red robin would seek the scattered rosehips. A little poem had been going around in my head while I was in the garden and I felt an urgent need to put pen to paper, so I sat in the shack by the French windows, watching the birds, and wrote it down:

The Ballad of Tessa

So plump and so shiny she preened her plumage of
  nut-brown;
On a branch on the plum tree she pranced up and
  down;
To the window she looked most of the time
To observe the family as they sat down to dine.

Woe betide an intruder who dared muscle in –
Thrush, bluetit or robin, even that big wood pigeon –
They were all scared of Tessa as she pounced on
  the wing.
This was her territory, this was her patch;
No other bird her crumbs could snatch.

Through all the four seasons Tessa stayed put
In her nest in the honeysuckle, in the eaves of
  our hut.
When a small fledgling, she had been caught by
  our cat
Who damaged her tail feather and left her dying on
  the mat.
I made her better, then set her free
But Tessa was content to stay on in the plum tree.

She grew so beautiful, all shiny light brown,
Her new tail feathers so long they swept the ground.
For many years she was part of our scene;
We loved to watch her patter across the lawn so
  green.
In winter she braved the snow and the cold,
Welcoming us with spring songs so happy and bold.

Last year when the plum tree laid its carpet of
  golden brown
We said *au revoir* little Tessa, we are returning to
  town.
The silver frost spread over the green lawn,

The oak trees were sleeping until spring would be
  born.

In spring the robin came hopping to the sill,
But no sign of Tessa: all was silent and still.
When we found her cold and forlorn, we saw
The brave heart from her breast had been torn,
For the new development had come to our patch,
Brought all kinds of enemies, including well-fed
  cats,
Who savaged our lovely, beautiful Tessa
Who was so wild and free and left us only a sad
  memory.
Goodbye our brave Tessa, we will not forget thee,
Our lovely tame blackbird who swung on the plum
  tree.

Later I went to visit my friend Beryl in her new
bungalow called Janton that was still being built. She
was full of gossip about the new people on the estate
and her trip to the town hall to protest about the new
road; the people of the woods were all opposed, but
they could not stop them from taking a strip of our
land. Beryl is one of my oldest friends in the woods.
She is good for me, because she won't let me feel sorry
for myself. We both knew this was only the beginning
of the great change to our woodlands, but we enjoyed
ourselves, reminiscing about the old days in the woods
that kept our children safe; in those winding, unkempt
lanes a stranger would soon be spotted, and you could
let your kids roam free, something you could not do in
the town. She showed me around her bungalow and cut
me a lovely bunch of late summer roses to take home
with me.

During the years that followed there was a lot of
disruption in our woods and we had to say goodbye
to a lot of our friends.

One year I began a garden of memories. It might seem a macabre idea to name my flowers after all my friends and relations, but it is my way of remembering them. For Pete and Tricia, Kelly and Shaun I planted a lovely pale-pink rose. I also planted a rose for Fred's brother, who had died; it was called 'Uncle Walter' and was a deep scarlet. Some years later, I heard the tragic news that Maureen and Jim's daughter Denny had been killed in a car accident. She was only seventeen, but already she had devoted herself to working for the housing charity, Shelter. That summer I planted a yellow rose for Denny called Liberty Bell, and on warm summer evenings when the scent of the rose pervades the air, I think of her as a child, climbing in the tree-house that Jim made at Dunroaming and dancing with us on the lawn under the night sky. I carried on buying roses for every little patch I cultivated – it was my way of keeping my memories alive.

Slowly Fred and I settled back into our life in the woods once again. It was usually just the two of us at the shack, as the kids had their own ideas on how to spend weekends, but we slowly made new friends and became relaxed and happy again. We started to visit the club at Cliffe village – it was great fun and the people were so friendly.

As I neared fifty, I lost my slim figure and started to slop around in old slacks and jumpers and my old shoes, but I was still reasonably healthy and happy.

Angela went off to Spain to work and after she returned she got back together with her first boyfriend, Alan. I wasn't happy about it for they were like chalk and cheese. Although he came from an East End family, his background seemed completely different from hers. Angela had been brought up in a close family, had gone to a Roman Catholic school, and now had a good job typing in an office. I couldn't understand why she wouldn't stick to her own circle, but I knew by the gleam in her blue eyes that he was the one for her. They were only seventeen, but you couldn't get through to Angela once she had made up her mind about something.

I moped about and my friends worried about me, saying I was getting very neurotic. Fred lost his temper with me and said, 'Pull yourself together! Leave her alone and she'll soon get fed up.'

So we went off to the woods to let her get on with what she wanted to do, but my guess had been right, and love blossomed as does the fruit on the trees.

I was worried about Keith, too. He had ditched his job and said he wanted to be his own boss – he just seemed unable to settle.

I started scribbling again, this time short stories. While the girls in the factory shouted their heads off across the track, I put down on paper them and their antics, writing in the first person as though about myself.

All through those years of hard work and worry, I would find comfort and peace in my beloved woodland, and now, as I sit under the oak tree at Five Oaks, a wave of nostalgia takes me back to all those happy years we spent here. I can see my Angela dancing up and down on her long thin legs amid the tall trees, her golden hair flying as she pranced and jumped around. And I see Keith in his tree-house, making his bow and arrow and whispering and giggling and going off to the shore to fish. We were a very close family, but I felt it was these woods that protected us and kept us together.

With the closing of the year the great oaks shed their acorns and the elms and beech grow red and fiery like the setting sun, and my little shack looks so lovely it seems destined to be the last to remain. I cannot help but shed a tear as I recall the desecration of so many acres of woodlands and with it the community that is lost forever. Yet I comfort myself as I look across my land at my beautiful rose garden. It has been the work of a lifetime, and whenever I come here I feel I have come home.

Book II

The Writing Bug

Chapter One

Maggie

The years have passed so quickly, yet yesterday seems closer than ever. I gaze dreamily across the room at the little Christmas tree that stands in the corner of my house at Wellington Road. My eyes rest on the little fairy that sits lopsided on the top of the tree; her glitter has now faded and she looks very forlorn in the aftermath of Christmas. But I smile up at her and think, 'Don't be sad, little fairy, for all that glitters is not gold.' I say this with irony, for I know only too well the price of fame. I am now termed a successful and wealthy woman and my family laugh as I tell them, tongue in cheek, 'I am the goose that laid the golden egg.'

All my life I had two dreams: one was to have a cosy bungalow in my woodlands; the other was to become a famous author. It is strange how when a dream materialises there is often another presence to spoil it, something that you had not foreseen in your vision. But I must not be sad, for to achieve both those dreams in one lifetime is more than most people ever get.

My thoughts wander back down the road, to when I first came to this house fifty years ago and to the many Christmases we celebrated under this roof. Even as old Hitler dropped his bombs we danced until the floorboards rattled.

As the sound of 'Auld Lang Syne' drifts in from the street outside my thoughts come to rest on one particular New Year's Eve when we celebrated the coming of the Seventies. The pattern of my life was about to change and I was to take a different pathway that was to lead to my recognition as a writer, something I had been yearning for ever since I was a girl. I was pleased to say goodbye to 1969; it had been a bad year. I had undergone an operation for cancer, but God was good to me and I survived it. That year Fred did not find a Christmas tree with a root to take down to the woodlands to plant on our lawn with all the others, but I was glad, as that was a year I did not care to remember.

My children had grown up and no longer needed me so much. Keith had grown into a tall, upright young man with a confident manner, though he still had that mop of red curls. Our neighbours in London used to say that he looked just like a doctor, going out to work with his briefcase. Angela had married Alan, the East End boy she had fallen in love with, and I now had a grandson, Baby George.

To get through my illness I filled my life with my writing. It was not an easy path, for I was just an ordinary little woman and stumbled many times, but I often wonder whether it was a path I was destined to take.

In the spring of 1970 Fred and I went back down to our woodlands. We had been at odds with each other in Wellington Road, which seemed to close me in and I felt like a prisoner. We had been back and forth to doctors and the radiotherapy clinic in the Mile End Road. He tried his best for me, but did not seem to understand that all I needed was my woodlands. I knew that if I could relax under the green branches of my oak tree and sit out on my lawn, I would get better. In the end Fred relented and let me stay the whole summer at the woods that year, while he commuted each day to London.

When I was alone I went down to the little wood at the bottom of the garden. It was still in its original state, just as it had been when we had arrived nearly twenty years ago. Tall trees obscured the light; brambles and ivy grew in profusion and there were small patches of brown earth where the grass and the wild flowers struggled out towards the light. The tall ash and the elms met, making an archway like the entrance of a church. I prayed hard for my life to go on, for there was so much I wanted to do. In this tangled undergrowth I was filled with a sweet sense of hope, which swept over me as I looked up and saw the trees rustling, almost as if they heard my voice. That beautiful feeling of peace that only this place could give me was inside me once more: filled with emotion, I put arms around my trees and felt their vibrations, then murmured those words that I had recited when I first entered these woods all those years ago:

'If you stand very still in the heart of a wood,
You may hear many wonderful things,
The snap of a twig, the wind in the trees,
And the whirl of invisible wings.
If you stand very still and stick to your faith
And wait for a voice from within,
You'll be led down the highways and byways of
  life
From this mad world of chaos and din.'

They say that faith can move mountains and perhaps that's what happened to me, for each day in my lovely woodland I grew stronger. Keith was good, and would call down and take me out in his smart car for a ride to Allhallows where we would breathe deep the healing essence of the sea.

While I had been in hospital I had begun to read a book

that was to change my whole life – *Hoxton Childhood*. As
I read it it made me recall my own days in Hoxton as a
child, and having then that time to 'stand and stare' I had
the idea for a story of a strong woman who would be
like me and my daughter, but most of all like the strong
women I had known. She would endure much and come
smiling through and her name would be Maggie. I was not
sure whether I would come out of that hospital ward,
but I concentrated my mind on Maggie, who came, like
me, from the streets of Hoxton. I promised myself then
that whatever happened to me I would record the times
I lived in and part of my own experiences, because my
time might be very short and I could not bear to leave
this world without leaving something behind, even if
the only people who read it were my grandchildren.

So it was that after that period of convalescence in
my woodlands, and feeling more confident about the
future, I joined a creative writing class, which was held
at a local school, with my daughter Angela. With all my
notes that I had on Maggie I began to piece together my
novel. 'She's got to be a woman who will cope against
all odds,' I told Angela. 'I want her to experience all the
social problems of the age.'

I decided I would give Maggie four sons: one a
communist, one a criminal, one a drug addict, and
one her illegitimate half-caste son. It was strange how
all these ideas flocked to me, because when I had first
had the idea for Maggie I had wanted to put my own
personality into her and write about my own life, but
she gradually took over and I felt excitement well within
me as slowly that strong character went her own way.
She was a mixture of several people that I had known and
loved and she flowed from me without any difficulty; it
was as if I knew her personally.

Angela encouraged me, hoping that while I was
enjoying my writing and making up all these characters
I would not be thinking about the cancer that could still

be there. She was always arriving with my grandson Georgie, who gave me so much joy, and Angela and I spent much time together discussing my writing, and taking Georgie out to the park or shopping. But it was at the classes that we went to once a week that my confidence really began to grow, and I blossomed from the contact with other people whose mind was akin to my own. They wrote poetry and short stories but no one seemed to get anything published.

We were given little stories to write and I noticed that while the others were writing a few lines and were all apologetic, I would have the story complete. Each week in the class we would all read out a little of our work, and I began reading *Maggie*. Gradually I realised that each week the other members would be waiting for the next instalment. I'll never forget the look of surprise on their faces, for I'd had no formal education and had only worked as a cleaner and in the local factories – they probably wondered how I could make them laugh and cry with my writing.

There was a strange mixture in our class: housewives, intellectuals and drop-outs. One night we were joined by a young boy called Robert who was a shock to us all. He had a skinhead haircut, which he informed us he had just paid 7/6 for, and was very pale, with horn-rimmed spectacles and a pair of dark eyes that stared wildly out of them. He wrote and thought of nothing but space and a thing called the fourth dimension. I hadn't got the faintest idea what that was about – I never liked it and couldn't concentrate on his space story. But we would have to listen and Angela and I couldn't help giggling.

'Mad Robert' read out the latest part of his fantasy, which concerned a genetic throwback who lived 2,000 years ahead. It was about a thing with pink knobs being intimate with another thing with green knobs and two sets of eyes, and I must admit, it really appealed to my sense of humour. I had to laugh and Robert looked very austerely at me saying, 'I hope you're not getting sexy.' I wondered how anybody could be aroused by a spaceman and a tadpole getting married and when I said as much, the effect on Robert was disastrous – he almost foamed at the mouth. It was filthy on this planet, he kept repeating, and I could not help saying, 'Well, Robert, if it's so marvellous in space you'd better find some means of getting there.'

Joe, the teacher, shut me up with an acid comment and Angela shot to Robert's rescue: 'Stop it, Mum, it was his first attempt and it's not bad at all.' Robert then proceeded to dissect me in a most violent manner, and Angela giggled, and to retain order Joe asked Robert to continue his reading the next week.

After the class we would all go to the local pub with Joe, who was half American and half Polish. He told us that he had never got any work published himself as it was all such a closed shop. I got on very well with Joe, who was a little eccentric, as perhaps I am sometimes. I remember how he laughed one day when he asked me whether I had much experience at writing and I told him I had always been a scribbler and kept it all under my bed.

Joe asked me and Angela to come along to his writers' weekend that he ran on a boat along the Thames. I would have loved to have gone, but Fred would only have sulked, still being a bit old-fashioned at heart. He'd been disgruntled of late with all this writing but was generally indulgent to me because of my illness, so I didn't want to take any liberties. If I could have got away with it I would have gone, for to be accepted by these intellectuals to discuss all the books I had read, and to talk of history and politics, was to enter a world that I had always wanted to be part of.

One night after the class Joe said to me, 'Lena, you're a natural, but your work does need discipline.' When I asked him about getting my work published, he just smiled and said in his American drawl, 'Well, seeing your work in print is another story – it happens to one in a million – but there's not much I can teach you about writing; you leave us all behind.' Joe certainly gave me confidence in my abilities, and I will always be grateful to him for that.

The next summer I started a short story about the Cliffe marshland. Angela came down to Five Oaks for a visit with Georgie. We went up to the village, taking Georgie in his pushchair, and walked about the old church then went and had a drink in the local inn, called the Bull. I had been there before and recalled sitting listening to the locals' tale about a ghost who haunted the pub after midnight. The inn dated back hundreds of years and at one time had been a well-known meeting place for the smugglers and sailors who drifted into the shores and creeks. It was of Tudor design, with high brick ceilings and black beams, and a gateway out the back that opened on to a cobbled courtyard with an oak bench.

We sat in the courtyard, but as I walked through the dim passage to get some drinks from the bar I stood and lingered for a while and thought about the history of the place and wondered if it was haunted. I could hear mumbled voices from the bar but my mind was far away, and before my eyes came a picture of a sailor. I could just see him in my mind's eye, with his brass-buttoned uniform and square-shaped hat.

I must have looked in a real dream when I collected the drinks, for I was thinking about my sailor. I decided that I would call him Bill and that he had been press-ganged aboard a ship in Nelson's time, to return from battle with only one leg. I had always had a fertile imagination that often got me in a lot of trouble, but I knew Angela would understand. I went outside and told her all about 'Bill Davis', the spirit who had come to me and had one leg, and we both had a little chuckle. I was glad to see the smile return to her face, for she had been miserable when she arrived, having had a row (one of many) with her husband.

We sat there sipping our cool drinks and talking about the sailor. When I said, 'I think he haunts this place and taps his wooden leg on the ceiling,' Little Georgie's eyes lit up and he demanded to go inside to hear the tapping. We told him it was just a game and with another bag of crisps he quietened down.

We were sitting in the shade of a willow tree, its leaves sweeping down on to the cobbled yard. The swifts and the swallows flew low around us on their way out to the marshland, and despite Georgie playing up for attention, we became lost in our own creative world and Bill Davis came alive for me. He was crossed in love and returned to haunt his rival, the proprietor of the inn, who had stolen his wife and child.

Georgie tired himself out running around the yard and trying to climb the tree, and Angela settled him in his pushchair and rocked him back and forth until he dozed off to sleep as we talked over ideas for my story of the sailor from the Battle of Trafalgar. Angela listened breathlessly and spoke in hushed whispers so as not to wake George. She confessed to me that she had forgotten her problems and how relaxed she felt listening to me create that story, and I confessed to her that I had discovered that creating stories stopped me from worrying.

And so began the story of *The Swift and the Swallows*. It was the first short story I completed and I really enjoyed writing it.

The landlady who served us our drinks that day walked out on to the marshland one day and drowned herself in one of the dykes. She was in her mid-forties and everyone put her suicide down to the change of life, but I often wonder if that place was not really haunted after all.

The next day Alan, my son-in-law, arrived in his car, looking for Angela. Fred stayed down at the bottom of the plot, digging a hole. He always stayed away from trouble and seeing 'Apples', as he was called, arrive, Fred soon disappeared. Angela's face lit up when she saw him and she said, 'I knew he would come looking for me.'

They stayed for dinner, then the pair of them went for a walk over to the orchard opposite to collect fruit, leaving Georgie with me, and returned some time later, looking very dreamy-eyed.

Alan had been in and out of prison since he'd left school, and he knew that I never thought him good enough for my Angela, though he did have that real Cockney humour that I love and when he had money was very generous with it.

'Changed a lot down here,' he said. 'Where's all the shacks gone?'

I told him what had happened to my woodlands and the next thing I knew he had gone off to look around, coming back with lead from roofs and bits of copper pipe, informing us that this was all worth money. 'Wish I had a lorry,' he said, 'there's loads of new bricks up the top.'

'They belong to the builders,' Fred said in a disapproving tone. 'They don't like looting down here.'

But he shoved all his scrap in the boot of the car and Angela helped him, her gold hair hanging loose and her face and clothes all grubby. I was only hoping the neighbours wouldn't see and I was thankful to see Alan and Angela drive away, though I would miss little Georgie, who waved from the car calling 'Bye, Nanny.' I was glad to be alone after they had left and to sit under my oak and feel the peace and beauty once more.

Chapter Two

The Haunted Hamlet

The next summer I was stronger and *Maggie* had been finished in longhand. I had also completed several short stories and my confidence was growing. Everywhere I went my creative mind was working.

Fred and I made new friends, Sheila and Arthur, the proprietors of the Railway Tavern in the nearby village of Higham. The inn stood on high ground above a railway line, and my friends informed me that once a canal had run in place of the railway.

With my usual curiosity, I began to investigate the history of the canal. I found out that in the nineteenth century the barge people carried human sewage up the canal to the Thames, where it would be dumped at the dung wharf, to be filtered away by the tide. The barges also carried bricks from the cement works that stood out on the misty marshland, where dykes and inlets flowed out to the sea. As well as bricks, the cement works manufactured the tiles and sanitary pipes that went towards the creating of new mansions for the rich and of factories to make yet more wealth, all on the bent backs of the common working-class people. The works employed young children under the age of thirteen, who were made to carry up to 14 pounds of wet clay on their heads.

I became so fascinated by all I heard and read about the cement works and the canal that I used to wander around the village, asking endless questions. Eventually I found a book by a man called George Smith, who had been an MP at that time and who fought in parliament for new legislation to abolish the slavery of these children. Eventually he managed to get a bill passed that changed the minimum age of employment to thirteen.

On reading his book I found that the little children were paid only for the perfect bricks they turned out. There were pictures of these children in his book, showing them trotting back and forth, stripped to the waist. They had deep scars on their hands from handling the hot bricks from the kilns and sores on their legs from the irritation of the clay. There were no safety precautions, and drink was allowed, which resulted in terrible accidents, such as the time when a huge pile of hot bricks tumbled down on a group of children. It was a hellish existence.

It all fed my imagination, and inspired me to begin my novel, *The Haunted Hamlet*, which I set in the times of the Napoleonic Wars. I became very wrapped up in it all, and when we went to the Railway Tavern for a drink on Saturday nights, in my mind's eye I would see a canal in place of the railway. I called it Hollinbury Hamlet, and as I sat in the inn a host of characters from the brickfields and the barges would venture into the bar. I decided that two sisters would run the inn and it became the central stage for the violence and disgrace of the times.

I was also inspired by the sincerity of George Smith to write about the beginnings of the Salvation Army, and in my mind I created the character of George Gibbs, who would start the first mission. I had a lot of reading to do on the founding of the Salvation Army and the Napoleonic Wars and Fred left me alone in my dreamworld, doing a lot of the heavy gardening while I sat under my lovely oak tree with my books.

We still had visitors down from London, who would look very surprised to see me looking so well. Instead of keeling over after my operation, I'd become a book-worm and, as I told them, I had the writing bug and nothing was going to stop me. Fred always insisted that I cooked the Sunday dinner, but otherwise my time was much my own. Fred and I never spoke about my illness and I know in his mind he blocked it out – he was always an ostrich. He would just carry on digging in the garden and never speak of it, but we remained close and were settling down in our woodlands, making new friends and making the most of what we had left.

Later in the summer Angela arrived with her husband, and little George on her arm, while I was busy making the Sunday dinner. Fred pulled a face as if to say 'Not another Sunday afternoon of their racket!' and made his exit, exclaiming that he was going to empty the toilet. Angela's face was sullen and little George was into everything, trying as best he could to help me mix up the batter pudding, making a real mess. Angela snapped at him and looked upset, then she said, 'I've told Apples that I want him to give me driving lessons, but he can't be bothered. He's been out all night drinking with his mates – no time for me.' Her lips were twisted in a tight line and those big blue eyes were sullen.

'Come on,' I said, 'let's have a walk around the garden while the dinner's cooking. I'll show you the rose I've planted for Georgie.'

Apples had been fiddling with his old banger outside, but now he pushed Georgie on the swing that was rigged up under the oak tree – a long rope with a knot in the end. George screeched with glee as his father ran up and down in his boyish manner, twisting up the rope and letting it go.

I showed Angela the pink rose that I had planted for George just by the fish pond that Fred had made so nice for me with long bullrushes and water lilies. 'It's not really a good time to plant roses, late summer,' I said, 'but I think it's taken.'

She touched a small pink rosebud and her warm smile returned once more. As we walked around the garden she told me that the TV man had come and taken the TV back.

'What?' I said. 'I thought you had a slot meter and put the money in.'

'Well,' she informed me, 'we never put any money in the slot, because every time the money ran out Apples bashed the TV and it came on automatically.'

'Goodness,' I said, 'you mean there was no money in it when the man arrived to collect it?'

'That's right, and he had a row with me and took the set away.'

'Well, I'm not surprised, dear,' I said, half seeing the funny side of it, but Angela moaned on about Georgie playing up because there was no TV. I couldn't help saying that Apples was bloody lucky the man didn't come and bash *him* after him bashing his TV. With this Angela managed a grin and I said, 'Never mind, dear, Apples will get you another one somewhere or other.'

We wandered round the garden for a while and picked some of the plums from Fred's miniature orchard at the back of the hut. It was the first crop from these trees that he'd nurtured and with wonder we sampled the luscious purple fruit, sitting at the end of the plot where the trees arched overhead. The only sound we could hear was the birdsong, and the smell of a bonfire drifted over to us from where Fred was burning some wood.

We sat and talked about *The Haunted Hamlet*. 'I really think you are a great writer, Mum,' said Angela. 'I've been looking at the paperbacks in the shops and they're not as good as your books. Why don't we try and get *Maggie* typed up properly and send it off to some publishers?'

'All right, dear,' I said, feeling rather proud.

'Right then,' she exclaimed. 'We'll make a start soon. I'll get some typing paper and you can read the story to me while I type it.'

We walked back to the shack. 'You never know, darling,' I said, 'I might even become famous.'

'Yes,' smiled Angela, her spirits restored. And so we held that little dream inside us, giving us both direction and hope for the future.

After dinner, the sun went in and the sky stretched red and yellow in the distance. It was late summer and a few leaves were trickling down from the oak in the cool breeze. I closed the doors of the shack and stoked up the fire with logs. Little Georgie was covered up in the armchair as he dozed off and Angela and Alan informed me they were going up to the top of the hill where he was going to give her driving lessons. He'd evidently given in and jubilantly she strolled off with him towards their old banger.

'Be careful,' I called after them. 'It will be all muddy and there's lots of holes up there.'

Once they were out of the way, Fred ventured in and sat and read his paper very sulkily, asking when they were all going home. Eventually he dozed off, but was very annoyed to be woken up by Angela shortly afterwards when she returned in tears. Her husband stood leaning up against the gate outside, his arms akimbo and looking very angry.

'What's up?' I asked.

'He kept shouting and hollering at me,' she sobbed, 'and in the end I went right down a ditch and we can't get the car out.' I'll never have a driving lesson with him again!'

Fred got very annoyed and told them to go home if they were going to argue and with that, little Georgie woke up and started to cry. I worried about how they were going to get home without a car, while they continued to stand and row at the gate, with Alan waving his arms and screaming back, 'What about my bleeding car? Can't get to work now!'

I was glad when they left some time after, with Angela still doing her Sarah Siddens act, saying he should be more concerned about her than the car. I watched them going down the lane, Alan walking in front in a huff and Angela trailing behind, refusing to speak, little Georgie on her arm.

'Don't worry,' said Fred as I closed the shack door looking upset, 'they'll get a train — it's still light and they're young.'

'Well, at least little Georgie had his dinner and a play on the swing,' I said.

'You worry too much,' he muttered as he opened his paper and settled down again to read.

I wondered how it was all going to end, but I got out my notes on the haunted hamlet and my mind drifted back to the nineteenth century, to the little inn on the marsh, and in this way I survived as I had always done, shutting out the pains of life that went on around me. Even as a child in the backstreets of Hoxton I had escaped from my troubles by reading my favourite books and when all the kids around me had a fight I would think of a little character I called Kitty Dailey, who I would pretend was part of me. She was my comforter, and I gave her all the things I didn't have myself. On days when the squalor of the street got too much for me, I would dream I was Kitty Dailey. She went to boarding school and wore a real gymslip and navy-blue knickers, and all the girls admired her party dresses. I gave her a friend at the school — Bessie Bunter, whom I had read about in comics. Kitty rode a horse and had lovely days out in the country — all the things I only dreamed of having. If I saw her today I would recognise her with her blonde corkscrew curls and bottle-green coat that fitted her perfectly. Whether she lived in my creative mind, or *was* my creative mind, I am not sure, but this little character was within me in all my quiet fantasy moments. I have never forgotten her, although she did fade when I began writing seriously.

The other kids used to think me strange, as I was always going to the library to read. I remember one of my favourites was *Little Women*. I loved the character of Jo, who became a writer. By the time I was thirteen I was reading Shakespeare and loving every minute of it. *A Midsummer Night's Dream* was one of my favourites: it spoke of the beauty in nature, the deep secretive side that I now have in my woodlands. When my Georgie cuddles up to me to go to sleep I often recite those unforgettable words that I discovered as a child, 'I know a bank where the wild thyme blows, Where oxslips and the nodding violet grows, . . . There sleeps Titania sometime of the night, Lulled in these flowers with dances and delight.' His little fair face chuckles and his little soft fingers touch my face. 'You are funny, Nanny,' he says.

Chapter Three

The Dandelion Seed

That autumn I went back to my writing classes. Those classes gave me plenty of food for thought, although I never stopped voicing my own opinions. We studied the Middle English of Geoffrey Chaucer and the thoughts of Mao Tse-tung, and had long debates – and often disagreements. As a sort of penance I have been reading T.S. Eliot. I am forced to admit that he's very clever, but way above my head, and I still maintain that this kind of poetry is morbid. This is a beautiful world, and we are not here very long, so if we see only unhappiness and misery we are wasting our time on this plane and I believe it is right to reach for the next one.

It was not long before I had a new idea for another novel. It all started one evening at our writing class. The nights had suddenly started to draw in with the coming of autumn, and the moon was low in the sky. I left the class to find the ladies, but somehow must have taken a wrong turn, for I found myself lost and wandering along corridors in an annexe of the school that was now out of use. I called out a few times, lost in a maze of dim hallways, and every door I tried was locked. I kept walking up and down the cold stone staircase, looking for a way out, but in the end I gave up and sat down on the steps to rest. I must have been exhausted, as I fell asleep where I sat.

As I slept, a vision came before me of a serving girl who was running from this very place as it burned to the ground. There were bright flashes of fire before my eyes, and I fought to wake up, but I was drawn deeper under in the strange dream, hearing the distant cries of people.

I knew no more until I felt someone shaking me. As I came round I saw before me an elderly man who told me he was the caretaker. He tugged at my arm to get me on to my feet. 'You all right, luv?' he demanded, looking concerned. I was still in a daze, but I realised that I had probably had one of my strange sleeps, and I knew I must have been making some strange faces. The caretaker looked at me very oddly when I said, 'I'll be all right now you've earthed me.'

I had found that whenever I had these sleeps if someone touched my flesh I could awaken. Often my old dad would wake me up during the war years by pulling at my big toe. It was in the war that these strange experiences first started to happen to me. The doctors put it down to the Blitz, and I did have a very bad time when I lost my first baby. I had been down the air–raid shelter on a night London was being badly bombed and I was nine months pregnant. The crowds were so afraid and panicked that I got pushed to the ground and hours later my baby boy was stillborn. Who knows, perhaps the bad things we go through in our lives leave some kind of permanent nightmare inside us. I have got used to living with my strange sleeps, as I call them, and they are a lot better now that I am older and have the creative outlet of writing, although they often return when I am overtired or under stress.

The caretaker led me back to the class and listened with interest as I told him all about my weird dream of a fire here many hundreds of years ago. He had to admit that this place gave him the creeps too and that he had heard some strange tales. He informed me that the school building was once a great house known as Brook House, and that it was believed to have belonged at one time to the notorious Guy Fawkes.

'That's odd,' I said, 'seeing he was burned to death.' The caretaker grinned nervously and looked over his shoulder. By the time we got to the class the caretaker had told me all he knew about the famous house and I felt a stirring inside me as my imagination began to take over. I said goodbye and thanked him – I had really enjoyed our little chat and I told him I was going to write it all down and that I had great hopes of becoming a novelist. In my mid-fifties, I was no spring chicken, and he probably thought me a little odd, finding me on the steps making all those strange faces. As Angela arrived in a huff asking me where I had been, he said with a grin, 'I think your mum's been a hundred years away.'

I returned to the class and Angela nagged me, saying it was now almost over, but I did not care. My mind was miles away, making up the character that I would put in that fire scene in this very house. There was a young woman in our writing group who was so timid that I always called her Miss Mouse. She reminded me of a little bird, with her long, pointed nose and twinkling blue eyes, and I looked at her across the desk with new eyes. I was placing her in this story as my serving maid, called Marcelle de la Strange, a lovely young girl with ambition and tragic circumstances, my ghost of the east annexe. She was to be one of my main characters.

I could not wait for the next day, thinking how I would go into the library to research Brook House. After the class I insisted on going over to the little pub across the road called the King's Head. The caretaker had told me there was a portrait there of Charles I, who was said to have stayed at the house. I was so excited when I found the picture and Angela and I walked around the back to explore some old stone buildings that I felt sure were once the stables of the inn where the King had tied up his horse.

The setting for my story was taking shape already and on reading further at the library I found that Brook House was used as a refuge for priests at the time of the Reformation. I spent that winter reading about the history of the house during the reign of James I, and found out that the owner of the manor at that time was a Sir Faulke Greville. I also came across a piece describing a night when the house was burnt to the ground. Add to that the battles between the Roundheads and Royalists, and I had a perfect setting for my novel that was to become *The Dandelion Seed*.

I was feeling so much better in myself at this time, giving myself no time to think negatively – my writing was becoming part of my life. Angela would come over most days and I would read out my stories. *Maggie* was by now finished and typed up, and we sent the manuscript off to the publishers Victor Gollancz, but to no avail – it was returned with a rejection slip.

One evening Maureen, my old friend from the shack Dunroaming, rang me to ask if I wanted to go down to her evening classes in Hainault, where she now lived. She told me there was to be a writers' evening and that the writer Celia Fremlin, well known for her crime stories, was going to give a talk. I thought this was a good opportunity to meet a writer in the flesh and hear her ideas, so I accepted Maureen's invitation. It was a good evening, with lots of Maureen's friends from the Communist Party, but I had expected that and there was never a dull moment. It beat sitting round the TV with Fred, and I loved to be with people who spoke their minds and had something interesting to say.

After the talk Maureen pushed me up to the front to talk to Celia Fremlin about my books. She seemed very interested and said she would read *Maggie* for me. I waited impatiently to hear from Celia, and when I received a letter saying that the book was very good and that I should try and get it published, my confidence, undermined by the rejection from Victor Gollancz, was restored once more. The encouragement Celia Fremlin gave me in her letter went a long way as it was the first time I had met a real author and I believed she would be honest with me. There was no holding me back now and Angela and I sent my work off to publishers and spent a lot of time together typing up the stories and watching for the postman each day to see what work was being returned.

I was always reading a book at this time, usually a biography or a history book, and I would often have pinned up on the wall a family tree, perhaps of the Tudors or Stewarts, or whoever I was interested in at the time. While Angela was working with me I introduced her to my favourite works, wonderful stories that always remained with me, such as *The Whiteoaks Chronicles* by Mazo de la Roche. How I loved the main character of Adelaide, the old woman who ruled her family with an iron hand in a velvet glove. She was rich and powerful in her black dress and veil, even though she walked with a stick. I can still picture her sitting out on the verandah of the big house of Whiteoaks, her big, happy family flocking around her. How I would love to have been like Adelaide – she was the kingpin of her family. I had always dreamed of having that big house in the woods and sitting on my verandah, rich and powerful with my family around me, but so far it does not seem to have happened.

Chapter Four

Autumn Alley

The following winter was a mild one and Angela and I got into a little routine of going down to Roman Road Market on a Tuesday, as there were lots of bargains mid-week. We would take Georgie and sort over the dresses on the stall then have pie and mash. On our trip there we used to pass Bow cemetery. They were in the process of building a new motorway and the bus would be stopped as the workmen held up the road. As I looked out of the window I couldn't help thinking of all those graves that were being dug up – all those old East Enders who had lived and loved – and I wondered if they would be forgotten forever. I didn't want those people or the hard time they had lived through to be forgotten and I found myself thinking of my own grandparents, who were buried in unmarked graves. They were such lovely characters, and I wanted to let the world know they were once here.

I recalled how my grandfather had come to England with his cousin, Dandy Fitz, across the Irish Sea in a little pig boat. They walked from Liverpool to London, and slept in a dosshouse in Middlesex Street; then they settled in a back street in Bow, where a small Irish community soon sprang up. They had come looking for gold in the streets, and they ended up working on the Blackwall Tunnel.

As I walked down the market I thought of the inner city decay and the reconstructions that have scattered the old communities. I wondered whether these people had departed this world without leaving anything behind them. Then I saw a little backstreet, called Autumn Street, with a pub on the corner and three bollards at the end where they used to tie up the horses. I stopped and lingered for a while, imagining a canal running along the bottom. I decided I had to go and investigate this little alley.

There were only four houses there and as we looked up at the front doors I was thinking of four families that I could place in those houses. 'One could be a Cockney family,' I told Angela as we wandered around, 'and one an Irish family; and in the other two houses I could put a Jewish family and a religious family who would always be quoting the bible.' I had it all worked out there and then, with a sudden inspiration, and I could not wait to write it down. Angela searched for a pencil and I found a scrap of paper in my bag, and Georgie played up as I drew a sketch of the alley, writing above each house which family I thought could live there. We both had to laugh at the tatty little sketch, but we also had to admit it looked very authentic, and Angela added names to it as I thought of them. I decided I would place this site between Bryant and May's, the factory where I used to work as a girl, and the Regent's Canal.

I was so taken over by this place and the characters I saw before me, that I talked and created as we walked on. The lives of all the families in this little alley would touch upon each other, for were they not already in my mind, waiting to be born? Now they were talking and living and coming to life – and so came about the birth of my new novel, *Autumn Alley*.

Angela listened and shared my excitement as I created,

although she did remark, 'I thought you were writing *The Dandelion Seed* – you can't start on another novel now.'

'Why not, darling?' I said. 'I can go back to that one later.' She just shrugged – she knew she couldn't stop me once I had started.

As we waited for the bus home I got out my little sketch of the alley and we talked about the Cockney family who would live at number three. We laughed together as we realised how reminiscent they were of her in-laws: Apples' father, a good-hearted man, who hung the fish up in the hall on a line, and Lil, who kept her house spotless and sat on the window-ledge, gossiping. On the journey home I thought about how I could also make some of those old characters buried in Bow cemetery live again in my story.

Autumn Alley took a long time to complete, because it was the first book I had written that had so many characters in, spanning three generations and many years, but it was like sending my ancestors out to the rest of the world.

The next spring I contented myself with my research for *The Dandelion Seed*. I had completed *The Haunted Hamlet*, and *Autumn Alley* was coming along nicely. Fred had taken me for my six-monthly check-up at the hospital for my illness, and all was well. Somehow I felt it would be, for I had my writing and I rarely thought about my condition. I shuddered when I saw the sad, yellow faces of the patients sitting in the waiting room who were not as lucky as I was. Each day was a bonus for me and I took such pleasure in the beauty of nature around me.

We now had three dogs, and we took them on walks around the lanes to see what new neighbours we had. We had found these dogs in one of the factories at the back of our house in Wellington Road. There was a mother dog and five puppies and I brought them all in and was able to find homes for three of the pups, but Fred and I were left with the rest of the brood. He wasn't very happy about it, but gave in to me as usual, knowing that I'd tried very hard to find them homes. They were mongrels, but looked as if they had some labrador in their parentage. The black one, whom we named Pudsey, was totally mine from the beginning, and would take to no one else, snarling at the least provocation if I spoke to anyone. Then there was Sandy, who was golden coloured and a lot more docile, and she took to Fred. The mother dog, Dolly, was a cross between the two and would run off all the time.

We had a few mishaps with them and Keith got very annoyed one day when Pudsey went into his room in Wellington Road and pulled his trousers off the end of his bed, chewing up three ten-pound notes from the pocket.

Keith had recently become very successful, having started up his own business – Elm Transport – and constantly walked about the place with a file under his arm. The business was growing bigger and when Keith landed a contract with the army, transporting the army officers' personal effects to new barracks in Dusseldorf Fred informed me he would be accompanying him on his trips to Europe. I wasn't going to worry – I always had Angela.

The little boxroom in Wellington Road was made into an office and was taken over by Pat, Keith's girlfriend, who had helped him in the business. She only ever talked business – anything else was a waste of time. Angela and I would be downstairs typing out my stories and she would venture down to make a cup of tea in the kitchen and look at us in dismay as I read out my work aloud and Angela bashed it out on the typewriter often we would laugh and cry as the story unfolded, and I must admit I often tested out my ideas on Angela and knew by her reaction whether or not I could touch people's emotions with my story. But as far as Pat was concerned lorries were the main topic of conversation. She thought I was very odd, wasting my time on such nonsense as stories, and couldn't stand Angela with her emotional, gossipy way. So the division of stories downstairs and lorries upstairs grew as time passed.

I became used to Fred going off abroad with Keith and was very proud when Keith moved into offices along the road and I saw his lorries, with a big Union Jack on the front, coming along the main road. At about this time Keith and Pat got married and bought a new house in Kent. Keith had taken to flying, and bought himself a plane – as well as lovely presents for me.

Angela and I still plodded on but had no success. She now had a part-time job and Georgie went to nursery school. One late-summer afternoon, while Fred was away, she came down to Kent to spend a holiday with me. Georgie ran to me, putting his arms around me, and we danced around the lawn singing, 'All a bunch of sugar' as we'd often done. He was now able to hold a sensible conversation and told me that his mother had run out of petrol on the way down and that they'd had to walk miles. I looked at my daughter. She looked better since she had started her job: her long, golden hair was now permed and she took more interest in her appearance, buying herself a new outfit every payday. I was glad she was confident enough to face the motorway, but she was just the same calamity she had always been since Fred had given her the nickname of Calamity Jane as a kid.

Chapter Five

Owen Oliver

With the passing of the seasons, my strength grew and the more I wrote the easier it became.

I had always loved the works of Dickens and it hadn't taken me long to discover that Cliffe was near Dickens country. Fred and I would often go for a drink at the pubs that had been Dickens' old haunts – the Falstaff and the Leather Bottle at Cobham, even the railway tavern at Higham, and at each place I seemed to feel the spirit of my favourite author. Fred would grumble, saying, 'Can't see the point of going to all these places – that bloke's been dead for years.' He did not understand and I did not need him to, for I would never have been able to explain my feeling that the spirit of Dickens still roamed the marshland, and that I walked beside him.

When Angela and Georgie came down for a week one summer we rode out to the little church of St James on the marshland of Cooling, the setting for the church that Pip had visited in *Great Expectations* to see the graves of his parents and brothers. I had always wanted to visit this place and as Angela was full of woe as Apples had been in yet another fight, I tried to take her mind off her problems.

It was a beautiful spot, and there wasn't another soul around. It wasn't long before we were discussing

Dickens and this lovely place that had inspired him. I knew that Dickens had once lived not far from this spot, in Gadshill near Chatham, where he had a chalet, transported from Switzerland, that he used as a kind of summer house to sit and write in. I was enthralled by this idea and dreamed that one day, when I built my big house, I could use my little shack as my own summer house. Georgie thought this a lovely idea and he listened intently, his little face lighting up, saying, 'Can I come in this writing house, Nan?' as though he thought it would be a very special place to play. He skipped off with glee to climb over the low stone walls of the ancient church and followed us as we strolled around the old gravestones and read the inscriptions.

'I wonder who old Esmerelda was "Who fed the Sheep",' I pondered, looking closer at the weather-beaten stone.

'I wonder if she found any happiness with a man,' said Angela.

'Well, darling, as Gray said in his elegy, "Full many a flower is born to blush unseen, and waste its sweetness on the desert air", but I expect even Esmerelda had her day.'

'I hope so,' said Angela, as she memorised the words from the poem.

We also came across a little line of heaped stones that marked the graves in *Great Expectations*, where Pip was captured by the escaped convict. I felt the salt breeze over the marsh and knew that I loved this spot, and that somehow, like that great man, I too had some sort of destiny here.

As Angela and I looked out across the marshland, where the tall grasses blew in the breeze that swept from the river, I pointed out that the convict had come across those marshes to hide in this very graveyard, and that the blacksmith's forge where Pip worked was not far away, in Higham. We became lost in Dickens' world for a while and I admitted to Angela that sometimes I felt spiritually inspired by Dickens, for he wrote about ordinary people, like I do – he would take the poorest person and give them character.

'Perhaps he does inspire you,' returned Angela wistfully.

'You know, darling,' I said, 'I have a story going round in my head right now, to do with Dickens.'

As we drove on to Allhallows-on-Sea I told her of the idea I had about a young man who had lived in the village of Higham and had a great gift for art. One day the young man met Dickens and became his illustrator. Dickens did actually have an illustrator, I explained to Angela. He was called Phiz, and he used to accompany Dickens round the schools up north, drawing little sketches of the children. Dickens was a great one for fighting all the social evils of his time, and he wanted to find out about conditions in the schools, so he went round pretending he was looking for one of his sons.

Angela listened with interest as I told her all I knew about the famous man, for I had been reading many books on his life. I told her that I would fictionalise Dickens' life and that my hero would be named Owen Oliver.

'You know, Mum, you have so many stories going now that I don't know how you are going to cope,' she said.

'But I love it, darling,' I said.

'When I get stuck with one, I go on to another.'

'Well, I wish the world would see your gift, Mum, but even if they don't, I think it has helped you get well.'

'Thank God,' I said, and touched wood.

We drove through the winding country lanes to the sea. The trees were covered in blossom and pink and white petals drifted in the wind.

At Allhallows we walked with Georgie along the sea wall to the fishing lake, where we sat and watched the sun go down. The sky stretched in shades of crimson

in the distance and a golden light shone on Georgie's
fair hair. Low in the sky was a round, red shape and
Georgie asked, 'What's that?'

I stared up at it for a while and, screwing up my eyes
said, 'I think it's a spaceship, and if you look up like
Nanny you could see it too.'

Little Georgie screwed up his eyes, his little freckled nose all wrinkled, until he too decided it was a
spaceship.

All the way home Georgie quizzed me about the
spaceship and I went on to make up a little story that
I called 'Moonecticus'. In this story, some spacemen
who had special powers to cure people who were sick
landed on the marsh. I called the spacemen Eenie,
Meenie, Minie and Moe, and although we laughed
about this on the journey home, it really turned out
to be a touching story.

The next day, while Angela took Georgie into
Rochester to do the shopping, I sat and wrote it
down properly. The spacemen landed at a cottage out
on the marsh and were befriended by the woman who
lived there. In return they cured her cancer.

That week we spent the warm afternoons sitting out
on the lawn, talking over my ideas. I made notes in
small exercise books for the Dickens story and read
more on his life, passing any interesting findings over
to Angela. She loved me to read my stories to her and
would lounge back lazily to listen, with the occasional
tear or smile crossing her face.

Chapter Six

Kate of Clyve Shore

Lately Angela had been taking some of *Autumn Alley* to work with her to type it up on the electric typewriter – it was so much quicker. We discussed the publishers we'd send it to, hoping we'd have more luck this time, and laughed about her friends at work who had been waiting patiently for the next instalment. As Angela typed it they kept picking it up to read – it seemed they couldn't put it down and no one got any work done. Angela had told them how I made it all up when I did my hoovering. They couldn't get over this, and they phoned the local paper, who said they would come down to interview Angela and me.

Later that summer we visited the Norman church of St Helen's, in the village of Cliffe. It overlooked the wide, windswept marsh and had a peaceful grandeur all of its own. On entering the church we became very solemn and gazed up apprehensively at the old ragged banners hanging overhead, the tall columns and arched roof and the magnificent brasses. Beside us was a low stone shelf. We admired a small carved bust of a young girl that stood on the sill. I picked it up and held it close, fingering the small, plump face and parted hairline. 'She reminds me of a little maid that worked at the castle,'

I told Angela as she took the little head from me and examined it.

I placed my hands on the grey stone walls and a dreamy feeling came over me as if I could see the life of the girl whose bust sat on the sill. I said to Angela, 'I think she used to live in this village and I can just see her walking down the winding lane from the castle, carrying the washing.'

Angela looked at me, her eyes soft and distant, and I knew she could also feel that strong emotion that was always with us when my creative imagination took over.

'I think I will call her Kate,' I continued, 'and some-how I feel that she carried a child of royal blood in her womb.'

Angela held the little head close to her and placed her hands on the grey stone, as slowly I pieced together the life of Kate. I could see her as rich and rosy as nature, walking by the strawberry fields. I told Angela she would be my 'Kate of Clyve Shore', as I knew Clyve was the Old English name for Cliffe. Suddenly we heard the wind blowing like fury and the rain pelted down on the stained-glass windows and we hurried from the church. But we were nourished and as we went home I sat dreamily thinking about Kate. I knew I had the seeds of a novel, but I wanted to read about the life of King John before I went any further.

It was some time later that the story of Kate finally unfolded. Angela had come down for a few days. She was very glum and didn't stop eating, and somehow I knew she was pregnant again. 'You're not eating for two?' I enquired as she tucked into her dinner, and a smile broke out across her pale white face.

'I wondered when you'd ask,' she said.

I sat down beside her for a moment and tried to give comfort, but I wondered how she was going to cope with another child. She had been happier since she

father, Cornelius
n Kennedy, born
1874 in Co. Cork,
land, died 1958.

Me with Auntie Mary, who used to look after me when my mother went to work.

Me as a young girl (*left*) with my friend Rosie on a
trip to Southend-on-Sea.

Me aged about seventeen outside the local shop,
run by Mrs Appleby, where I worked.

As a young working girl, proudly wearing my new coat
with a beaver collar acquired through the 'Provi'.

Me and Fred on a day trip to Brighton during our courting days.
Brighton was a favourite spot of ours and where we spent our honeymoon.

On our wedding day. My sister Molly was my Maid of Honour.

With Fred in the garden of Wellington Road during the war
years when Fred was home on leave. He was stationed in
Egypt with the Tank Regiment.

I sent this photo
of me to Fred in
Egypt, inscribed
with the words
'The dawn is not
distant, nor is the
night starless'.

This was taken after the war when Fred came home.

Happy camping days at Allhallows-on-Sea.
Me with Keith and Angela.

The early days at the shack: Fred sitting on the step with Angela and Keith. Fred's home-made ladder is proudly displayed.

Later years at the shack, showing all the hard work had paid off.

At the party to launch *Maggie*. To my right, with his arm on my shoulder, is Joe Wolowski, my first writing teacher; and to my left is Maureen Burns;

At the same party talking to Alan Sillitoe.
On the far left is John Marquezi, my first publisher.

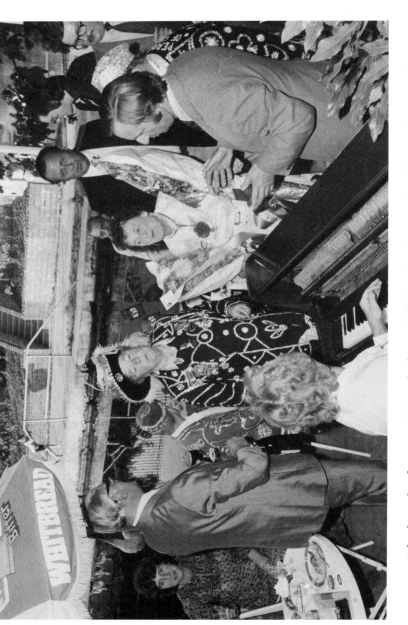

The launch of *Autumn Alley*, which was held by the Regents Canal. Fred is seen beside the pearly queen, clutching a bottle of bubbly, and I am at the piano,

At a signing session for *Lily, My Lovely.*

Fred and I took the aunties on a day trip to the cottage in Essex where Angela lived with her family. *From left to right:* Angela, Aunt Theresa (Mary's sister), Aunt

Fred and me on board the *QE2* en route to New York, pictured here with fellow passenger Telly Savalas. .

Taking time ou
on my tour of
Australia to fee
the birds.

On a trip to
Jersey with
Fred.
Pictured
here with
my beloved
Pudsy and
Sandy.

dressed up,
t before the
omen of Our
ne' lunch,
ich was held
the
chess of
oucester
ecially for
men who
d achieved
mething
ecial.

Proudly holding the award presented to me by the
American Romantic Novelists' Association.

Pictured with Eamonn Andrews and
my grandson Horatio on *This Is Your Life*.

started working and having extra money, but then I remembered Fred's wise words to me that you cannot live another person's life. With a faraway look in her eyes she told me how pleased Apples had been when he found out she was pregnant.

With my lips tightly sealed I went to put the kettle on. Angela then went on to tell me how shocked she had been a few nights before when a policeman knocked on the door to tell her Apples had turned a car over.

'I was all upset, Mum,' she said, 'but the policeman said there wasn't a mark on him and that he wondered if he was Batman, because the car was found upside down in the main road and anyone else would have been killed.' I could see the funny side of this when I thought of Batman Apples, though I wondered however she put up with him.

We soon forgot our worries the next day when we visited the Old Rectory. I had been longing to visit this place since I had discovered in my history books that it had been a secret meeting place for King John and his bishops before the Magna Carta was drawn up at Runnymede. It was not far from the castle where my Kate would have worked and I felt that here I would find the connection I needed.

Tall elms bowed low and hid the Rectory from the road. We pushed open the rickety black gate and walked around the grounds. It was obviously empty and overgrown with shrubs and tall weeds with pretty mauve flowers. Fuchsias bordered the hedges and hung in red and purple bells, and tall yellow sunflowers leaned against the ivy that grew up the stone walls.

We peered through the windows at the dusty low oak beams and dark interior. I could just imagine King John and a group of men gathered inside around the table, arguing about the Magna Carta, and Kate's frightened little face as she brought them clean laundry from the castle. I felt that now the final pieces of the jigsaw had come together and I could write my novel, *Kate of Clyve Shore*.

The next day we went into Rochester and saw the old curiosity shop that was another setting for one of Dickens' novels and looked up in awe at the blue plaque overhead. Angela must have read my thoughts, for she remarked, 'Perhaps you'll have a blue plaque one day, Mum.'

It was my greatest wish but we had recently had so many disappointments – just the week before, *Autumn Alley* had come back from the publishers with a rejection slip. But I would press on. I enjoyed my writing so much that I couldn't help it.

'Never mind, darling,' said Angela, taking my arm as we walked on. 'Nothing or nobody will stop you writing.'

'I know,' I smiled, 'I think I've got the writing bug.'

'The writing bug!' exclaimed Georgie. 'Can I have one of those?' and we both laughed.

I had been feeling a bit down that week, what with the rejection and my anxiety about Angela being pregnant, but my spirits lifted a little when Angela said, 'Don't worry, Mum, that seems to be the thing I can do best – having kids.' A little ray of joy flickered in my heart when I thought of another grandchild, and I prayed my health would hold out to hold that baby in my arms.

Back in Wellington Road we had the long-delayed visit from the local newspaper. I had almost given up hope of them coming down and I had a feeling that the pleasant young journalist was filling in an empty spot at the last minute. He asked me where I got all my ideas from and I told him and added, 'As you get older, the road back becomes clearer, you know.' He looked at me oddly, and couldn't believe the amount of books and stories I had written. He took our photographs, with me sitting at the typewriter and Angela standing behind me and thoroughly enjoying the journalist's attention. Of course, she had to let him know she was pregnant and made a thing about holding her tummy in.

When the article eventually came out it said that perhaps there would be two births – the birth of a novel and the birth of a baby – and went on to say how close our mother and daughter relationship was.

I was not surprised when Angela later came storming home from work to say her boss had seen the article and paid her off, seeing that she was going to have a baby. I comforted her and we both agreed eventually that 'it was an ill wind', for she couldn't have kept the job for long.

It was a good photograph of us and the neighbours talked a lot about it, but it did not help us in our plight to get my work published.

Chapter Seven

The Comic Publishers

While Angela was pregnant we got a lot of work typed up. Most days she would arrive after dropping Georgie at school, full of complaints about feeling sick and mooning around with a long face. Somehow I would manoeuvre her behind the typewriter, where I would read out my handwritten drafts of *Owen Oliver* and she would type them up into manuscript form. She would moan about the shiny paper, saying it put her teeth on edge. This paper Fred had brought home from work for me, as typing paper was expensive, and I cut it to size and was quite happy with it, though I was never sure whether it was actually wrapping paper. Even the old manual typewriter had seen better days and had a few keys missing.

Lately even Angela had moments when she lost faith in me, for I had successfully completed four novels and many short stories but so far had only received rejections. But my writing was like a gnawing inside me and I could not stop, and the more people looked on me as an odd bod, the more I carried on.

I had started reading Galsworthy after seeing the dramatisation of *The Forsyte Saga* on television and had found out that he started life as a lawyer. I'd got Angela reading Compton Mackenzie's *The Four Wings of Love*, and we discussed how you can love in many different ways. I felt that the truest love of all was mother love. I also read the lives of Byron and Shelley, and on cold winter days we would sit around the fire with little Georgie, who would cuddle up to us as we discussed the Romantic poets.

Often I would disappear to the library, taking with me my magnifying glass, and would be gone for hours, reading about the lives of the great writers. I could not lift the large research books and the helpful young girl in the library would bring them out to me. I would get deeply involved and would arrive home late with the shopping. Fred would look very annoyed at having to sit and wait for his dinner, but I would feel as though I had drunk a double scotch, for the nourishment from the great works of literature was all I needed.

Angela had sent off some of my short stories to magazines, but one after another they came back through the post. I didn't dare open the letter from the magazine until she arrived and would place it on the mantelpiece, where it would glare at me all day from among the photographs of Dad and other relatives.

When Angela arrived we would open the letter and my heart would miss a beat, but it was always a disappointment. With a very dismal expression on her face, Angela would say, 'All these lovely stories you write, Mum, and no one wants to know. I don't know how you carry on.'

'Well, darling,' I would say, 'when I was in hospital I expected to die, and when you survive a death sentence it gives you a whole different outlook on life. For the first time in my life I am doing what I always wanted to do: to write is my destiny.'

On those days Angela would lounge around, refusing to do anything, the loss of hope written all over her face, but somehow I would lift her spirits and we would talk of the characters in my latest book. Before the day was out we would both be back in front of a typewriter, and she would be back with me again.

When I think of those days, when Angela and I were in the dark about the world of publishing, and how we'd struggled on, losing hope but somehow getting it back to fight another day, I realise that we shared a dream, and I think of the saying that it is better to travel hopefully than to arrive. We might have been hard up, but we had direction and we share our lives.

Often Angela would get very irritable with me when she couldn't find the next chapter, as my papers were piled high around the room, and looked very messy. But I would know every word I had written and knew exactly where to find it.

'Don't know how you find anything in this mess!' she would declare, tossing over the pages, and glaring sullenly at me as I looked for my glasses to find the passage we had mislaid. But whenever I read the first and last line of a page as I searched through the manuscripts I would know exactly where I was and what I wanted to say, and Angela would type on as I read aloud, cutting bits here and there, and replacing them with new ideas as they came to me, which never failed to surprise my daughter.

In this way I survived the winters in Wellington Road, for my life without my lovely garden in Kent would otherwise have been very dull. Fred would get a bit fed up with Angela sitting around eating and little Georgie under his feet when he came home from work.

I was pleased to hear from Angela that Apples was doing well. It seemed he had given her money for new clothes, and new furniture had been bought for the house – I was relieved he was looking after her. She told me that he was working down on the old railways and had found lots of scrap metal. 'Well, you never know, dear,' I said sardonically, 'perhaps he's found himself a goldmine.'

One day Angela admitted with a worried expression that he had recently cut through a cable and nearly blown himself up.

Typical Apples, I thought and nearly said as much, but when I saw her sad little face I decided not to. She had told me that he was rarely home since he had had money in his pocket, and she didn't like some of the mates he was hanging around with. I only hoped he wouldn't get into any trouble just now.

Sometimes I pushed myself too hard with my writing and I would get overtired and need a rest. At these times of mental rest I would turn to another outlet: my crocheting. After about two weeks, the whole family would be presented with woolly hats. Georgie would refuse to wear them, but Angela, trying to be kind, would wear the long scarves I made. Even Apples had a scarf made for him. I remember I presented Fred with a jumper one winter that had an animal on the back, but he couldn't make out what kind of animal it was. He passed it on to Keith, who decided it was some kind of beaver. My crocheting was a standing joke and Fred would say, 'I'll be glad when you get back to your writing – you always did have a butterfly mind.'

I gradually realised that weaving in my writing and knitting those characters together was far easier than weaving that wool.

It's strange how fate eventually took a hand in getting my work published. These things have a way of happening when you least expect them to. The road to publication took several avenues and the first one began when Angela decided that she was sick and tired of seeing the work returned, and that we would no longer waste our time by sending it off – we would get in the car and go and find those publishers and talk to them.

We started by looking up their names and addresses in the telephone directory. By this time Angela was heavily pregnant and her Apples had gone to stay inside for a short time in the care of Her Majesty's servants. This had been an upset to us, especially as she was pregnant, but that was another story and nothing to do with our road to fame.

So rather depressed about life, with Angela's stomach bulging, we set out one day in the old banger. We had picked out the publishers that were nearest, in the East End. As we drove around we passed the street where Apples used to live, and Angela got very melancholy.

I said to her, 'You have a lonely road to walk, darling.' She gave me a knowing look as my mind began to work on a little story called 'The Lonely Road', about a girl who came from a middle-class family but married a man involved with the criminal fraternity. She often felt she belonged nowhere when times got hard. I wrote this story in the next few days, and Angela shed a few tears as I wrote down her close feelings, but she told me she thought the story should be told.

On our search for a publisher, we got a few doors slammed in our faces as we stood, manuscript in hand, but one day we met with a more sympathetic reception. A tall, elegant man came down to meet us and listened carefully as we told him that the manuscript belonged to an old lady who had a suitcase full of scribbles under her bed. Then, with a gentlemanly smile, he took the manuscript and told us we would be hearing from him soon. We gave him my phone number, then set off home, very excited that someone was taking an interest.

'Well, *Maggie*'s a great story,' said Angela with a smile. 'I'm sure he's going to like it, Mum.'

So, with all our old dream restored, we chatted all the way home about the things we would do if we got the book published. I revived my old dream of having a house built at Cliffe, and Angela talked about travelling the world and owning a cottage in the country.

A few weeks later the kind man returned the manuscript with a very long letter, saying the thought it was a marvellous story but unfortunately he only published comics. Angela got very irritable and could not understand how we had made such a mistake, but I just tried to see the funny side of it. Fred thought it a right joke and he and Keith teased me, saying, 'You're a right pair of comics, you two.'

Chapter Eight

Susan

During Angela's second pregnancy, I am unhappy to relate a division arose in my family. Angela's circumstances had made her very bitchy and Keith was becoming more and more successful in his business and they fell out over a stupid little incident. They were both so obstinate that they refused to speak to each other again. This was no five-minute wonder, for fifteen years later they were still not on speaking terms.

I suffered many scenes in Wellington Road when one would arrive and the other would leave. It broke my heart, for I had only two children and now my family was divided. Fred stuck more to Keith and I to Angela – she seemed to need me more than ever now.

I was very glad when Angela got a lodger to stay in the house with her and Georgie, for I had been worried about her being alone. The lodger's name was Samantha, and from the beginning I got on with her.

As Angela's time drew near, I frequently called in at the house in Leytonstone where she lived. Often I would find the house in chaos. On one particular day little Georgie informed me on my arrival that Apples' father had been outside the house upsetting Mummy. He had arrived with a truckload of old machinery and then stood arguing outside with his son Tommy. Georgie told me how the two men had argued and screamed at each other, for as soon as one put a piece of machinery on the back of the truck the other threw it off. It seemed that this scenario had gone on all day and in the end one of the neighbours had threatened to call the police. The two men then quickly made it up and were away as thick as thieves again.

I found this very amusing, although my daughter continued to complain and shot me a black look as I remarked to Georgie, 'It must have been old Steptoe and Son.' A smile crinkled his face as he climbed on to my lap, grabbing my bag to search it for sweets.

He then informed me, pointing to the dog Mandy, that she was going to have lots of babies too, just like Mummy. I looked at the black mongrel who sat and glared up at us, waiting for one of the sweets. I could see her swollen belly.

'Not again!' I said to Angela. 'She's already had three litters. Can't you keep her in?'

Little Georgie then told me that her boyfriends waited outside and Mummy would try to keep her in, but she would just jump over the wall.

When the pups were born Georgie insisted on calling them all 'bad dogs'. I could only suppose it was Mandy's behaviour that gave credence to that name.

I looked at my daughter, heavy with child, and she looked very fed up, but I made her laugh as I related the story of the time my father came home drunk and my mother refused to let him in and aimed a flowerpot out of the window that landed right on his head. 'It's a shame, dear,' I said, 'that you can't aim one at your in-laws next time they visit?'

Angela showed me the letters she had received from Apples. She was lonely without him, but had been spending her time reading Wordsworth and, with a dreamy look in her eyes, would recite the words, 'You gave me eyes, you gave me ears'.

*   *   *

It was while Angela was in hospital having the baby that Samantha and I really got to know each other. I was staying at her house and looking after Georgie, and from the beginning this girl inspired me. She was in her late twenties and good looking. She used to go to work looking very smart in a suit, but in the evening she would have a whole personality change and would go out looking very glamorous in mini-skirts, and would not return till very late.

I quizzed Angela about this, who was a bit naive and told me she was no trouble and had a good job, but I thought there was more to this girl and I found myself weaving a story around her. We had long chats and she told me about her past life, and the two children she had left behind, who were being looked after by her mother.

As I listened to her story I was remembering a young girl who used to play with my children when they were small. She lived just along the street from us and was an orphan. She would often call to see me, as she did not get on with her adoptive parents, and I still have the bible she left here after Sunday School one day. The inscription reads 'from my loving mother and father', but the handwriting was hers, and I felt very shocked as I realised that the child had written those words to herself. One day she was molested by the park keeper. Many years later she returned to Wellington Road to tell me that she could not cope with the world.

It was from the recollection of that girl and how she was a victim of circumstances, and the inspiration of the flamboyant Samantha that the seeds of a new story were sown.

When I was out shopping a few days later I stopped and looked at a little sign in a window that read 'third floor: Susan'. Here was the final link that I needed to spur my creative imagination to produce *Susan*, the story of my own little orphan girl who had a bad beginning and never had much of a chance.

The story of *Susan* begins in a convent and this inspiration came from my own children's schooldays, as they went to Catholic schools and would walk in religious processions, accompanied by girls from the convent. These were girls who nobody wanted except the church: they were outcasts from society. To this day I am still haunted by the lovely face of a young girl who walked with them, and I can remember wondering why she was there.

In the months that followed *Susan* took shape, the story of a West End prostitute, an orphan girl who was a victim of circumstances. I had to draw a lot on the past, but I was lucky that I had always been blessed with a good memory.

Book III

Distant Memories

Chapter One

Family Life

Georgie would constantly ask after his father. Angela had told him he was away working on a ship and he would cuddle the little Action Man that I had given him, telling him that his dad had sent it to him.

One day he sat snuggled beside me on the settee, rubbing his eyes, and drowsily asked me if I had a nanny too. I tried to tell him all about my own grandmother, but his voice was getting far away as he quizzed me and the warmth in the room was sweeping over me. Like a warm blanket, sleep came over me and I felt my eyes flicker.

I was remembering my lovely Nanny Murphy, and my mind drifted back to the steps in Hoxton where I used to sit with her. I would run home from school to join her there, and on long summer evenings we would sit and watch the goings-on in the street, and Nan would say, 'Look at that silly lot, darling,' as we watched the women and kids fighting.

Hoxton was a very poor slum quarter of London, though many famous people were born there.

I hated it all – I hated the school, the street, caring for my sister and brother, the ragged old clothes we wore. There was a girl in my class called Violet Kenny, whose mother had a shop, and she had a different silk dress on every day – funny, I hated her too because of this. Would the wisdom of psychologists call this an unhappy childhood?

Being Irish, we were Catholics, and I found this to be my one solace in life. I discovered the peace and beauty of the church at a very young age, and it has stayed with me all my life.

Originally Hoxton was just a collection of poor streets – twenty or thirty, that's all – with a pub on each corner and several churches all around, but it was alive, not only with boys but also with original living Cockneys, as the rest of the world calls them.

Amidst that maze of poor streets ran Regent's Canal or the Cut, as we called it. The Cut belonged to our way of life. On summer evenings the boys swam in there and schoolchildren and little toddlers would fall in and get drowned. The old folk used to get fed up with life and throw themselves in the Cut and the kids would stand and watch as they pulled the bloated bodies out with a hook and put them in a barrow to take them to the mortuary. We all used to march along behind, chanting, with groups of children following up behind. If there was anything unwanted around, like a cat litter, the poor little things would be thrown into the Cut. Old mattresses were chucked in and the stink was terrible on a summer evening.

Hoxton looks very different now, because Hitler's buzz bombs demolished most of the houses and the council finished off the rest. All the original inhabitants have gone on their way or live in twenty-storey blocks of flats.

I was what was known as an Irish Cockney, from a poor Irish family who emigrated to London because of the bad times in their own country. My mum came of Irish parents but was born in Hoxton; but my father came straight over from the 'Leary Pond', as they used to say. He was a big, strong, red-headed Irishman, born in Banteer, County Cork.

I was very fond of my father, but could not understand my mother, who always seemed harassed and had no time for conversation. With my dad it was different: he would talk about politics, religion and his home in Ireland. I loved to listen to him and took everything he said to heart. I remember one particular saying he had, 'Then there's currants for cakes and reasons for many things'. Having a strong Irish brogue, he made reasons sound like raisins, so in my school essay I wrote it down as raisins. I always used to feel very proud, walking along with my dad in my smart dress. When we came home our mum would cook the dinner, and it would be nice to sit down to a meal with a cloth on the table, as we always had newspaper in the week. I wondered why my mother never went to Mass and used to think she was wicked, but I realise now how hard her life was, for she was out at work from six till six every day, and only had the weekends to do all the work at home. She did her best for us, but hard work and shortage of food and four kids all helped to wear her out.

On Sunday evenings the Salvation Army would come down the street and form a ring with a drum and trumpet and a couple of cymbals. All the kids would gather round and sing along. Often they would get carried away and put their own words to the hymns. But the Salvation Army were good people and they pretended not to notice as they were ridiculed.

In my earliest recollection of my home, I remember nice lace curtains and roses on the wallpaper, but that must have been when I was very young, because our home had sadly deteriorated by the time I started to go to school.

When I was about eleven years old we lost our youngest brother, Billy, a happy little boy. My poor mother – it broke her heart and she only lived another two years herself.

I remember the night he died. We all lived in the one room in the winter because it was cold and damp in the other, and we could only afford one fire. I sat there with my nose stuck in a book, as usual, while my mother took the baby to the doctor's. He was a drunken Irishman who told her, 'Just the tummyache – nothing to worry about.' But the poor little boy had a ruptured appendix and it killed him.

I can see my mum and dad sitting watching him while he rolled about in the bed. Suddenly my dad ran off and came back with the doctor, who filled the room with an overpowering smell of whisky. He took a look, then, 'He's dead,' he said, and held out his hand for seven and six. My poor mother. Now I know how terrible it must have been for her.

There was a postmortem and the little coffin was placed in the room where we slept. I got up and looked at him one night and could not forget that little face for a long time.

I don't want to make you sad – I'll try not to – but it was there all the time, this sadness, you could not get away from it.

After the baby died the house deteriorated. The bugs got worse and nobody bothered about us – we were left to ourselves more and more. I used to run around to Nan whenever I could, because there was always warmth and love there, something that was lacking in our home.

Nan was my mother's stepmother, and although we had no blood ties, I loved her better than my mother. She lived in the next street; number thirteen, Harvey Street was a dear little house, always bright and clean, with lots of plants in the window and virginia creeper growing up both sides of the front door. Nan had a little gardening can which was precious to me. She would allow me to help her water the plants and tell me all their names.

When my grandfather married her he was sixty and she was thirty. She was a French Canadian and had been in service in Canada until the people she worked for brought her to London with them. Nan Murphy was a lady and even the rough streets of Hoxton where she had been for thirty years made no difference to that. She had black hair and little bright brown eyes, and a lovely personality.

There were lots of books and games at Nan's house, and we used to play dominoes and draughts together. In the summer we would sit on the doorstep and she would make me laugh and giggle about all the funny people who lived around.

She also told me tales of the Wild West of Canada and all about the many books that she had collected and read. She inspired in me a thirst for knowledge, and even then perhaps that small part of the brain that produces creative energy was being stimulated, for she fulfilled something in me that no one else did in my childhood.

I will never forget the day when I came running home from school to find her no longer sitting on the steps. Then I found her inside, sitting there telling the fortunes of the ladies from the big houses where she used to work. I ran to her afraid and worried, but those warm arms came round me and she said, 'Don't worry, darling, it's just a little pocket money for me, and I'll teach you to tell the cards when you're older.' I think she must have been very good, for the ladies would often pull up in their carriages to see her.

I used to dread going home from Nan's, especially on dark nights as we lived over a stable and I had to cross a yard full of mysterious creepy things before reaching the rickety stairs that led to our flat above.

I would always go to Nan with my troubles. There was always a warm fire and something would be cooking in the oven, and we would talk about Canada and Quebec, where she came from – there was no end to the lovely stories I could get from Nan. I learned little French songs and read books on English history, in which she was very interested.

Nan died when I was about fifteen years old. It was a great loss for me, and I've never forgotten her.

My grandfather was ninety years old when he died. He'd had fourteen children by his first wife and seven by Nan, the second. I can see him now, sitting in Nan's kitchen in a wooden armchair, with his long white hair and the red spotted handkerchief with which he used to blow his nose very loudly. His birthday was on St Patrick's Day, and we would all be sent round with a box of sweets, a packet of black twist tobacco and a big red spotted handkerchief. My sister and I would wear our best dresses, with green bows in our hair, and we would stand in a line with Ted, my brother, to offer our presents.

He would give us all a kiss then we had to dance for him. He would bang his stick in time as we danced an Irish jig and my skinny legs would be revving, going up and down, and I would be afraid to stop till he gave us permission. Curtseying to him afterwards, we would all be given some money, then off we would go.

He had a cousin whom we used to call Dandy Fitz, a little man with a long ginger beard and a sort of squeezed bowler hat. Dandy was a Fitzpatrick, and he had come from Ireland with my grandfather. Later, Dandy's grandson went on to build roads and is now a millionaire.

In those days my grandfather and Dandy Fitz were partners in a little stonemasonry business. They used to get drunk and argue and sometimes fight. They would sing all the Irish songs, some of which had fifty verses, and woe betide anyone who spoke a word while this was going on. He was a grand old man, my grandfather, may God bless his soul.

*   *   *

There were a lot of rows at home after my little brother died. My mother had become very depressed, and I always thought it was her fault though now I know how difficult it must have been for her. The old man would dodge out to the pub whenever she started to lay down the law.

I was thirteen when my mother died; she was forty-six. She had not seemed well that year and she had thought about giving up her job. She told me 'Be a good girl and help me, and I'll give up work at Christmas. Then when you come home from school I'll be waiting with the tea ready.' To me this would have been wonderful. For years I had come into a cold deserted house every evening, and had had to light the fire and give the kids their tea, so for the first time in my life I began to feel happy and content, with something to look forward to.

But at the end of November Mum fell ill. That Sunday Dad said, 'Don't go to Mass. Stay with your mother.' Feeling very upset, I cooked the Sunday dinner and she showed me how to make batter pudding and apples and custard, holding on to her side all the while.

On Monday the doctor came to see her. I had never seen her lying in bed before, and she looked terribly tired and drawn.

When we returned from school the next day the bed was empty – Mum was in St Leonard's Hospital. We went to say goodbye, but I was scared and ran out when I saw her. I stood in the cold hospital corridor, my head against the wall, and sobbed.

When I got home I found Dad standing at the stove frying sausages for tea. I went up to him and said, 'I'll take over for you, Dad,' and from then on I was their little mum.

We managed as best we could over the next two years, but Dad was drinking more than ever. During that time I never went to school. A man from the school board would come and knock at our front door, but would get no reply. The home deteriorated as things wore out and were not replaced. Some of the neighbours offered to help, as my mother had been well liked, but I was very proud and would tell them, 'No, you hop it. I'll look after my dad.' 'Saucy little cow!' they would say, and leave.

I found it hard to accept my mother's death. At first I thought that it must have happened because she was so upset about Billy and that she needed a rest, so I convinced myself that she would come back someday. However, I was determined not to let my dad suffer, so I took up the reins and ran the household with a rod of iron.

The idea that I might see my mother again lingered on. Just a few years ago I saw a poor little woman shivering in a shop doorway in London, and right away she reminded me of my mother.

I must have been calling out in my sleep. I woke in a cold sweat saying my mother's name, to find little Georgie shaking me and pulling at my jumper saying, 'Who's Billy, Nanny?' He threw his arms about me, warming me with his little kisses.

When I had recovered from my bad dream, Fred came in and told us in his calm way that little baby Alan was born. I only hoped he would have a better beginning in this world than I had, and I decided that I would fight to see that he did.

Chapter Two

Down Our Road

Recalling my childhood brings the memories flooding back – not just of my family, but of all the other people I grew up among.

There were some strange characters living in our street. Across the road was Charlie Nelson and I don't think that I have ever seen an uglier man in my life – enormous, with a thick, mouldy sort of skin, and lots of little bumps on his face – but he had the most charming personality, and was always laughing and singing. He was the knocker-up. This job has disappeared in the age of alarm clocks and telephones, but without Charlie, those who had a job would never get there. He used to go round with a long pole, knocking at the windows at the time that you wanted to get up for work. For this you paid about threepence a week. He used to knock at our window at 4:30 each weekday and then would come back at 5 o'clock in case we had overslept. Most of the men drank very heavily, so without Charlie, I doubt that they would have got to work on time.

Around the corner in Piley Street lived Mother Ryah. She was quite a legend in Hoxton: no one knew how old she was; in fact, my mother said she looked just the same when she was a girl. She was a funny little woman. We used to say that she had dogs' paws and a

horse's head – this may not have been true, but certainly
she was a funny shape. She wore a man's straw boater,
and a long black mane, just like a horse's, hung down
her back. Little paws stuck out of the sleeves of her
long raincoat and she waddled from side to side like
a duck.

All the children used to follow the poor old lady and
call out 'Ole Muvver Ryah!', but as soon as she turned
to chase they fled in droves, screaming their heads off.
What the mystery of her birth was and where she went
when the bombs came, no one knew. She was very
fond of the police, and used to stand on the corner
talking to the copper on the beat.

In Hoxton this was a strange thing to do: you did
not hobnob with policemen, but kept them at a distance
unless they caught you hanging about, then a solid pane
of glass would go swinging through your ears. Boys
would charge through the market, nicking things off
the stalls. Stealing was something that was expected
in Hoxton, but policemen did not arrest children – I
suppose it was left to their parents to discipline them.

Further down the street was a terribly rough family,
the Carhiccis, who fought each other with knives and
choppers and sometimes guns. We children would stand
in a crowd and watch while they nearly murdered one
another at weekends. No one came forward and said,
'You must not see all this violence; it will spoil your
character when you grow up.' It was part of our
everyday life, but I don't think my generation were
as vicious and violent as young people are today, and
I sometimes wonder if it's not better to grow up the
hard way.

I remember some other neighbours: Greg and Gladys
Goring, an elderly couple who always sat together on
the window-sill. He was fat and burly had been a carter
– you only had to look at him to know he owned horses.
He had retired when I knew him and would sit there on

the doorstep with a quart of brown ale at his side. As soon as it was empty one of the kids would be sent up to the pump for another one.

The old lady, known as Gran, would sit placidly next to him in her clean white apron, until she was summoned out. A little child would come running up: 'Would you please come? Muvver wants yer.' Then Gran would get up, pick up her carpet bag and set off to help a new little babe into the world. She was the best midwife and brought all the local babies into the world. There was no training for this sort of thing – you did it if you liked it, and Gran did. She must have been in her sixties when I was at school and she was still going strong after I left Hoxton.

The sad thing was that so many little ones were born and yet so many little ones died. Every family had lost some little brother or sister – if they got to five years old, you were lucky. Diphtheria was the chief killer, then there was TB. I remember the Robinsons, down at the bottom of the street – all these nice little fair-haired children, just getting buried one by one. We used to stand around and watch the funerals. All our entertainment was free – just watching the pattern of life that went on around us.

I particularly remember Freddie Robinson. He was about my age and used to sing 'Hark the herald angels sing' in a beautiful, high-pitched voice. When I saw his little white coffin being carried out I thought of him as a little angel with wings.

There were some great characters at the market. This was held in a long, winding road, narrow at the top and widening as it went down towards the City. On each side were stalls of all descriptions: second-hand clothes stalls that did a roaring trade, fruit stalls and raffle stalls. On Saturdays the stalls stayed open till 10 or 11 o'clock at night, lit by gas flares that hissed overhead. You could get nice and warm hanging around these stalls, as most of the street kids had found out.

Behind the stalls were the shops: pie shops, sausage shops and fish and chip shops – there were a lot of windows for hungry children to feast their eyes on.

Right down at the bottom of the street was the Britannia, a theatre of sorts, which I used to pass every Sunday on our way to church. I longed with all my heart to go there. Dad told me that he'd been to the Britannia to see Marie Lloyd and other celebrities, and that when he got a winner up he would take me there.

By getting a winner up he meant the gee gees, for what little spare money there was often went in that direction. The street bookie, a seedy-looking character, used to stand on the corner of the street, with one or two other men posted to watch out for the cops.

There was a strange kind of class system in that little tight-packed square of street, bursting at the seams with squalling, shouting humanity. If you were a publican or a shopkeeper, you were somebody to be respected. Next on the list was the respectable church-going family, and last but not least were the stallholders – the costermongers.

These last were a breed apart – they even had their own language. For instance, they would say 'apples and pears' to mean 'going upstairs'; or a bloke might say to his mate, 'Can't go to the flicks, me whistle and flute's up Uncle's' – this meant he couldn't go to the cinema as he had pawned his best suit.

Uncle, as he was known down the street, did a roaring trade. Every Monday morning you would see some child or other sticking his head out of the front door and looking up and down the street. He would sidle out with a parcel tucked up in a sacking apron, then set off to the pawnshop with Dad's Sunday suit. From each house would come the little parcels, and they'd march up to Long & Doughty's with the three brass balls over the door. Sometimes there would be a couple of kids with a pramful of parcels, if they were really hard up. Then on Friday night, when the old man had brought home his wages, there would be a queue outside Uncle's waiting to draw out the pawned articles.

I used to have to take Dad's best trousers. The poor man never had a complete suit – just a pair of flannel trousers for weekends and a jacket from the second-hand stall. When he was at work he wore corduroy trousers with a little strap bib like the sort kids wear, and his clothes would be covered with grey cement dust.

How our parents must have had to struggle to keep up any sort of respectability.

We were the only Irish family in our street, for most of the Irish families lived at the other end of the market, near the Roman Catholic church of St Saviour's. Dad's pals used to come up to the Barley Mow for a chat, and on these nights there would be a good deal of excitement dished out to us children sitting outside. They would have a good drink up, sometimes ending outside the pub doing jigs and reels and swinging around the bollards singing Irish songs like 'The Rose of Tralee'. It did not always end happily: the Irish used to get into arguments with the locals and it would end up in a big fight with lots of yelling and screaming and police whistles blowing. My Dad would join in, sparring up to someone in his shirtsleeves. It used to scare the life out of me, and I'd run home and hide under the table.

On one occasion they were all taken down to the Old Street police station, and the story goes that on being asked their names, my Dad and his mate told the constable that their names were Connie and Florrie. The policeman did not find this amusing and said, 'OK, girls, no bail. Go back to the cell and try to remember your real names.' The funny thing was that my father's name being Cornelius, he was known as Connie, and his workmate Florentine was known as Florrie.

Chapter Three

Schooldays

School was a dreadful place and I have nightmares about it to this day. Gospall Street LCC School was a tall, grim building, with stone stairs and marble walls. I remember there were two calor-gas lights at the top of the stairs, but it was dark at the bottom. There were about forty kids in each class, with dirty, white little faces, thin legs and a terrible fear of the teacher. How anyone managed to learn the three R's I shall never know, though it is strange but true that more children could read at an early age then than can today, in spite of the bad conditions.

Looking back to when I was seven, I remember I had a teacher called Mrs Cornish, who wore a brown dress with a high white collar, just like a uniform, and a black cross on a thick cord around her neck. She was very quick to bring order, with a crack and a whack from the long, heavy ruler that she always held. But she was fanatical about history, and the compelling stories she told have stayed with me to this day.

I was a terribly nervous child and I dreaded playtime. We would all charge out into the tarmac playground, taking two pieces of bread and marge to eat, if we were lucky. The boys would charge about, knocking everyone down who got in their way, and the girls would gather in a group and tell dirty stories. I never seemed to be interested, though. For one thing, I was very small for my age, and for another, somehow I had nothing to say to them.

At 12:30 I would tear home to my brother and sister to get their dinner ready, as my mother would be out at work. She went out at six o'clock every day, leaving us two plates of cold faggots. I would peel the potatoes, then boil and mash them up with the faggots for the kids. Sometimes I would have to get the coal in from the yard down the road, hump it home and lay the fire for the evening, wash the kids and take them back to school – and then I could go back to that prison myself.

I didn't always have time to wash my hands after cleaning out the grate and black-leading the hearth, and I remember another teacher, Miss Victoria, who used to look at my dirty hands then look away with disdain. One day, when I was about eight, she called me up to the front of the class when I got back to school after the dinner hour. 'Come out, Lena Kennedy,' she said. 'Why, your hands are dirty. Look at your fingernails!' She made me stand out in front of the class, holding out my hands for everyone to see for about an hour. I felt terrible, with all the other kids grinning at me, my only crime being that I had laid the fire in my lunch hour and did not have time to wash my hands after taking the other children back to school.

There was one teacher who eventually took an interest in me when I won an essay competition, and she lent me books, but Miss Victoria continued to look down on me. When it came to getting my testimonial on the day I was leaving, she asked us what we wanted to do with our lives. Most girls said they wanted to get married and have babies, but I stood up, stuck my chin out and said, 'I want to travel the world and write books.' It was pathetic, a pale-faced ragged kid daring to be so ambitious. I was squashed flat as usual, with a sort of sneer. She dismissed me coolly with a wave of her hand, saying, 'Sit down, Lena Kennedy. Next girl, please,' and there were sniggers from my classmates, for how could a scruffy little kid like me expect to do such things? On my testimonial she wrote, 'unpunctual, unclean', and with a twinge of conscience, added, 'would do well at books.' I never forgot her snub and it only made me all the more determined to make it. When I became famous I often thought how I would love to tell her, but life seems to play odd tricks on us, for more often than not when we get our revenge, it's too late, and Miss Victoria was probably not in this world any more.

I remember always feeling unhappy at school, and think how lucky the children are today with their school dinners. My brother and sister and I were more fortunate than most because my mother worked, so we could eat at lunch time, but lots of children went hungry or down to Daddy Burt's for a free dinner. Once I went to 'Truss', as the kids called it, being short for Father Burt's Trusthouses. Father Burt was a great philanthropist who did much good work in that poor area of London and Daddy Burt's mission was part of the Ragged Union, a religious society that endeavoured to feed these hordes of hungry children.

First we all queued outside, then when the doors opened there was one big rush to get to the long wooden table and forms in the middle of the hall. Rough boys pulled your hair and fought and swore, and trampled over the little babies to get first seat. If it was full up you had to stand and wait hungrily for the next sitting. If you did get a seat, once you were all settled, a prayer was said. The famished children waited expectantly for the meal to arrive. I watched one girl of about twelve in charge of four or five brothers and sisters, and some of the families seemed to be made up of sixteen or even seventeen ragged little children. Finally a man came along and placed a tin plate in front of each child, and slowly women went round, dishing out meat

pie and mashed potatoes with a slosh of brown gravy
on each plate. At the word 'go' the kids scoffed down
the food like pigs at a trough. Those who finished first
larked about, shouting, pinching other children's food
and throwing around spoons and plates.

I never went again to Daddy Burt's but would look
after the children myself and forage for a dinner for
them. My poor mother would say, 'You're a good girl
and a great help.'

I was always a bookworm. To get away from the
children and the dirt and squalor of the street, I'd hide
away with a book – my favourite spot was Griggs' cart.
The Griggses owned the stables that ran underneath our
house, and when old Tom the horseman went to bed,
the pony-cart that he used to collect old Winnie would be
left in the yard, making a cosy little seat. Every evening
in the summer I'd be tucked up in there, with only the
snoring and muttering of old Tom from the stable to
disturb me.

Around the corner there were a few shops, and one
of these sold second-hand books and comics – you could
get a second-hand comic for a ha'penny. This was my
main supply of reading material and I used to rummage
around for hours in the pile of dusty old books. I read
Compton Mackenzie, Jane Austen and Jules Verne and
several more besides. The old boy would say, 'Gawd,
your mum will tan your arse if she catches you reading
these books! Have a nice comic, love.' No, I had to
have books. He used to lend me books free of charge,
because he knew I was poor and interested, and as long
as I took care of them I could go to his shop each week
for a new one. Ten years old seemed young to take an
interest in matters like war and sex, but these were real
stories of love, life and travel. I used to dream that when
I grew up, I'd travel the world and write lovely stories
about all the things I'd seen.

I began to hate school and whenever possible I'd pretend to be ill so I could stay at home and read. By the time I was twelve I had got through all of Dickens' books, *Tom Brown's Schooldays*, *The Swiss Family Robinson*, and many more. Rudyard Kipling's poems really interested me, and I recited 'If' to myself till it was perfect.

At eleven years of age I was small and thin, with a pasty face. Some of the girls at school chased after the boys, but I never looked in their direction, for I thought I was very ugly. My uncle used to say, 'Be careful, ugly duckly' and I was very hurt until I read the story of the ugly duckling.

I made a friend around this time whose name was Kitty. She was everythig that I wished to be, with her dark flowing hair in two long braids, glowing black eyes, and long legs in black stockings. Kitty liked the boys and would ask me to come to the park with her and have some fun. I used to go, but I never understood what went on there.

The park was in De Beauvoir Square, a stone's throw from where we lived. All the boys of our age would hang about there and Kitty was much appreciated in the game that they played. The boys would chase the girls around the park, and when they caught one they would push her against the park railings, and one boy would hold the girl's arms back while another would kiss her. The girls would squeal and giggle, but I never liked the game and would run back home, only to be chastised and told not to play with Kitty.

One night one of the girls was yelling and crying and no one went to her rescue. The next day I asked the other girls what all the screaming had been for and they whispered together and said that some boy was trying to take her garter off. This was all a mystery to me and eventually I went back to my books and lost my friend.

A few weeks later, Kitty's family were evicted from their little house. Kitty's mother was a cripple, and it was pathetic to see the little grey-haired woman sitting crying, her possessions all piled around her, while the bailiffs boarded the door and windows of the house. The neighbours gathered around in sympathy, offering cups of tea. Several of the men were drunk, complaining loudly about the Irish evictions, and one punched the landlord on the nose.

Eventually the family were taken off to the Bung House, or the Land of Promise, as it was called and Kitty was sent to another school, but I heard later that she'd run away at the age of sixteen.

All these families with their problems – sometimes it seems to me like a huge, complicated patchwork quilt.

Chapter Four

Out to Work

I was fourteen when I left school and the next day, carrying my testimonial from the headmistress, I went in search of a job. With my friend Mary I wandered through the narrow backstreets towards the City in search of a job in a clothing factory.

Mary was a large, blowsy girl with a grubby face, who already had a child at home – reported to be by her own father. I remember I hardly listened to Mary as we went along, as I was worrying about my brother Teddy, who had fallen on his arm that morning. I was feeling guilty, as I knew I should have taken him to the hospital, but I was so excited and anxious to get out and find a job.

We walked a long way before we came to the right address and we climbed a steep, smelly flight of steps up to the factory. I clenched my hands nervously as the boss, Mr Fox, looked me up and down. 'Yer don't look fourteen,' he said, as the sweat dropped from his broad forehead. He squinted at my testimonial, then declared: 'Books! Won't get much time to read books here! I'll put yer on bastings.' I was thrilled that I had been given a job.

A small, wiry man came into the office and took us off to the busy workroom, where he made us sit on a

low wooden bench next to an enormous old lift. The
cutter and tailor stood nearby, snipping material with
large shears and making jokes about us. A pile of coats
grew all around us, and as fast as I could manage, my
fingers picked and pulled at the strong white basting
cotton amid the whirr of the sewing machines. Life at
the sweatshop had begun.

At six o'clock the hooter went, and with stiff legs
I started down the flight of stairs. What confusion on
those steps in that homeward rush – boys tore past,
jumping two at a time, fat women carrying large
handbags waddled down, everyone pushed and shoved,
having a desperate urge to get out into the cold air.

Outside I stood watching the trams trundle past. I had
no money, so I set off on foot and flinched nervously as
I passed the dim street corners where the unemployed
men loafed about. On my way I relived my first day at
work in my mind, and the thought of returning there
the next day made my heart sink.

I was glad to reach my own street. The kids were still
playing out in the light of the streetlamps, yelling and
shouting, but I found it a refreshing sound after the dull
humming of the sewing machines in the sweatshop that
seemed still to ring in my ears.

When I got home I got the fire blazing and put the
heavy iron kettle on to boil, and then scrubbed the
potatoes – Dad loved spuds boiled in their jackets. When
the chores were done I settled down with my books and
became immersed in medieval England at King Arthur's
court, picturing the beautiful ladies and their courteous
knights, but my daydreams were suddenly shattered by
the noisy arrival of my younger sister Molly and my
brother Teddy.

Little Ted looked pinched and pale and he had a big
woollen scarf wound around his arm. 'Teddy's arm
don't 'alf 'urt 'im,' Molly declared. 'Mrs Brown said
yer ought to take him up the slope.' ('The slope' was our

name for the hospital, since the entrance to the hospital in Kingsland Road was a steeply sloping ramp.)

'Disgraceful, she says it is,' Molly continued, 'a little boy going about crying all day.' His arm looked twisted and swollen, and his lashes dripped with tears.

I took him to the casualty department of the Metropolitan Hospital. It was quite a way down the main road and Teddy whined all the time. We had to wait a long time and finally, when we reached the door of the surgery, he began to vomit. A nurse ran up with an enamel dish and the doctor arrived, saying, 'Great Scott! This child has a broken arm – why wasn't he brought here before now?'

I started crying and I told him I had been at work. 'Oh dear,' muttered the doctor, wiping his brow, 'where are your parents to let a little lad suffer all day?'

'My mother's dead,' I told him 'and Dad's not home from work yet.'

'The doctor looked bewildered but his voice became kinder as he said, 'Take this girl to the canteen and get her something to eat while I fix up this boy.' Eventually with Bovril and biscuits inside us and Teddy's arm in plaster, we trotted home, but my legs were so weary that all I wanted to do was to get home and sleep.

I had started work in the same old black dress that I had worn for my mother's funeral. It was long and hung around my legs unevenly, since I had lost the tie-belt. One day, however, I arrived at work in a white blouse and black skirt – it was the same old black dress, but it had been turned into a skirt and washed, ironed and shortened, and the blouse had cost three shillings from Levi's, the local shop. It was snow-white with a Peter Pan collar and three pearly buttons down the front. I was so proud of that blouse.

I had looked at it in Levi's window for a long time before getting up enough courage to ask the price.

Mrs Levi told me it was three shillings – and I only had two shillings. Seeing my disappointment, she said, 'You can pay me the two bob and I'll keep it for you, and the next time you come in you can pay me the rest,' then added kindly, 'and you're gonna look real nice in that white blouse – gonna be a pretty girl when yer grown a bit.'

I felt so excited, and the next weekend I paid off the rest and cut out my skirt and put elastic in the waist.

On the Monday morning, when I took off my shabby coat, and walked leisurely through the workroom, the cutters and tailors all stopped and stared. 'Hey, look at our Lena!' they declared, 'what a pretty girl!' and the forelady said, 'My, my! Very nice, dear.' All through that day I wallowed in the pleasure of being admired; it was something that had never happened to me before.

You can imagine my horror when I went home one day to find my sister Molly dressed in the beautiful white blouse, playing tag up and down the street with a mob of kids. I was so overcome with rage, I dashed at her and tried to pull the precious garment off her, but Molly was sturdy and fought back until the blouse was in ribbons. She howled and struggled under my grip as a neighbour yelled, 'You spiteful cow, Lena, leave your little sister alone!'

Before Dad reached the entrance to Griggs' yard that night he was informed of the scrap by the nosy neighbours in the street.

'Dearie me,' he said to us later, 'little birds in their nests don't fight, and so brothers and sisters must love and respect each other.'

We stood before him red-eyed and ashamed and said sorry to each other.

On Saturdays I'd try to clean up the week's accumulation of mess, but the lace curtains hung down in holes and had turned a musty yellow, and the long leather sofa at the back of the room now had the springs hanging down to the floor and bunches of horsehair protruding through the leather, as Teddy had used it so often as a horse in his wild games of Buffalo Bill.

Saturday was also bath night, and I'd place the old tin tub in front of the fire, filled with water that had been carried in buckets from the end of the yard and heated on the stove. First Teddy would be dumped in and washed, and then Molly, and finally it would be my turn. When I had got dressed I would collect more water and wash all the vests and pants, socks and shirts, and hang them about the fireplace, where they dried in no time.

It was at about this time that I made friends with Rosie Smith, who introduced me to the baths. Rosie lived in our street, and she came from a family of thirteen children. I used to wonder how they all managed to squeeze into their two-roomed house and scullery.

Mr Smith, the father of the family, was seldom home, as he worked long hours as a French polisher in the furniture trade, and when he did eventually come home there seemed scarcely to be any room for him to sit down because there were so many children. He was a tiny, softly spoken man. Since his house was crowded with his own children and their friends, he would often clamber up on to the stone copper in the corner of the scullery and, with his chin on his hands and his elbows on his knees, he would try to sleep amid the clamour of all the young ones sitting and playing on the floor.

Mrs Smith's family were always very clean and their back yard constantly displayed long lines of snow-white washing. She spent most evenings in her front room, ironing. She would heat the flat iron and spit on it vigorously before pressing all the small trousers and shirts.

I often saw Rosie Smith hurrying down the road on a Sunday as I walked to church, and I wondered where she could be going. One day I gathered up my courage and caught up with her.

'Where are you going?' I asked her.

'To the barves,' she replied primly. 'I go regular every Sunday.'

I asked her if I could go with her.

'Well, you're supposed to take your own soap and towel,' said Rosie, 'but if you've got tuppence you can hire them, and you'll need another tuppence to get in.'

I decided to take a chance and go to these 'barves' that Rosie seemed to enjoy so much.

I remember the first time we went together to the large, grim-looking Victorian building. Inside, the green and white tiled corridors echoed coldly as we walked. Rosie bossily guided me through the turnstile and an irritated-looking woman glared at us from a small window. 'First or second?' she snapped.

'Second class,' Rosie replied and the woman handed us the tickets. 'My friend wants soap and a towel,' said Rosie.

I handed over the extra tuppence and was given a hard white linen towel and a small square of green soap. We joined a row of people on a long wooden bench and sat there silently. One by one they got up as the word 'next' was called. When it came to our turn, we went into another room, from which came lots of noise and clouds of steam, and finally into what looked like a marble cell. In the middle of the cell was a huge, deep bath, and steaming water rushed from a pipe, pouring into the bath at a terrific rate.

A stout woman with a purple face, the sleeves of her overall rolled up to the elbow, snapped, 'Don't dawdle and don't lock the door – you kids lark about too much.'

When I was left alone with all that water I tentatively dipped my big toe in – it was very hot. Suddenly Rosie's voice came over the walls of the cell: 'What number are you in, Lena?'

'Number five,' I returned, looking up at the number on the door.

'I'm next door – number six, she informed me.

'I can't get in – it's too hot,' I called.

'Well call out for more cold, you silly cow!' cried Rose, and she demonstrated in a loud voice, yelling out, 'More hot for number six!' then, to me, 'Now you call out for cold.'

I timidly asked for more cold and Rosie roared with laughter, but it had worked, for the attendant's voice growled 'say when', as a great volume of cold water shot out of the pipe into the bath.

Soon I was immersed in the steaming water. All round I could hear intimate conversations going on between the other people in the cells and much singing of popular songs. I splashed the hot water over my skinny limbs and lifted one leg high in the air to see the effect – why, my skin looked a different colour! I suddenly felt relaxed and I lay back and felt the lovely warmth get right through to my bones. For the first time ever I experienced the satisfaction of a good, hot, luxurious soak.

From then I went regularly to the barves and I started to take quite a pride in my appearance. After my weekly baths my skin felt fresh and clean, and I set my hair with clips and made a small kiss curl stuck down with sugar-water on my forehead. The finishing touch was a round slide that I had bought at Woolworth's. Although I was very slim, my breasts had grown and my hips had filled out.

The terrors of working in the sweatshop became less great, and I became quite used to most of the other workers there and didn't mind the cheekiness of the cutting-room boys who joked and flirted with me. When I left work the boys on the corner would give wolf whistles as I walked past but I ignored them and strode on – no low life was going to influence me, I had decided.

I also made a good friend at work. Her name was

Kunner – yiddish for Anna – but everyone called her Kunner in such an expressive way it sounded like a rude word. This was probably because she was generally disliked by her workmates – she was classed as a sweater because she was greedy for work, always on the lookout for an extra penny.

Kunner was an odd-looking woman, in her early thirties. She sat on her high stool with her head down, her shoulders rounded, and her short legs crossed as she worked. She always wore red: a red high-necked jumper, a tight red skirt, and smart shoes. Silk stockings with seams down the back completed the outfit, and before leaving each night she'd spend a lot of time making sure they were straight.

She was always gracious to me, offering me matzos spread with white butter, which I found strange but very appetising. Kunner was a fine needlewoman and expert at her job. She was also very involved in the Union. At that time unions were frowned upon by many workers as well as by the bosses: the defeat of the general strike had left its mark, so anyone who had a steady job would hang on to it at all costs. However, the tailors' union was growing in strength. Many of its members were Jewish, from the East End, and had strict socialist principles. Kunner's views were influenced by the Russian Revolution and she often made herself unpopular with her argumentative ways and strong support for the Union.

She took me under her wing and remarked how bright I was. 'Lena, my little treasure,' she would say, 'go down to the basement and ask Nick for his union dues. Do it quietly and don't tell anyone, and on Friday I'll give you a tanner.' So I collected the union dues and recorded them in a little book she gave me and gradually collected more from others that Kunner had recruited. It had to be done secretly as the Union was forbidden in the factory.

During the lunchbreaks I would sit and talk about socialism with her. I was curious about other people and different ways of thinking, and wanted to find out all about this movement that gave equal rights to rich and poor. Kunner loved to educate me and one night she asked me to go with her to a meeting in Bethnal Green. I found the evening very enjoyable. A lot of people made speeches from the platform and during the interval everyone was served with buns and a cup of tea. The atmosphere was free and easy and, even though I didn't understand much of the talk, I found it very stimulating – and I also liked the buns.

I went to several more political meetings, and I liked the warmth and community spirit of the Party, although I was still not sure of their ideals. I loved the history of the kings and queens of England, the colourful clothes they wore and the victorious battles they fought, but these folk did not believe in such stuff, so I kept quiet about my interest.

Kunner always carried a book with her and often spent the lunchtime reading. She belonged to the Foyles' Bookclub and for the price of two shillings a month would receive a copy of the current bestselling novel. 'Don't make them dirty and I'll lend them to you,' she said to me one day.

I wallowed in the new excitement of fiction and politics, but when Dad heard that I had been going to these meetings, he went wild. 'Is this the sort of company you've been keeping all this time, Ellen Kennedy?' he roared. He stamped and shouted but I stood my ground, even though I hated to upset him. It was only when he started yelling that he was going to find Kunner and give her what-for that I got scared.

I rushed out of the house and went down to find the parish priest, Father Blake. He was understanding and kind, and suggested that I should keep myself occupied on Friday evenings by coming to church meetings. I had no intention of going round the church in a long blue cape and white cap, so I compromised and said I'd give up my job. My sister Molly was now getting on for fourteen and was leaving school to go to work at the match factory, which meant that there would be no one at home to look after Teddy when he came out of school. Dad said he'd do some overtime and we'd manage, and it was better I stayed at home, although he was sorry he'd upset me once he'd got over the shock of it all.

So I left the sweatshop. I did feel a slight pang of remorse as I climbed down the steep flight of stairs for the last time. I had made some good friends there, people who had been kind and looked after me.

But Dad was pleased about my staying at home and looking after the place. There was another consolation: I discovered the local free library that had now come into operation, so I'd spend afternoons huddled in the old armchair reading until Teddy came home from school.

When Teddy was old enough to be left alone after school and Molly was more independent and settled at her job, I decided to go out to work again. This time I found myself a better job, in C & A modes. I gradually worked my way up to become a buttonhole machinist and was very proud of my position.

Some Friday evenings on my way home from work I would see a little crowd of boys standing at the corner of the bank. These were the Islington boys, a little crowd that was one up on the lads from our street and held in a certain respect. I noticed one boy in particular: he wore a white collar and was tall, with dark hair and a lovely broad smile. He would look over at me as I passed and a friend told me his name was Fred. From then on I made up my mind I was determined to get him.

One day he spoke to me as I got off the bus. We talked about our jobs, and he told me all about his work as a trainee cameraman at Gainsborough Studios. Gradually we got to know each other and we developed a little routine: every Friday evening after work he would be waiting for me at the bus stop and we'd go and have a drink and a chat and then we'd say goodbye, so I could go home and get Dad's supper and see that Teddy and Molly were in.

Fred came from a nice family – his father was a carpenter and they had a nice house at Islington. His family seemed staid in comparison to mine – he had been given a Victorian type of upbringing – but in Fred I found great values. He was loyal and dutiful, and it seemed he had made his mind up on me too, but that was Fred. He had the loveliest blue eyes that would change colour according to his mood – I could always tell whether he was unhappy or not.

One Friday evening he came back to my scruffy little house and helped me get the fire going, and Dad was so pleased that I had found a homely young man.

After that we spent many hours touring the country side on Fred's motorbike. It got me away from the streets of Hoxton and he was a nature lover, like me. Sometimes we'd ride out to the sea. Brighton was a favourite place, and we'd walk along the beach and sit and watch the sunset. We were so happy together. Fred began to spend more and more time at my house, helping me to make it look nice and look after the family. Whatever problem came up, in his calm, capable way he would put it right, and so I became Fred's girl and he was always there to look after me.

Book IV

The Road to Fame

Chapter One

Queenie

Not long after baby Alan was born we took him to see his father. Little Georgie stayed with the in-laws and Angela tucked Alan into the carrycot, then we set off on the train from Waterloo to the Isle of Wight. She was very excited about seeing her husband again.

The porter on the train provided hot water to heat the baby's bottle, and a few nosy women chattered to Angela, admiring the baby and trying to find out where she was going, but she would not say.

On the ferry crossing we soon got talking to some of the other wives who were going to the prison, and they pointed out a little group of women who were going to the top security prison. We also met an affluent gentleman who told us he was a television director. In our naivety, we told him all about my books and he gave us his name so we could write to him at the television centre. On our return we did this but got no reply.

However, something positive did come out of that visit to the prison, for it gave me the idea for another book. The subject was to be a man who was unjustly convicted. So far I had written mainly about women, but I did not seem to be having much luck with my women's stories, so I decided I would try another point of view.

While Angela went in to visit Apples, I sat outside in the small waiting room. The musty smell of stale cigarette smoke lingered in the air, making me want to heave, for since my operation I had given up smoking. I sat and watched the comings and goings of the visitors and the sad faces of the women with children who came to visit their men, and all the while my mind was creating.

A vanload of prisoners stopped outside by the gate, and their hungry faces peered hopefully into the waiting room as their names were checked on a list by a prison officer. These men were being brought in from the fields after a morning's work. Among the group was a face that stood out: an intellectual-looking man, with a lean face and a little beard. He looked up at me with an anxious expression, then bent his head in thought. His face reminded me of Joe, my lovely teacher from the evening classes who went back to America, and I wondered why he was in prison.

I began to imagine an educated man, unjustly convicted, who would spend many years fighting for his freedom. Dreamily I sat in the musty waiting room, the face of that prisoner before me. My thoughts were interrupted when Angela came back, but I knew I had the character for my next novel.

On our way home Angela was tearful, her voice sometimes breaking as she talked about the visit. Apples had given her a lovely painting, and she told me that he had given up all his supply of tobacco to another prisoner to paint this for him from a photograph.

As she looked dismally out of the train window at the fields and I fed baby Alan, I tried to lift her spirits by talking about Oscar Wilde, who wrote the *Ballad of Reading Gaol* and was himself imprisoned. 'You ought to tell Apples to get that book from the prison library,' I told her, but she was only half listening to me.

Thinking of Wilde and the marvellous literature he

wrote while he was in prison sparked my imagination, and as the train made its way to Waterloo I was placing my new character, Joe, a lonely intellectual shut up in prison.

Time was a great healer for Angela and she coped well. The WRVS contacted her and offered her a pram when baby Alan was old enough to sit up. We went to collect it, but it was so old-fashioned that Angela refused to use it.

Alan was a happy, contented baby, and when his father eventually came home he put his chubby arms around him and said, 'Daddy'.

Apples said he was now a reformed man, and they seemed very happy together. They talked about moving out to the country and Angela would dreamily tell me how she would like to live in a cottage with lots of pets and ducks. I would listen to her plans, wondering privately how they would cope. Country life was grand if you had money but treacherous in wintertime if you didn't have a car or a job, and I hoped it was all just a passing fancy. Moreover, I could never imagine Angela getting Apples to move far away from his East End family.

When the family settled down again and all was back to normal, Angela's dreams of a country cottage soon faded. It was not long before she and I began looking around for some new evening classes to attend, because although we enjoyed the class at Hackney, none of our classmates ever thought about getting anything published. Eventually we found another class in Leyton.

By this time I thought myself quite an adequate writer, even though I was still unpublished. But after listening to the female teacher lecturing at the new class, I wondered how ever the others managed to create a story at all, there seemed to be so many rules and regulations. She set us a story to write and I was very

taken aback when the next week my little story was
returned to me with a very low mark. The page was
full of crossings out and red correction marks.

I came out of the class saying to Angela, 'I'm
not going back there; she's completely destroyed my
confidence.' Angela comforted me and took me for a
drink at the pub to cheer me up. But I continued my
tirade: 'Perhaps my grammar is incorrect? Perhaps I'm
wasting my time, trying to be a writer?' I was full of
self-doubt. The teacher had accused me of overwriting
– I wasn't even sure what that meant.

However, after a few drinks I calmed down enough to
notice a fair young woman sitting on a stool at the bar.
She was well made-up and looked like the manageress of
the bar, from the way she gave orders. Her small, astute
eyes did not miss a trick as she surveyed the room.

I was also thinking of 'Joe', my prisoner who had
been with me for a while now. I noticed how the
blonde at the bar fussed over a man who came in with
a little brown paper bag and I thought, perhaps he has
just come from prison. I could not help staring as I put
the character of Joe in his place. She fussed over this
man and soon took him off into a little back room.

As Angela and I sat there enjoying our Guinness, I
found a scene unfolding in my mind. I decided I would
call the manageress Queenie, and I would put her in a
pub down by the Tower of London. Upstairs in the
pub I would have a little office where all the crooks
would plan their jobs and my character of Joe would
go there when he was free to clear his name.

I told Angela my ideas and we talked it over, then
she changed the subject to the painting Apples had
given her. Suddenly an idea came flooding to me and
I knew I had the missing link: not only would Joe
write poems for the other prisoners to send to their
wives, he could also paint pictures for them . . . and
what if he was to paint the beautiful Queenie, only

to discover later that she was the key to proving his innocence?

I found I had already forgotten my bad experience at the new evening class, for now I had discovered Queenie. I declared to Angela: 'I think I'll make Queenie a nymphomaniac,' and she started to giggle. I was glad that the blonde who sat hunched up on her stool couldn't hear us.

Angela shook her head in disbelief: 'I don't think anyone will ever stop you from writing, Mum, because no matter what that silly teacher says, you have a rare gift, and one day the world will see it too.'

Chapter Two

A River Outing

A year later the novels of *Susan* and *Joe* were completed.
We saw an advertisement in a magazine for a crime
story competition. It specified that the story must be
no longer than 20,000 words, and we spent hours going
over the manuscript of *Joe*, trying to shorten it. After we
had sent it off, we waited each day with anticipation for
the postman to call, but *Joe* came back with the usual
cold noncommittal rejection slip.

I lost interest in seeking publication – it all seemed
so soul-destroying – and decided to settle for the sheer
joy of my art. Angela was fed up with the rejections
too, and she went to college to study for 'O' levels.

She put hours into writing essays, getting very
harassed. I would find the essays very interesting,
but the lecturers would return them saying that they
were too emotional, or that she should stick to the
facts. We would have little disagreements over this, as
I would tell her that I felt that academic training could
destroy any creative gift that was already there. I did
not want to be unkind and tell her she was wasting her
time, but I really did feel that the pattern of academic
training had a way of holding your mind down, and
that if you were to be a writer it needed to be free.

That summer at Cliffe we had the usual visits from

the family, but often Angela and the children would arrive at the same time as Keith and one of them would have to leave, as they were still not speaking to each other.

This always upset me. Fred was beginning to talk about getting away somewhere different for a few weeks, as he was getting fed up of being caught in the middle between Angela and Keith.

One day Keith arrived, his face beaming, and told me that he had just bought a boat. I was very proud of him. Every one called him the Whizz Kid, and I nicknamed his business 'The Elephant Line' after the successful TV series, *The Onedin Line*.

We walked around the garden, and he talked about building a lovely big house here for us, with three loos and two bathrooms. What would I want three loos for, I asked him, but that was my son – he always had big ideas.

My heart would have broken if they had pulled down my little hut and my lovely trees, but Keith understood the way I was, always clinging to old associations.

It was a luxury to stroll around the garden with my lovely son. Little bunches of golden marigolds smiled sweetly at us, and he helped me collect seeds and put them in trays so that I would have lots of late summer flowers. His burnished gold hair shone in the sunlight as he chatted eagerly about his new boat with a Mercedes engine. I preferred to remain noncommittal about the boat, since I was worried that they might try to get me in it – I preferred to keep my two feet on the ground.

Later Keith discussed the new boat with Fred. I had to laugh when I saw Fred lifting the tarpaulin off his boat, which had sat there on the lawn, unfinished, for twenty years. I could not help whispering to Keith, 'Take no notice, dear, that's Fred's Noah's Ark, and you definitely won't ever get me in *that*.'

Keith, as always, saw the funny side but when he

insisted, 'You'll be safe in my boat, Mum,' I wasn't
so sure.

Before long my old friends Maureen and Jim arrived
with their daughter Denny. I was very pleased to see
them return to the woods and we sat around the table
on the lawn and drank some home-made wine and
talked of old times.

Jim, politically minded as ever, spouted on about the
bourgeoisie that had moved into the woodlands – 'all
cleaning their bleeding cars on Sunday afternoons.' He
hated the little box-like houses that surrounded us and
I was glad when the wine took effect and Keith turned
the conversation to boats.

It seemed Jim also had a boat and although it was old,
it was still seaworthy. Before long Keith and Jim had
become engrossed in their conversation and Maureen
and I looked on, astounded, as a trip down the Thames
was planned. It was decided that Jim's boat could take all
the camping equipment and could be towed if need be
by Keith's boat, which had a more powerful engine.

To my surprise, Fred was all for this venture. Keith
was ready to organise the whole thing, saying he
thought it was about time Mum had a holiday like
this. I was not so sure, and got very panicky when I
suddenly remembered I couldn't swim very well, but I
thought I'd better keep quiet, as they were all so keyed
up. Maureen and I just poured ourselves a big glass of
wine and hoped it would all come to nothing.

It was nightfall before I said goodbye to them at the
gate. The scent of honeysuckle pervaded the air and the
moon lit the path with a silvery light. Maureen clung
to my arm as the 'Captains Courageous' shook hands
at the gate on their deal. 'Well, Maureen,' I whispered
as she got in the car, 'we'll either sink or swim.' She
was still laughing as I waved goodbye, but it seemed
that our two-week river holiday was planned.

★   ★   ★

A month later we met at the quay at Gillingham, all set
to launch our boats into the rough sea. The men made
several attempts to launch the boats and then stood there
arguing, so Maureen and I decided to leave them to it
and sloped off to the Waterman's Arms, feeling very
cold and fed up.

Some hours later the men turned up, moaning and
groaning that we had made them miss the tide and that
we now all had to go by car to Teddington Lock.

After much debate it was decided that Keith's boat
should tow Jim's little boat with all the camping
equipment up to Teddington and we would meet
him there.

By the time Keith arrived at Teddington, wet and
dishevelled, we were all freezing and fed up with waiting and Maureen exclaimed, 'It was bleeding quicker
by car!'

How we got on to the boats I'll never know, but I
felt very apprehensive as I waved farewell to my son at
the quay. I was beginning to wish I had never ventured
from my books, my garden and my old haunts, for this
holiday was turning into a catastrophe.

Should you have been standing on the banks of the
Thames one Sunday evening in late July, you might
have beheld the strangest sight. Along the crowded river
chugged our little blue motor boat. Fred steered the
boat with a grim expression on his face and I, wearing
a large, floppy sunhat and an outsize yellow life jacket,
clung grimly to the sides. I looked back anxiously for the
Buccaneer, the small boat that we were towing through
the crowded river. Maureen and Jim's boat was loaded
with bundles and passengers. Maureen clung frantically
of an umbrella and Jim, the with-it Dad in his straw
hat, stood beside their two young sons.

The small boat careered from side to side, oblivious
of the hooting of the other boats. Grandpa Fred steered
steadily on while Grandma Lena looked anxiously to

find the small boat that had disappeared under a huge willow tree that hung over the river. Suddenly it appeared again, all its occupants lying flat and camouflaged by the leaves of the willow. Grandma gave an anxious wave, then suddenly she disappeared and a pair of black-clad legs shot up in the air. For a brief moment her floppy hat and yellow life jacket seemed to float on the water. Then, with a prodigious heave, she pulled herself up into the boat and down under the deck into the hull.

When I reappeared I felt very dazed and could not help but cross myself. The passengers aboard the *Buccaneer* held their hands to their mouths in consternation while Fred steered steadily on. He was so proud to be taking this boat out, and nothing or no one was going to deter him from making steady progress up the Thames.

Gradually the cortège made its way upriver, Grandpa dodging in and out of a small fleet of sailing boats steered by men in life jackets and little else. It seemed the language of weekend sailors was no better than that of weekend motorists but by now I had recovered and proceeded to return their swearwords, word for word.

Then I heard shouts coming from the *Buccaneer*: 'Mind the rock!' I shouted a warning to Fred, but before we knew it the smaller boat had swung round in the current and was caught against the rocks, unable to move, as we drifted alongside them. I can only remember clawing and hanging on to those rocks, pushing with all my might to try and stop our boat being smashed against them, until I heard Fred's calm and austere voice commanding me to let go. We glided back out into the river and I looked behind to see Maureen waving and calling 'It's OK,' as their boat followed.

At Richmond the river scene was reminiscent of Petticoat Lane on a Sunday morning: small boats came at us in all directions; large boats created a terrific wash that nearly drowned us; and small boys swam precariously across the bow, but still Sir Chichester Smith sailed steadily on.

We arrived at Chertsey Lock all in one piece, little realising that the hazards had only just begun. I clambered up a slippery wall and aimed a coil of slimy rope straight into the face of the lock-keeper, then I held frantically on to a long, green, slimy chain and saw the water disappearing beneath me.

I began to think I'd almost got my river legs, but there were still another hundred locks to pass through and I can't say I was looking forward to my annual holiday of being the fat grandma on the boat, for I still had the task of camping on the towpaths, cooking and shopping to look forward to.

I was relieved when we pulled into a quiet place where the trees hung over the water, with only the sound of the birds to disturb the peace.

There was an inn nearby and we went for a drink. Later I lost myself for a while in my writing and wrote a little short story called 'The Three Chimneys'.

'You at it again?' Fred asked as I sat dreamily with my pen and paper on the bank, looking out towards the inn with the tall chimneys.

Before long, we made headway along the river, but Maureen's twins got very bored and slumped on the deck refusing to do any work.

I looked up at the land over the bank and spied red buses going by – Maureen and I could not believe that after all this hard work we could just get a bus home. I looked at Sir Chichester Smith with deep sympathy as he moved slowly on, but I must admit, it was a relief when the twins played up so much that we decided to call it a day and head back down the river.

Chapter Three

Auntie Mary

We continued to spend a lot of time at Cliffe. One visitor who was always welcome was Auntie Mary (Nanny Murphy's daughter and my godmother). She was always smiling and pleased to see me, and we would catch up on all the family gossip. We shared the same love of nature, and she wrote beautiful poetry. She was almost eighty years old and the only person I knew who didn't grumble about the toilet in the days when we still did not have the water mains connected outside. She would shuffle across the lawn, saying how very pleased she was that she didn't have to climb the stairs as her legs were bad.

Auntie's hair was silver-grey and she wore it in a long plait down her back. She had a natural ladylike quality. She never had any children, but each year her husband Mick would present her with a piece of jewellery, and her diamond rings sparkled like her mind, which ticked over very quickly. She had the same twinkling brown eyes as my lovely Nanny Murphy, and the same wisdom and understanding of people and, like Nanny Murphy, loved to tell the tea leaves.

When she came to stay each summer after her husband died, she would look around the garden for the lilac rose, called 'Blue Moon', which I had planted for her Mick.

She would cup the full bloom in her wrinkled white hands and declare how beautiful it was, and admire my rose garden. There was now a rose tree for baby Alan, the newest member of our family.

Auntie had often inspired my work as she was the one who told me all about our Irish ancestors, and my novel *Lizzie* was based on my aunt's many tales about her working life as a forelady in the factories. As we sat on the lawn and I read to her my stories which she loved to hear, I could feel her mind sometimes straying to the past and memories of her beloved husband.

Some mornings Auntie would wander around the garden to feed the birds, when the dew still carpeted the lawn, wearing only open-toed sandals and no stockings. I would call after her to wrap up, but she took no notice, saying that she loved the open air – it was the gypsy in her soul. 'If it wasn't for my legs I'd be all right,' she would declare. Some days her legs were very bad, and she would tell me, 'they just will not work'. I would smile to myself as I watched her make the sign of the cross on her forehead, for once Auntie had done this her faith would be restored and she would be walking again around the garden to explore the beauty of nature, almost forcing those legs to work.

Auntie loved her annual holiday with me and many visitors would come to see her, for she was very popular. I remember one particular incident that still makes me smile to myself when I recall it.

I had a friend called Beryl, who lived around the back in Tennyson Avenue and would often call in on us. On this particular day she arrived with a cutting of a willow tree she'd promised me, for I had often admired the long trailing branches of the willow that swept down over the steps of her smart bungalow. Beryl was pleased to see Auntie and asked her if she was going to tell the tea leaves this year for her.

While Beryl looked around for the right position for

the willow, I put the kettle on and Auntie was left in charge of making the tea. Beryl in her commanding way decided the willow should go in straight away while it was moist, saying, 'It will look nice beside the fish pond, so let's put it there.' I followed her round to the back of the shack, and doing as I was told I picked up my trowel to dig the earth. We stopped for a while as she admired the water lilies that Fred had planted in the pond. I was very proud of the lovely white flowers that seemed to float on the water, and couldn't help showing off a little, but Beryl was looking down at my odd socks and I noticed a flicker of a smile cross her lips. I said, 'They say it's lucky, don't they, Beryl?' and her face creased with laughter, for however smart she was, I know she loved my easygoing ways. I had got used to her meticulous ways too – she was not untidy like me when I worked in my garden.

We returned to the shack soon after to find the garden table covered with a nice white tablecloth and set with the best cups, a milk jug and a plate of biscuits. Eagerly Beryl sat down for her tea and said to Auntie in her haughty way, 'I hope you're going to tell my tea leaves and tell me something nice.'

I knew Auntie would do as she always did – she had an acute understanding of people and always told them just what they wanted to know. It was only ever done in fun but it was very entertaining.

Auntie, very pleased with herself, poured the tea from the best teapot as Beryl and I nattered on. I was pleased Auntie had laid the table so well as I liked things to be just so for Beryl. But when I tasted the tea I found it had a most unusual taste. I looked into the cup and could only see a thick black liquid with lumps in it – what on earth was it? I looked at Auntie in disbelief as, in her ladylike way, she sipped the liquid, and agreed with Beryl that she only liked to drink from bone-china cups. I could not help noticing that Beryl was pulling the strangest face and then she quickly got her hanky out to wipe her mouth.

Not wanting to embarrass poor Auntie, I kept quiet, and slipped inside the hut to investigate. I was not surprised to see an old battered tin of coffee beans open on the side that Fred had put in the cupboard twenty years ago. He insisting on keeping it, saying, 'They won't ever make coffee like this again.' I began to think he was probably right, because I had never tasted anything quite like it.

Without a word about this awful mistake I went out to ask Beryl if she would like another cup of tea, but she looked at me very oddly, and in a very cool, precise tone said, 'No, thank you, I really must be going,' and went on her way, not waiting for her tea leaves to be read. Her unfinished cup of twenty-year-old coffee beans remained on the side. Afterwards I couldn't help saying to Auntie, 'I hope she didn't think we were trying to poison her.' Auntie kept apologising but I soon got her to see the funny side of it and blamed Fred for being such a terrible hoarder. I went and dug a hole and chucked his coffee beans into it, then put the tin back in the same place, hoping it would be another twenty years before he looked in it.

During that holiday Fred and I took Auntie for a day out. We eventually ended up at a place called Jeanie's Inn, near some disused cement works. It reminded me of a Spanish castle, I am not sure why. The inn was ancient, but the huge white towers of the cement factory surrounded and overpowered it. It was a warm summer evening, and a full silvery moon outlined the tower, creating a weird shadowy atmosphere.

The landlady was Scottish and had often told me the story of how she had married a Campbell against her family's wishes. As I sat there looking out on to the eerie scene – the tall white towers that dominated the inn, the derelict cranes that decorated the skyline, the huge crater full of water – I thought about Jeanie and my mind began to stray to the bloodthirsty battles between the Macdonalds and the Campbells.

As I closed my eyes and listened to the sea beating monotonously over a broken-down jetty, somehow the silhouetted figure of a man walking along the jetty came before my eyes. His kilt waved in the breeze and the plumes on his bonnet moved agitatedly. His plaid was red, mauve and green – the tartan of the clan of Macdonald – and he played the bagpipes, a fierce warlike tune. As I screwed up my eyes I could see his iron-grey hair and huge whiskers.

'You're miles away,' Fred remarked as he brought us out our drinks, but Auntie understood and knew I was thinking about a story. I told her how the black-hearted Campbells fought fire and brimstone with the Macdonalds on the Flodden fields. I was thinking of a story about a Macdonald returning to haunt a Campbell, and before long, as I sat there under the night sky, the wild marshland around us, I could hear the tune in my head of the bagpipes that would return to haunt the proprietors of this inn.

Auntie, her mind in tune with mine, listened with interest as I created this story, but Fred's blue eyes were twinkling with amusement. 'Let's go home, girls, before I start hearing the flipping bagpipes too.'

The next day I was still thinking about my wandering piper, out there on the marsh, returning with fury to haunt the Campbells. 'Well, I hope he don't come here,' Fred remarked drily before informing me he was going off for the rest of the week with Keith to Germany on business.

I enjoyed that week with Auntie – we didn't have to worry about cooking and I could write when I wanted. We lazed under the oak, the dogs besides us, while little Marigold the cat crouched in the long grass, her yellow eyes glaring up at Percy and Pauline the pigeons, who sat defiantly on the fence. When the sun went in we went inside the hut and lit the wood burner. Most nights I got out my books, and read up on Scottish history to help me with my story of the Wandering Piper.

One evening the electricity went out, but determined not to be defeated, I found some candles and placed them on the table in front of me while I wrote. I loved the shadows the flickering candlelight cast across the room and the brightly coloured moths that buzzed around the room, attracted to the flame. I smiled to myself as I watched the flames flicker; it reminded me of the old days when we first came here and only had an oil lamp. Auntie dozed contentedly in her chair beside the stove while I read and wrote by candlelight into the early morning hours.

Late one evening she woke with a start and said she had had the most vivid dream. She told me that she had seen my books all in a long line on a shelf, with my face on the front covers. 'It was so real,' she said, 'that it seemed more like a vision. I knew they were your books, because your name was written on them in big print.'

'That was a lovely dream,' I told her, 'but I can't see it ever really coming true.'

'You must not be despondent, dear,' she returned, 'for it will, I know it – when I dream in colour it often comes true.'

That was certainly a comforting thought for me just then. I had many finished novels behind me, but so far not a sign of success. I told her that my novel *Susan* had been rejected like so many others, and that I was wondering whether I should go on or not.

'You must go on,' exclaimed Auntie. 'You have a destiny, you just wait and see.'

One sunny morning before Auntie left, I heard the noise of children's laughter outside the shack – Angela had

arrived with the boys. The three of us hugged and
sang 'All a Bunch of Sugar' as we always did, but
when I looked at my daughter's face I saw it was
pale and sullen. Before long she broke down and we
listened to her tale of woe: Apples had lost his job yet
again. We eventually calmed down a distraught Angela
and listened to the latest saga about my son-in-law.

Auntie in her wisdom consoled Angela and soon got
her talking about her college work, and it turned out to
be a lovely afternoon discussing books and poetry under
the oak tree while the children played.

Angela told us a poem she had written about Keith
and herself, which made me feel rather sad:

My Brother

I clasp that useless, fumbling hand,
Impatient at its dependent clinging past,
Damp legs and grimy face I found,
Wandering, searching, relying, in the queue always
    last.
Our bikes one red one white,
Through the woody prickly lanes we rode,
Dark and lonely, roaming, watching, looking,
The bats flapping, clinging to the shadowed leaves;
Where is the way, he says.
So much we took, perhaps it was just a needy phase;
My flesh I sacrificed for principle,
Luxuries we call them now, why was I such a fool?
How I long for that love that turned sour,
Where is this pretence that we take as it seems,
Who is this tough material man, with a fake suntan,
Who doesn't know my means? I only have the lean.
I watch my sons take each other by the hand;
Will the commercial carnival bring them to differ-
    ent lands,
Will life make them incapable of its source,

Will my brother remember, forgive?
For I cannot forget when we lived,
Wild and free, no pretence, no values, only need,
For look beyond, my dear brother, and you will see.

We were silent for a while as this made us feel very
melancholy, thinking of the situation between her and
Keith. That love was still there – you could feel it in the
air as she read her words – but how they were to come
together as brother and sister again I did not know.

Yet again, Auntie showed her wisdom, comforting
my daughter, and later on telling me not to worry about
her, for she was just a bit immature and found it hard
to cope. I knew I had brought her up to be gentle; no
doubt that was why she had an aversion to the hard life
she now led. 'She will grow strong,' said Auntie, and I
only hoped she was right.

Auntie also took a great interest in the children,
cuddling and fussing over young Alan, or Ali, as I called
him, who was a plump, fair, contented child. He would
snuggle beside me on the step, while I invented stories
for him as I had done for my own children. It was a
creative gift that never left me, no matter what the closed
world of published literature threw back at me.

As I sat there on the steps peeling runner beans, my
eyes strayed to my grandchildren: two little brothers
who skipped on the lawn and played on the swing. I
remembered the lovely dream I had always had ever
since coming to these woods, of seeing my grandchildren playing in this spot. Even though I didn't have the
lovely bungalow I wanted, and the dream of becoming
an author had not come to fruition, at least I had these
two lovely healthy grandchildren, who gave me such
joy as I watched them play.

Chapter Four

The Fun Palace

The next year I was very pleased to hear that Maureen and Jim were feeling better and had found themselves a new interest. This interest would turn out to play a very important part in my journey along the pathway to fame.

It all started when they rang one evening to say they had been to the Theatre Royal at Stratford, where they had seen a poster in the foyer asking for help from local people with a project run by Joan Littlewood. The project was to help local poor children, and Maureen told me there was to be a meeting at the theatre, and asked if I would like to come along.

When Angela and I went to meet Maureen and Jim in the small theatre bar, little did I realise that this was to be a landmark in my life, but if I had not gone to that meeting I don't suppose I would have become a published writer.

At the meeting was a cross-section of the community: mothers from the nearby tower blocks, would-be writers, entertainers and actors. It was all very informal. I was thrilled to be in the company of that well-known director, Joan Littlewood, whose current production was all about pirates. Several members of the cast wandered in and out of the bar, dressed in turbans with gold loops in their ears and blackened faces. We looked on, completely enthralled at being in such company, and afterwards bought a programme and felt very important as we pointed out the well-known actors we had met that night.

With a little navy cap on her head and continually smoking her French cigarettes, Joan told us how pleased she was to get all of our support, while a young actress with feathers in her hair handed out leaflets that told us all about 'the Fun Palace'. I had already read about Joan Littlewood and admired her very much: I knew she had come from very humble beginnings, and thought she was like the strong women I loved to write about. I watched her with interest as she spoke from her heart about the local kids who never had a chance to go to drama school and who mostly left school early to work in the local factories.

I guessed a lot of Joan's own childhood struggles were behind her strong views and sincerity. We listened intently as she told us of her plans for a fair that would be held just outside the theatre on some waste ground. Any proceeds from this would go to build a theatre club for the local children, where they could learn art and drama. This sounded like a wonderful idea.

During the winter months that followed, there was a meeting each week, with more members joining each time, until there was quite a gathering. In the spring the project really took off. The pop group, The Who, donated funds for two prefabricated buildings on the site, where music and drama classes were to be held. Famous actresses came down to the site and planted shrubs outside the new buildings that Joan was so proud of. She had helped many young actors and actresses on the road to success, and now they were returning to help her. The donations kept pouring in until there was enough money to turn the wasteland into a children's playground.

A fair was arranged for Eastertime, and we all had
our assignments. Jim and Maureen were to arrange a
float and after much debate decided to portray the
cast of *Oliver Twist* – and what a sight it was to
see Jim dressed as Fagin and the twins as two Artful
Dodgers. Angela got all dressed up as Nancy, but was
late as usual, and came running up behind the float
to be hauled in headfirst by Jim, revealing a mass of
petticoats and two skinny legs. But she did her party
piece and once aboard sang in a sweet voice 'As Long
as He Needs Me'.

During the meetings she had made friends with a
girl named Ann Murrey, who wrote plays, and Ann
played the piano that was installed on the lorry. Crowds
lined the roads as the procession from Hackney Town
Hall made its way to the theatre. Angela's thin voice
sang out above the chaos of the float, while the artful
dodgers tried to drink from the crate of beer and Jim
struggled to keep control as the young urchins got
bored sitting still.

I stood watching the floats pass by with Apples and
the two boys. Georgie had refused to go on the float
in case his schoolfriends spotted him. We were all very
pleased when the *Oliver* float won first prize from the
well-known playwright, Lionel Bart, who was there
to judge the display and had himself presented *Oliver*
in the West End. Unfortunately, when we all looked
for him afterwards, he seemed to have made a quick
getaway and I wondered if the real artful dodgers had
anything to do with it.

We all drank in the bar till very late and all the
members of the 'Fun Palace' scheme got together with
the actors and writers. It was a world that I had never
entered before, but here we were with no barriers,
talking and singing songs while Angela's new friend
played the piano.

The fair went on all through the bank holiday, and

the next day tents were rigged up on the playground and the local kids put on shows. My part in all this was to raise money by telling people's fortunes. They parked me in a tent that was on uneven ground and the stall I sat on kept toppling over – my turban, too. I wore a gypsy tiered skirt and long dangly earrings, and put black pencil round my eyes.

I stared into the eyes of my customers, enjoying every minute of my role as mystic, but when it came to the crystal ball that I was supposed to concentrate on, I wasn't so happy – I was much more at home with the pack of cards that Nanny Murphy had taught me how to tell. However, I tried to look the part and turned the cards over, and before I knew it there were queues outside my tent. The next problem arose when the local kids all got over-excited and tampered with my tent, then giggled their heads off as my stall toppled over and I landed on my backside on the stony ground. I picked myself up and carried on, and many of the professional actors sneaked in to get their cards read, for word was travelling fast that I was good at it. It was a day I will always remember.

Joan's plans for her Children's Village came to fruition and it was successful for some years. Sadly, her husband Gerry died suddenly after the Easter fair. She never got over the loss of Gerry and eventually went to France to live, a country that was very close to Gerry's heart.

That summer, Angela's new friend Ann got her a job at the Children's Village, so while Georgie was at school Angela took young Alan to the theatre and helped out in the office a few days a week. She loved her job and some of her old sparkle returned. Often I would go and see a play there and would get all the gen from Angela on the acting world. We laughed when we saw little Alan following Joan around her office and messing up

her papers, but she treated him very graciously and
took it all in good part.

One Sunday afternoon Angela came tearing down
to Kent to tell me some good news. She had been in
the theatre bar one evening at one of Joan's publicity
ventures and had got talking to a publisher called Terry
Oats. I knew that she had driven everybody mad in
the theatre, talking about her mum's books and how
wonderful they were – and at last it seemed she had
found someone who actually wanted to listen.

It all came out in an excited rush: 'When I told him
you had written about seven books he couldn't believe
it. He said, "Do you actually mean your mother still
writes all these books, even though she gets rejections?"
and I told him how talented you were and I asked
him if he would read *Maggie*. He was very interested,
and would you believe it, his own mother's name is
Maggie!'

This did seem a promising coincidence and when I
heard that he was originally an East End boy who
had got on I began to think perhaps he would take
an interest in my work. We were so pleased about this
break that we got carried away and danced around the
lawn, talking excitedly about how we were going to
travel the world with all the money we made when
the book was published.

Fred gave us some very strange looks, and just went
to dig his hole at the end of the garden as usual. But
that did not deter us – we were over the moon.

The next week, with young Alan in his pushchair, and
Maggie tucked safely under my arm we set off on the
tube to see Terry Oats.

When we arrived at his West End office Angela left
young Alan with me and went up in the lift. She
returned a few minutes later with a dismal face. Terry
Oats' secretary had informed her that he was not in,

and told her to leave the manuscript and her phone number. Angela was disappointed that she had not seen him and warned me: 'Perhaps he wasn't serious, Mum. We mustn't get our hopes up too much.'

However, she rang the office when we got home, and spoke to Terry Oats. To our surprise, he said he was very sorry to have missed us and how pleased he was that she had brought the novel in.

Once again our spirits were lifted, until I looked at his card again: 'Do you realise that it says Music Publisher, and not Book Publisher, dear?'

'I know, but he's very successful. He knows all the writers at the theatre, and I bet he mixes with all sorts of people who publish books.'

I knew he was our only hope of getting *Maggie* noticed, but a little doubt crossed my mind as I thought of the comic publishers that we had found on our trek around the East End before – we both laughed as we agreed we didn't want another one of those.

Chapter Five

Penelope

The months passed and we did not hear from Terry Oats. Angela phoned him and he said how wonderful he thought the book was, but it seemed he had not done anything with it. 'I can't keep phoning him,' she declared, 'and what else can we do with it?'

So we left *Maggie* with Terry Oats and our dream of instant success went out of the window for a while. Angela continued in her job at the theatre, where she seemed to be very happy, and she was getting on better with Apples. I continued with my writing, and that winter I wrote several short stories and typed up *Owen Oliver*.

By the following summer we had not heard any news and I was glad that I had kept a copy of *Maggie*, even if it was only in longhand in my notebooks. Angela seemed to have lost interest a bit and every time I asked her about it, she just said, 'Well, you may as well leave it with him. You never know, he might do something with it one day, and I'm fed up with sending it off to different people.'

Whatever disappointments I had in my quest for publication, my woodlands always gave me the strength to go on, and I began to think of a new story.

It all began when Angela came down to Kent one day

and we took the children out to a little inn on the marsh. The Sun Inn was an old-fashioned little pub, dusty and filled with bric-à-brac, and it looked like someone's front room that had not changed from before the war. There was a big pond ouside with ducks and the kids had fun chasing the ducks over the grass.

The inn stood at the end of an unmade road called Bull Lane. Black and white cattle grazed at the side of the road and obstinately wandered into the lane, preventing visitors from passing. There was a tiny hamlet nearby, consisting of a few workmen's cottages.

The owners of the inn were the most unfriendly proprietors we had ever come across. They served us begrudgingly, and only spoke to a few locals who came in from tending the farmland around. We giggled as they gave us dark glances and grumbled about the kids running in and out.

I found myself picturing this place as it was many years ago. I had not written a story about the occult before, but here was the very place that such things could happen. The whole scene took shape before my eyes: the graveyard was just opposite, and I pointed out a little pond to Angela: 'That's where they'll dump their victims.'

As we left I told her 'There's an old saying – to sup with the devil you need a long spoon.'

'Bet they've got plenty of those,' she replied. 'They're a strange crowd.' And so began the story of *The Long Spoon*. I imagined a witch who would stir her cauldron with a long spoon bringing back to earth the spirit of a beautiful young girl who would cause havoc in this quiet, unfriendly little hamlet.

Around this time we joined a new writing class. The other members of the class were elderly professional ladies – doctor's wives and ex-governesses – and I looked a bit out of place. But I had paid my fifteen shillings to join and there was no way they were going to elbow me out. At first they were very sceptical about me, but as I read my work out to them I slowly won their respect.

One day we held a competition in the class, based on the idea of us all writing a story and using a nom de plume so that nobody would actually know who had written each story. I wrote a sentimental story called *The Willows Wept with Me*, and when it was chosen as the winner they all nearly fell off their seats.

One day one of the old ladies came up to me and said, 'Here's an address for you to send a little story off to, dear. It will be a little bit of bread and butter for you until you get a novel published.'

A lot of the old ladies had worked on magazines, so they knew all about the magazine market. The address I had been given was for *True Romance* magazine, and I decided to write a new story, but Angela suggested that I send *The Lonely Road*, a story I had written about her. I decided to follow her advice and we hoped it would bring us luck. It did, and when I received £30 from the magazine and saw my first story in print it made me very happy.

I was less happy to hear that Angela and Apples were planning to move out to Essex. They were going to buy an old cottage and live the country life she had always dreamed of. I wondered how they were going to cope in the country – Porchleigh, the cottage they eventually bought, was miles away from anywhere and there was little employment in the area – but the two of them were full of hopes and dreams. With the excitement of selling their house in London and packing up, our dreams of getting a novel published were far from our thoughts.

When Angela was settled in her cottage I started taking day trips to Essex as I missed her and the children.

I found out that there was a lot of history in the area. We heard many stories in particular about Leigh's Priory, a big house where a lady called Penelope Devereux once lived with her husband, Lord Rich, who founded the nearby public school of Felstead. Penelope was said to have been notorious for leading a rebellious life, but the more I heard and read about her, the more I felt it would be good to know her.

One day we set out in Angela's old banger for the priory. When we got there, we roamed the grounds, and I visualised Penelope walking there, picking flowers. As I looked up at the tall turrets of the priory her unhappy face seemed to smile down on me.

I later found out after much research that Lord Rich, Penny's husband, was the local magistrate. He was said to have been a very hard man and to have raped Penny on their wedding night. As I looked at his portrait I wondered what on earth had possessed the beautiful Penny to marry such an ugly man.

I went to Chelmsford record office and read up on the Tudor history of the area, and a new novel began to take shape in my mind. Penny was to become one of my favourite characters. I did lots of research on her family, the Earls of Essex, and discovered that Penny was behind Robert Dudley, the Earl of Essex, in his rebellion against the Virgin Queen, Elizabeth. Penny was quite a character, a rebel like her brother, in a time when you had to keep to your place in the Queen's court, or off came your head. She had many lovers and the same courage and spirit as my Cockney heroines.

I went to Lambeth Palace during my research, and there hanging in the picture gallery we saw a portrait entitled 'My Lady of Devon'. The dark eyes of Penny stood out from the canvas with a mischievous glint. She was obviously beautiful and fascinating, with auburn hair and white skin, yet her sincere smile told me that she was ruled by her heart instead of her head.

Penny is not mentioned much in the history books –
in fact, when I visited the library at the British Museum,
I found only one book written about her.

To further my research I visited the grounds of
Wanstead House, where Penny spent a great deal of
time with her brother, the Earl of Essex. The ancient
house seemed full of memories of ladies in long gowns
and men on horseback. There were giant tapestries
depicting the family in the gardens and I pointed one
out to Angela where I could see Penny sitting on a swing
in the garden, her saucy smile directed at a young lad.
Then there was the lake in the grounds, where I could
see her on a boat with her lover, Sir Philip Sidney, the
poet. With every step we took, Penny was there like a
ghost from the past.

It seemed as though we had brought Penny's spirit
to life for the world to see, even if I did seem like an
eccentric old lady as I wandered the grounds of Wanstead
House and the old churches.

Chapter Six

The Launch of Maggie

I was feeling very despondent with the whole world of publishing. The rejections continued as I sent my work off; the latest one being from *Blackwood's Magazine*, which dealt with stories of the occult. I had thought *The Long Spoon* would go down well with them, but they were not interested. I began to think I'd just stick with my *True Romance* stories – it was far less soul-destroying.

But fate had a surprise in store for me, in the form of my old friend Frances, whom I had first met at Allhallows camp. She often came to visit me at Five Oaks, and one day, as we walked around the garden together, she told me that she had heard all about the music publisher from her daughter Carol. It seemed Carol had been working at the Theatre Royal and had heard through the grapevine that Terry Oats had taken *Maggie* to read. I knew Frances had always been fond of me and I trusted her judgement.

When I admitted I was concerned about *Maggie* as I had not heard anything for a few years now, she reacted with characteristic firmness: 'Well, Lena, I think it's about time we got it back off him.'

She told me she lived just up the road from the music publisher's mother. 'It's a small world, and I've a good mind to go and sort it out.' She was a real sorter out, was Frances, and being a bit annoyed with him for not returning my manuscript, I was all for it.

Frances's word was her bond – she went to see Terry Oats' mother, who then got a message to her son. From then on everything happened very quickly. When Terry Oats got the message he immediately phoned me to say that he had been looking for me for two years. I could not believe it – did he not have my address? No, he informed me, he only had Angela's address and kept ringing there, only to be informed that she had moved and her whereabouts was unknown. He went on to say that a friend of his who was an agent had come to dinner at his house about a year ago. He had given him the novel to read and the agent and his wife had sat up in bed each night reading chapter after chapter, unable to put it down. He was almost sure the agent would still be interested and he would phone me soon. I could not believe what I was hearing and my heart was pounding.

I couldn't wait to tell Angela. She turned up soon after to spend a week in Kent, looking very miserable, but she soon cheered up when I told her the news. Like me, she could not believe that all this time they had been looking for us.

After we had got over the excitement of my news, we walked in silence around my woodland, both in our own little worlds, but I had the strangest feeling that my dream was going to come true, and so did Angela.

Back at Wellington Road soon after, I had a call from John Mann, the agent who had enjoyed *Maggie* so much. He told me how wonderful he thought the book was and that he wanted to come down and see me.

I made a little lunch for him in the front room of Wellington Road and I felt very spoilt as he seemed so interested in me as a person and asked me so many questions about all the books I had written. 'You are

an amazing lady,' he told me. 'After all those rejections
you still carried on.' I wondered if I was in a dream as
this lovely young man (an Oxford graduate!) looked at
me in awe and told me that he was sure he could find a
publisher for my work.

He asked me to sign something so that he would get
his cut and then he presented me with a cheque for £250.
As he left he told me that he would be in touch shortly
about the publication.

He took with him *Autumn Alley* to read. Many years
later he told me that he had left the manuscript on a
bench at the station when he got on the train. He
discovered the loss and went back, only to see it still
sitting safely on the bench.

I pinned all my hopes on John Mann. I was very proud
of my first cheque, which stood on the mantelpiece for
all to see, and even Fred looked up from his newspapers
to say, 'Well, you never know, it could happen.' Typical
Fred – but I was so happy inside that I didn't care, for at
last I was getting some recognition for all those years of
writing.

In the new year it all came together. John Mann
phoned me to say that he had found a publisher for
Maggie. The publishing company was called Paddington
Press, and was owned by an American couple, Janet
and John Marquees, whom he had met at the Frankfurt
Book Fair. They were delighted when he introduced
them to my book.

From then on I had many visits from John Mann
and Janet and John Marquees. They came to Wellington
Road and told me how wonderful they thought my
writing was. They were incredulous when I showed
them the drawer full of manuscripts, and told me they
thought they could make me famous and that my work
should sell well in America. I was over the moon and it
was not long before I was invited to their smart offices
to sign the contract for *Maggie*.

So on a fresh March day, full of the joys of spring, Angela and I walked down Bentinck Street in Mayfair, dressed in the new suits we had bought from C & A. It seemed like a dream come true.

When we arrived at Paddington Press we were treated like celebrities. I was introduced to Emma Dalley, who was to be my editor. I liked her from the start and from then on Emma and I had a good relationship. She was to visit Wellington Road several times to go over *Maggie* with me, but made only a few changes, telling me I was a natural.

By the next spring the book was ready for publication. Janet Marquees had chosen a photograph that she had taken from my little office on one of her visits, a picture of me at sixteen. It made me recall the time when I was very poor, and brought tears to my eyes. Janet saw my tears and in her warm way patted my shoulder and said, 'You'll be a famous lady now, Lena – don't look back.' She held the photo out in front of her and said, 'Now that is Maggie. It will go on the front of the book.' I didn't argue with her.

Janet had sent me a lovely review from the well-known writer Alan Sillitoe, who said, 'Such are Maggie's adventures, tribulations and victories that the what-happens-next of the novel never lets up.' I was thrilled that a famous writer had written these things about my Maggie. This review went on the first copy of the hardback publication.

We had a lovely party for the launch of the book at Bentinck Street. The morning before the party Fred brought the *Daily Express* to me as I lay in bed. Inside was a picture of me and a large piece headed 'It's never too late'. After all, at sixty-four I was no spring chicken, yet suddenly I was declared to be an up-and-coming writer. Janet had been very busy and had already sold the American rights in my novel. *Maggie* was declared an international bestseller overnight.

At the party were famous people like Alan Sillitoe and Derek Jameson, and many others from the literary world. The editor from the *True Confessions* magazine who had given me my first break was there, and my lovely teacher Joe from the evening classes.

The family were all there on my special day. Apples was dressed up in a snow-white suit, but he had one over the eight, and before long had disappeared with one of the publicity girls. Later, when Angela went to find him after not speaking to him all night, there was quite a to-do. But my lovely son looked very smart in a tweed suit, accompanied by his wife and their latest pet, a long-haired wolfhound. I felt quite long-haired myself, watching the escapades of Angela and Apples, but was taken far away from my cares when all the journalists gathered around me for my story – they were inquisitive about this elderly lady who had somehow made it. Janet gave a little speech to say how glad she was to have discovered me and that I wrote just 'like a naive painter' and that perhaps I had done a 'Grandma Moses' too.

I shall never forget the joy of that day – the day my dream came true.

Book V

The Goose That Laid the Golden Egg

Winter

The Last Of Autumn

The winter was coming;
The autumn leaves were falling to the ground,
Beautiful colours – red gold, copper and
I was standing on a carpet of gold.
The garden looked forlorn and
I gazed and saw a lovely snowdrop had pushed
Its way through the weeds;
It looked so strong and proud
My heart was full of joy.
They may change the world
But like old Father Thames
Mother Nature will live on for ever
And ever, Thank God.

Mrs Mary Clark (Auntie Mary)

Chapter One

A Famous Lady

Being a famous lady had its good times as well as its bad. I would continuously tell my family, 'I was the goose that laid the golden egg', and they would all look at me quite oddly, but I knew exactly what I meant and secretly would enjoy this absurd joke.

I had bought a fox fur coat, new glasses, and a diamond ring, and Fred took me to Harrods and bought me a gold necklace. It was a world that was quite alien to me. Although I had dreamed of recognition for my work, I had never thought that my first novel would take off the way it did.

Mine was a kind of rags-to-riches story, as I came from the streets of Hoxton, just like little Maggie in my first novel, who sat on the doorstep outside the pub, with holes in her stockings. But the streets of Hoxton were an education as well as an impoverished way of life and gave me the inspiration to write that novel. I would say to the youngsters today who have a poor upbringing, don't be ashamed of it; it gives you great values and helps you through life; just strive to get out of it. I was born in a depression and lived through two world wars, and in my books about London I wanted to record those times, to let my grandchildren know the kind of existence we had, as a kind of social document about the grim reality of a poverty that kids today do not know about.

I had never expected to sell the American rights for *Maggie* overnight, and yet there I was on the front page of the papers. When the American publishers, Pocket Books, arranged for Fred and me to go on the *QE2* to New York on a publicity tour of the States, we were thrilled. Telly Savalas was also on board with his beautiful young wife. Fred was quite amazed when I went up to Telly and said, 'It's all your fault that my uncle Mick died.' He looked at me with great surprise and exclaimed, 'Who's Uncle Mick?' I told him the story of how Uncle Mick (Auntie's husband) had been watching him on the TV in 'Kojak' when he had a sudden heart attack and died.

I loved being on the *QE2* at the captain's table with all the important people. I had bought Fred a dinner suit with a dicky-bow tie and I tried to twist his arm to tip the waiters. But he had always proclaimed: 'I have never bought a publican a drink in my life', and nothing would change him – he was my rock and my anchor, for I knew I could be very silly with money at times.

Being on the *QE2* took me back to my schooldays, for when the headmistress Miss Victoria went on a holiday to America, she sailed on the *Queen Elizabeth*. The name still lingered in my memory because I had felt so jealous when she told us the story of her trip to the United States. In the cold cheerless hall, we stood cheek to cheek, shoulder to shoulder, ragged, hungry kids, while she told us of the cosy voyage, the wonderful food, and the places she had visited. She wanted to impress all us poor kids, because she knew very well that we would never be able to do that kind of thing. It's strange how the young mind works: I was convinced that being born in poverty I would die in poverty, like millions of others before me.

It gave me a strange feeling when some years later

I went with Angela to see my paperback publishers,
Futura, up at Shepherdess Walk. We were going to be
entertained with lunch out and all the special treatment,
and as we approached the door of the publisher's office
I said to Angela, 'See that factory, Bryant and May's,
over the road? I used to work there.' It was as if the
other side of the road was one life and this side of the
road was another, and only the years of struggle between
had changed the few yards of distance.

I could not help recalling working in the tailoring
factory we called 'the sweatshop'. The rats would come
up the lift shaft and run about the factory floor as I sat on
my workbench, pulling bastings out. The men would
chase the rats with cutting shears and the women would
scream until the rat catcher was called. He would put
down a yellow, smelly jelly, which the rat would get
stuck to, and then its baby would come and join it. I
will never forget that rank, sour smell and could never
help feeling sorry for the baby rat.

But I must try and remember the good times, too. I
recall when I worked in the ammunition factory during
the war and the friends I made there. All us girls used to
use the little bits of wire that were left over from our
work as curlers. We would twist them into our hair and
later take it in turns to go to the ladies to take out our
curls, then we would all get dressed up to go out on the
town. I remember going to the Café de Paris with
the girls from work and on arrival seeing some of my
friends being carried out as the place was bombed. But
that was all part of the times we lived in, and we had
some very good times as well as bad.

I was luckier than most of the girls, as I received half
wages from Fred's firm, Unilever, while he was away.
My sister and my old dad remained in Wellington Road
with me, but before Fred left, my old dad said to him,
'Don't worry, Freddie boy, I'll take care of the house
and it will be here when you get back, and I'll take care

of the women, as well' – which he certainly did, and with a very heavy hand too. But there was a spirit of survival in those times. Dad and I would often venture out in the Blitz. We would walk up the local together, taking my Alsatian dog called Ginger. I would tie a scarf around the dog's eyes so he couldn't see all the flashes of light in the sky or the red dust that floated before our eyes. Because if you did not live for each day, you would not survive, and I would probably have ended up an old woman.

It was always important to me in my life not to be ignored – I hated that more than anything – and sometimes I think it was the exhibitionist in me that made me want to be a writer, for then I could act out all the facets of my personality. If I had not been a writer I think I would have made a good actress. I was always waving my hands about as I spoke, and my old friend Dolly used to laugh at me and say, 'You're just like Sasso Pits,' who was an old actress from the Thirties who spoke with her hands.

After I had been published, I would often meet Dolly up the shops and we would slope off for a drink together. It seemed my life was now a continuous round of radio and television appearances, and in the quiet spots I was always under contract to get another Cockney novel out, so sometimes I just liked to revert to my old self. I would tell Fred I was just popping up the road to get some shopping and off I would go to meet Dolly. Going along the street I passed the factory where I used to work in the canteen, and once I bumped into one of the workmen. He couldn't get over my success as a writer and kept telling me 'No one used to make bacon sandwiches like you did, Mrs Smith.'

Even though I loved the company of my old friends, they viewed me with different eyes now I was a famous lady, and everywhere I went with them, they would say 'Do you know who this is? It's Lena Kennedy!' and these people would look at me oddly, not thinking for a moment that this little woman with her shopping bags could be a famous author. But Dolly and I still had our laughs about the old times – that was something money couldn't buy. When I said to her, 'I think they'll name a street after me one day, Dolly,' she would grin and say, 'I don't know, Lena, you do make me laugh,' as though even Dolly disbelieved what had happened to me. I loved her company and that hearty laughter of hers that took my cares away, but I always rushed back to cook Fred's dinner. I used to talk about having someone in to cook and clean, but I guess we were too old to change this habit of a lifetime, and Fred liked me to cook his dinner when we were not out at the Savoy or somewhere similar having dinner with the publishers.

The socialising was a great part of being famous, but the contracts and agreements mystified me, so my lovely agent Caradoc King came to the rescue. I found out how he got that funny name – he was descended from the Welsh chieftain who rode with Boadicea. We got on very well, Caradoc and I: he shared my romantic turn of mind, although he was also full of money-making schemes and publishing ideas.

One week Angela came up, not looking at all well. She had been fighting with Apples. I had been fighting tooth and nail to keep a roof over the heads of my lovely grandchildren, but there was no quick remedy.

Angela and I were just popping out for a drink when the phone rang. It was the agent from Pocket Books in America, who said that she had been instructed to meet me. She didn't know her way around London, so I told her to meet me up West. The only place she knew was Claridge's, so we arranged to meet there at 4 o'clock.

Angela wanted to come too and rang her friend to make the boys their tea after school. So we got ourselves together, left the car at Leyton station, then went on the tube to Oxford Circus. We asked a taxi driver if he knew where Claridge's was. 'Certainly I know Claridge's,' he said with irony, then I realised it was that first-class hotel where celebrities dine.

'Oh dear there's nobody outside to meet us. We'll have to wait now,' I said when we arrived, but just then a man with an umbrella came to escort us from the taxi into the splendid hotel. We got our drinks – £3/10s for two – then sat and waited, watching well-known faces go back and forth to the reception area. We couldn't get over the price of the drinks but as Angela remarked, 'Well, Mother, you would never find a bar open now.' Soon we heard someone calling my name, and a young woman waved us over.

'This must be her,' I said, 'but we could have bought a whole bottle and got drunk in my own sitting room at that price.'

However, Karen was the most charming of all the publishing girls I have met over the years, and Angela liked her too. She was small, dark and petite, with sad, wonderful eyes of blue-grey.

We spent a nice long afternoon drinking and talking. The agent asked me the sort of questions that told me she was well informed about *Maggie* and my life. Eventually she invited us to have dinner with her.

'No, not here, darling, it's too expensive!' I exclaimed.

'It's quite all right, have it on Pocket Books – I'm on expenses.'

'Well, as long as it's on them, and not out of your own pocket,' I said.

'No, it's quite all right,' she assured me, and seeing that Pocket Books owed me all those dollars, I gave in. We had a really nice meal served in luxurious surroundings and the three of us had a good talk. Around us they spoke in hushed whispers, looking at us over the edge of their plates – well, I suppose they were used to it.

Karen ordered snails, then ate them, in a hesitant manner, struggling to get the little bits out. I thought of the winkles and whelks we used to eat – 'Used to cost a tanner a plate in the East End at Petticoat Lane years ago,' I told Karen, but she informed me that these were French snails – a real delicacy. Well, she was welcome to them.

Angela and I had a prawn cocktail, the menu being mainly fish. It was a lovely meal, ending up with coffee and *petits fours*. Angela busily wrapped them in a serviette to take home to Ali.

I was sorry to say goodbye to Karen. 'You're a great personality,' she told me. 'You'd be popular in the States – you must come out to see us next year.'

With the encouragement of Paddington Press I began to work on a new novel, *Nelly Kelly*. I decided to make the heroine a writer, but unlike me she would make it at forty. The sudden inspiration to write that book came to me when I saw the cover of *Maggie*. It was just out in the shops, and on the cover was my own photograph. It took me back to a very sad time in my life and triggered a desire in me to write the story of my own poor upbringing.

The sad time I was reminded of was when I left school and my mother died. After her death our home became cold and empty, although my dad worked hard, and I used to dread going home to the empty grate and the table littered with rubbish.

I had a friend along the street called Rosie. She always looked nice and one day, when I saw her in her best Sunday coat with a fur collar, I asked her where she got it from. 'From the tally man,' she told me.

Mr Mac, our tally man, was a very slick, smooth-faced gentleman who always wore a bowler hat and rode around the streets on a bicycle with his ledger book under his arm. I'd always wondered what he carried in his bag as he banged on the doors for his money.

I told Rosie that I longed for a coat like hers, but that Dad would not have any callers knocking for money. She told me I could have the coat delivered at her house and pay her mum the money. So I got my new coat. It was identical to Rosie's, except that it was a rusty colour, but both had fur collars – coney, according to Mr Mac, but I was so proud of that coat.

When I saw the photo on the front of *Maggie* of me wearing that very coat with the fur collar, it brought back those hard, sad times and made me cry.

I dedicated the book to 'my late father, Cornelius Erin Kennedy' who inspired the character of Dah – Nelly's father.

While I was working on *Nelly Kelly*, Paddington Press brought out *Autumn Alley*, so now I had two books in print. I was very proud to see it everywhere when I did my shopping in Rochester. It seemed strange going around the supermarket and seeing the paperbacks on the tray, but despite my new-found fame, I still kept to our old routine: I would wheel the shopping trolley while Fred picked out the bargains.

As an author I always enjoyed the acclaim that fame brought. I love meeting people and that kept me going though all the hard weeks of radio promotion and interviews with journalists. Sometime I felt sorry for Fred, when he was addressed as 'Mr Kennedy' or 'the minder' – after all, we were really Mr and Mrs Smith.

Chapter Two

Courtroom Drama

In 1981, my British publishers, Paddington Press, started to have financial difficulties and stopped paying money due to their authors, which was very frustrating for me because my books were still selling well. I had used up most of the advances from Futura on buying a caravan and looking after the family. It seemed that Paddington Press were also determined to hold me to the last year of the contract. I was very disappointed, as I had thought John and Janet were a nice, hard-working couple, but you can't be right all the time. When they went off to America with my advances and declared bankruptcy, the receivers stepped in, and for every pound that *Maggie* earned the receivers took their bit too – and so the legal tangle began.

At that time I was on a promotion tour of America for Pocket Books. Fred and I were living it up on the publishers, but a big shock was in store for me. I was on the Carson TV show the day that the bombshell hit me. When the show had finished I found a lawyer waiting to inform me that I was required to appear in front of the bankruptcy court of New York the next morning. I was told that I had been seen on the TV by Janet and John Marquees and that they had taken out an order to get me to the court. They were now settled in the States

and the previous month they had gone before the courts
and taken out a summons against me for 'unjust riches'.
I couldn't get over this 'Unjust Riches' claim – after all I
was still waiting to receive the money they owed me.

The courts served an order of attachment on all the
money due to me, and this was to be held in the States
with no funds to be transferred to England. What with
the receivers in England and the Americans holding my
money back, I wondered whether I was ever going to
see any of my earnings.

When I stood before the judge at the bankruptcy
court the claims against me were read out from John
Marquees' affidavit. They were claiming $75,000 dollars
for what was termed: 'the extensive work on the rough
manuscript of *Autumn Alley* and *Nelly Kelly* to transform
what were in essence a rough collection of notes and
drafts into a publishable novel'.

I could not believe what I was hearing. I was determined to stand up to them and fight for my rights and
for the future of my family. They wanted half of my
royalties on all my books, but I felt that surely it was my
right to have these royalties, as I was the one who had
written the books. It seemed they were trying to make
me out to be some silly old woman who could not write
anything, and that I had only given them collections of
notes instead of novels.

A lawyer grilled me for hours. He obviously viewed
me with utter suspicion, thinking that this elderly lady
could not possibly have written all those books. The
claim that my manucript was in 'extremely rough form'
and 'wholly unsuitable for publication' put my back up.
I knew what I had written. Angela and I had typed up
the novels many years ago, and there were many people
in England who could verify that the manuscripts were
in good form.

I told the court that these claims were not true. I
explained that Paddington had sent me an editor named

Emma Dalley, and that we had got on very well, but she had come to my house no more than six times to go over the manuscript of *Maggie*. She was a highly educated girl, and she had changed certain words, and taken out a few things here and there but nobody ever changed the storyline. Emma knew this – she often said that I was a natural and admired my work, and she above all people knew the truth. (In fact poor Emma had liked her job at Paddington and when they suddenly closed up and went to America she was unaware of the fact, and returned to work after the Christmas holidays to find nobody there and herself out of a job.)

In court it was like being grilled by the Gestapo. I was asked questions like, 'Did Paddington Press ever work on the paragraph form or sentence form of the manuscript?' I told them no, we just changed a word occasionally. Then the lawyer went on to question me about my education: 'What formal training in English grammar did you have?' I told him I had been to school, but this did not satisfy him, and he seemed determined to try and trip me up. He went on to ask me whether I considered myself to be an educated person. I thought about this for a moment, then returned: 'I am not uneducated. I read and I learn and I have lived my life; I am quite capable of writing and as to education, I don't know what you mean by that.'

He then starting asking me when I wrote all the books, quizzing me about dates and demanding that I be specific. I told him I had started to write *Maggie* when I went into hospital.

'What year was that?' he retorted.

I told him I couldn't remember offhand – 'I'm not a business woman. I don't know about dates and things like that – I write books.'

He didn't like this reply and said sardonically, 'You like the benefits of business.'

'When they pay me, I will,' I returned with equal sarcasm.

When they started discussing with the judge about me being a 'non domiciliary residing without the States' consent' I felt I wanted to get up and run out before they put me in the clink. But I decided to stand my ground because I did not doubt myself and knew my own capabilities, and if I hadn't they would have drained me dry. I knew that even though I was perhaps only a self-educated woman, I had a rare gift. This gave me confidence, and if the King of England had been standing there I would have stood up to him in the same way as I stood up to that court.

They flashed agreements and contracts in front of my face and asked me to identify them, but I told them I did not understand. They even wanted receipts for the caravan I had bought Fred, suggesting that Paddington had bought it for me. I couldn't help thinking, aren't I even entitled to a caravan after writing all those books? But the legal mind did not see it that way.

I never was very good with business matters, and I tried to explain this to the lawyer, but he just said, with an air of disdain, 'Do you consider yourself to be competent enough to handle your own business affairs?'

At this I wondered if they were going to declare me completely stupid and said, 'I am still capable and not in a bathchair.'

This line of questioning went on for three hours and I was getting very tired of it all. The more I told the lawyer I was not good at figures when he flashed agreements in front of my eyes, the more annoyed he became. When he turned to the judge, saying that I was needed for re-examination another time, I thought, no fear, and told them I was going home.

'Do you intend to return to the USA in the near future?' asked the lawyer in a threatening tone.

'No, not if I can help it!' I exclaimed.

The lawyer continued to pressure me and I was feeling upset but was determined they were not going to beat me. With my courage returning, I said, 'I have not done a crime, have I?'

He shot back sarcastically: 'You mentioned the word crime; I didn't.'

Finally, when he went on to ask me about the lawyers in England who were called Rubinstein, Callingham, I got very contrary. I don't know whether it was my nerves or not, but I suddenly wanted to laugh, and I couldn't resist saying, 'I don't remember their names exactly, but I think it was something like Frankenstein.'

With this remark he let me go, almost as if he gave up. He looked at me with a kind of disbelief when I walked from the stand telling them I was going home to finish *Lizzie*.

Fred couldn't help reminding me that an order of attachment could also be against property and I wondered whether I was going to lose my house over this. Caradoc King, my agent, was also served an order in London. Bills, receipts and all sorts of documents were requested, and much paperwork I did not understand. If I hadn't told the court that my son Keith would fly over from England and bring all this paperwork over and sort out my affairs, I don't think they would have let me go.

I was relieved when Keith arrived soon after with all the documents. He went to the court and to the lawyer's office and, after many lengthy discussions, Keith and Caradoc arrived at the fairest deal possible. Paddington Press were to have 50 per cent of the royalties on three books for a certain number of years, and on *Maggie* for life. Keith and I agreed it was all a sham – after all, I had written the books, but it was better than them taking the lot, and as I told Keith. 'I can always write another best-seller.' I just wanted to go home.

So we called a truce and I will always be grateful to my loyal son, whose clever business mind was good enough for those American lawyers. Keith also arranged for Emma Dalley to be a prime witness and give evidence on my behalf, which helped a great deal. Thanks to Keith, I could finally be released and go home to pick up the pieces and start again, as Kipling advised in his poem *If*:

Watch the things you gave your life to broken
And stoop and build 'em up with worn out tools.

I had found that people are not always what they seem. I remember how Janet pushed me to finish the latest book, although she must have been aware of the financial problems at the time. Yet, even now, after all the trauma of the court case, I can never dislike her and John Marquees. They had seemed such enthusiastic, go-ahead young people, and they really did help me to get my books on the map, but how they could do the things they did to me later, I will never know.

Chapter Three

The Publicity Bandwagon

After the ordeal in America, it came as something of a relief to be invited by the publishers in Ireland to a family reunion. They thought it would be a nice idea if some of my relations, the Kennedys, were invited to the hotel where I was staying so that we could have a little gathering.

I was still surprised when I walked into a room full of Kennedys, for it seemed the word had travelled, and because they were such a big family and all lived in a close community in County Cork, some having little shops in the same street, they had all decided to come.

The publishers, Rep, looked quite dismayed and hurried around looking very harassed, trying to make adequate arrangements for the crowd of Kennedys. Rep had only sent out a handful of invitations, but there they all were, sitting around the tables, waiting for the food and drink.

I was pleased to meet some of these long-lost cousins. It was a real Kennedy evening, and from that little gathering and the mystic beauty of Ireland I became inspired to write a story called *The Pig in the Parlour*, all about an Irish lad returning to his homeland to claim a lost inheritance. Perhaps I was also thinking of my own lost inheritance in America, for it was all still very much on my mind.

It took a long time for the Americans to pay me for my work, because all monies had been stopped while negotiations were going on and it was a good while before we saw any of it. It cost me $30,000 to fight the case and the taxman was on my toes. This all got too much for me and was proving a terrible worry, so Keith took over my affairs. I don't know what I would have done without his help, for although I was good at words, figures were beyond me and I got myself in a terrible muddle.

I also had another consolation for my worries, in the shape of my third grandchild, Horatio. Keith's son was a redhead, like his dad, and I planted a rose in his honour, called Milord.

I was still churning out the Cockney novels, taking only six months to write them at times, and each new publication meant several signing sessions from town to town. When I did the signings in London, friends and people I knew would often drop in. Old ladies with their shopping bags would come into the shop and look at me, afraid to speak, and I would love to draw them out and have a chat about the old London of my books that they loved. They would look at me as though I was a queen sitting there signing books, but I would only look back and remember it was not so long ago I was like them. They were my generation and the London I was writing about was slowly disappearing. Tower blocks now replaced the old slum streets, but the old ladies were lonely in these flats.

One day a woman came up to me and said, 'You've written about all the places in our London except for Canning Town,' and with that I began to write about Lily, who came from that district. *Lily, My Lovely* was my first Romeo and Juliet – a real love story of the war years that became another bestseller. It was the ordinary people like me I wanted to write for, and it was the ordinary people who inspired my work.

I remember how the title for that book came to me. I often pinned up bits of poetry in my little office, and as I finished the book I looked up to see a poem by my Aunty Mary entitled 'The Lovely Lily', all about a beautiful lily she had seen bloom in her garden.

During another signing session, a woman came into the shop and told me that she was once married to a man whose death made newspaper headlines. I got on well with her and found her a lively and interesting person. She came down to see me one day and had a cup of tea with me, and asked if I wanted to write her story. I told her that I never take my stories straight from life. But it seemed I was only just starting to realise the dangers of being a famous lady, for just being friendly to this lady landed me in a lot of trouble.

When my new novel of Cockney life came out she accused me publicly of writing about her life. This worried and upset me a great deal and the legal entanglement went on for a long time. Fred often warned me not to get involved, but because I loved to talk to people I let myself become wide open. 'You're a silly cow!' he exclaimed. 'You don't realise what people are like.' He was right, and I was certainly more careful after that episode.

I felt I needed to escape all these worries and strangely enough, the chance to do that came when I had to go to Old Street Court to pay a speeding fine that Keith had incurred. Noticing a court was in session, I decided to sit in and listen. The small circular court with its high ceiling and oak-panelled walls was very impressive. The magistrate sat on a high chair with a real leather back and presided over the proceedings. I sat in the front amidst the law students, an untidy-looking lot. Some stared at me, wondering, who's that old girl? Never seen her before.

The first case was a young man who was accused of stealing a car. He was about eighteen, tall and good-looking with long hair that hung down to his shoulders. He had a provisional licence that was two years out of date. The judge was very severe with him, and snapped, 'Can't you read? You lads that steal cars are menaces.' For the first time the boy showed some emotion. From where I was sitting I noticed he had his hands behind his back; they were nice, clean, well-kept hands, with rather long square-tipped fingers. It didn't look as though he had done much work. As the judge stopped to read the report of his past convictions he denied he had regular work, and I could see his knuckles gleaming white. I felt the atmosphere heavy with anxiety as we all waited for the judge to proceed.

Eventually he said, 'Because of your mother, who's very fond of you, I will not send you to Borstal. But you must pay a fine of £50. You will have help to get a job and then you must pay £5 a week out of your wages, and I don't want to see you again.'

I was a bit surprised at the conviction: after all, this boy was a thief, yet he had got off lighter than my son with his speeding fine.

I sat there and listened to the other cases. It was all food for thought for my novel *Down our Street* and all helped to inspire my imagination.

To this day I don't understand how individual people think I write about them in particular, because to me one person is not interesting enough. I may take bits of people's personalities and mould them with my imagination to make a character, but when people think they are just taken from life straight into a book, they are mistaken. I always say I put it all into a pot like an Irish stew and stir it up. I like to think that the people who have passed through my life and the times I lived through during my own lifespan have not been in vain, and that I have been able to record their kind of existence as well as my own.

Angela said to me one day, 'If you wrote something about my life, Mum, I would not mind, because then perhaps I would live on like you do in your work.' I dedicated my first book, *Maggie*, to Angela, as we had worked so hard together. It was not until seven books and many short stories later that I had any luck. We had many rejections, and Angela would say, 'I think we could paper the walls with all these rejections, Mum,' but I always insisted, 'You must be persistent, dear.'

If any of you people out there are writers who have never had any acclaim, my little story should encourage you to keep at it – 'never give up'. But do not expect money to bring you happiness, because it doesn't, although the recognition you get as an author is very special.

Just before a new book was due out, the publishers would always send me the cover to see if I approved of the way they had depicted my characters. This was always a special moment for Angela and me. We would look in wonder at the cover and discuss whether we thought it was like the characters in the story. Until that moment they would only have lived in our minds, but now their faces would stare out at us from the cover of a book, and they would seem like real people for the first time. This is a rare moment and makes it all worthwhile.

The papers have referred to what happened to me as a fairy story. I guess it was, but I also believe anybody can do anything they want. I always felt I needed to let the world know I was here; from when I was young I wanted to leave my mark. It is something that is not important to everyone, because I guess that to have happiness while you're here is of ultimate importance to most people, and I can understand that too. But the thought of passing through this life without being remembered afterwards troubled me, and I often thought of my lovely grandparents, who lived in this world for fifty years or more and lay in unmarked graves. In my books I felt I made some of my ancestors live again, especially my two grandparents. In *Autumn Alley* I recreated the lives of my mother's family, the Murphys, who came from Ireland to London, and in *Eve's Apples* I explored the lives of my father's family, the Kennedys, who went out to America after the potato famine.

It was a strange feeling when at the launch party for *Autumn Alley* the publishers tried to recreate the scene of the book. I was a bit apprehensive as I had had a long day of radio interviews. The party was held at the Cricketer's, a pub in the old Ford Road by the Cut, which features so strongly in *Autumn Alley*. We had a real Cockney party, with sausages, pease pudding, pie and mash and jellied eels. There were gay songs around the old Joanna, and they reconstructed scenes from the book, but I was numb, as though it was a last and dangerous glimpse of old London. The original slum streets I had written of had now disappeared and a motorway had been built in their place. The publicity girl said we should all sit by the canal, but I couldn't help thinking that in the old days you would never sit there, for they threw everything in the Cut, from old prams to dead cats.

But this was a grand occasion. I was treated like a filmstar; two bottles of bubbly were opened and TV cameras were there following everything I did. They pushed me into singing some Cockney songs like 'On Mother Kelly's doorstep', and with the support of family and friends, the evening turned out to be fantastic.

That party was for the paperback publication, but six

months previously the launch of the hardback publication had been somewhat of a disappointment. The publication of *Maggie* had been very jovial, but Macdonald Futura, my new publishers, seemed slightly more reserved. The publicity girl had lovely golden hair, but there was a coldness about her. Nevertheless I survived her superiority and on the day the book was published I had to go to Radio London on the John Dunn show, and she was with me.

'I have a little surprise for you,' she said. 'They are going to give you a little treat from the proceeds of Paddington.' I was looking forward to a real rave-up, but that wasn't to be. We waited for a taxi outside the radio station in the West End and after travelling through the heavy traffic we eventually ended up at Simpson's, a posh restaurant in the Strand.

I was given all the red carpet treatment in the foyer and shook in my shoes wondering what was going to happen next, but I felt a bit let down when we booked into lunch – just me and her. I am not accustomed to too much male company, but the thought of several hours with Miss Frosty Face was no inducement to me. She put on the airs and graces of a duchess, assuming that she was impressing me and letting me know how she was used to wining and dining.

The portion of meat that arrived at our table was a truly huge side of beef, and I thought it looked like a body. Frosty Face declined any alcohol but I asked for a glass of wine. She sat there chasing the black baked spuds all around her plate with her fork, and after waiting for my glass of wine I lost my patience. 'Sooner go up the fish and chip shop,' I said to her. 'Anyway, I thought we were going to have a party.'

She flushed up a bright red, and with a sullen face she asked the waiter to take the food back and cook it properly. He came over and looked at the offending spuds, and I found it very funny and laughed my head off. He came back with a dish of very nicely cooked potatoes with the chef's compliments and an oily smile. I was chattering away like a monkey, but Miss Frosty Face was still unappreciative, although I told her the rest of the potatoes were hers.

The lunch was awful, and ended with crusty stilton – what a way to spend a publication day. How happy I would have been in the pub with Angela with salad and beer; it would have been ample for me. I thought of her waiting for me at home all day, as I had promised to meet her, but Frosty Face had organised me and I went along with her plans.

The two gentlemen at the next table seemed very interested in Frosty Face. She was very beautiful, young and fresh of face, and I did not blame them. Then it occurred to me that as we were in Piccadilly, they probably thought she was some call girl dining out with her madam.

The waiter came over and said, 'That gentleman over there would like you to have a drink with him for his birthday.'

'Oh thank you,' said Miss Frosty Face. 'I will,' and I piped up, 'Well, it's my birthday too.'

So once more I looked like the madam, but that did not worry me and did not disapprove as the two gentlemen joined us for a chat and a drink. Miss Frosty Face had two admirers now and I was extremely interested to watch the young man, who was very attentive and kept looking at her most unnaturally. He reminded me of the white rabbit in *Alice in Wonderland*, and I found this very amusing, for after all, it was my publication day.

The other gentleman was older, a very quiet gentleman with a humorous personality. 'Is it your birthday too?' he asked.

'No, it's my publication day,' was my reply.

We began to discuss *Maggie* and her Cockney background. He had also been born within earshot of Bow
bells and was now a big shot at Scotland Yard, so
we had an interesting conversation about his youth
and the back streets of London. He told me he had
run a paper round to get extra pocket money to buy
books for the grammar school he went to. The other
gentleman soon joined in our conversation, and so a
good time was had by all except Miss Frosty Face,
who still had that cold, superior expression on her
sullen face.

The next day I went to the Waldorf, again with
Frosty Face. There was a little orchestra to serenade
us as we had afternoon tea and afterwards I had my
picture taken outside the hotel. Then I was taken to
do a talk-in chat show with Dan Damon at LBC radio;
Dan tried to cope with the different callers, who were
asking to speak to the 'cockney sparrow'. It seemed so
strange that with my lack of education, people were
asking my advice about books; until now I had always
been on the other side of the fence.

Later Fred and I went to stay down at Cliffe and,
together with all our friends, listened to the show
when it went out at 10 o'clock that evening.

As time went on and more books were published, the
publicity business became increasingly hectic.

For the party to launch *Lily, My Lovely* we had a
Pearly King and Queen to entertain us, and for *Nelly
Kelly* the TV people were there. I will never forget
that frantic day. It started at Radio Medway, then
we travelled home to Leyton to find some television
men waiting on the steps of Wellington Road, who
wanted to film us for *Arena*. It turned out that they had
heard Fred and me on the radio that morning, in a 'A
Happy Couple' interview and they enjoyed my chatter
so much that they decided to do a TV piece there and

then. With the help of a young girl on the television team I made the tea. We had a good conversation and I showed them all round my little office. I had arranged an appointment at the hairdresser's for later that day, and the charming young man who was directing the cameramen, David Wheatley, was very persistent about following me there.

When we arrived the old ladies were in a real panic to get their rollers out. They had all come for the pensioners' cheap day hair-set and had never known such excitement at the hairdresser's before. The shampooist was very pleasant about the filming and said, 'I'll have Vidal Sassoon coming up and offering me a job after all this.' So there I was, sitting under the dryer at the little hairdresser's that I had gone to locally for many years, with a team of nice young men following me around with their cameras.

From the hairdresser's they followed me home into my little kitchen in Wellington Road to film me while I made the tea and then waited outside for me to arrive at the party for *Nelly Kelly*.

To this day the old ladies at the hairdresser's have never got over it, and Wellington Road and my kitchen were on the News at Six, with Andrew Gardner saying, 'perhaps one day there will be a blue plaque on Wellington Road'.

During my years of fame, I met many well-known and talented people. I made friends and corresponded with some of them, and it was a wonderful feeling to know I was accepted as one of them. Although I had hardly any educational qualifications to speak of, I found I could talk on most subjects, especially literature and history, and could hold my own at social gatherings.

I often travelled on promotion tours with other artists, like the time I went on a train up north with the Roux brothers, and they told me of their small beginnings in a restaurant in France. I also met Donald Sinden – how I loved that cultured voice of his, and the way he had of taking my hand just as though I was a lady.

I loved touring the radio stations from town to town, stopping overnight at hotels. Often a journalist would come from the local paper to interview me over breakfast. I was tireless: I loved to talk of my life and to hear other people's life stories.

It was all just like the dream I had told my school teacher about all those years ago, of travelling the world and writing books. I was now in my sixties and got physically tired sometimes, but I was living that dream, something that it seemed my whole life had been directed towards.

In my little office in Wellington Road I put my special invitations up on the walls, like the one to the 'Women of our Time Luncheon', which was presided over by the Duchess of Gloucester. This was a celebration for women who had achieved something special, and I felt very grand as I sat at the table with Clare Francis, the lady who had sailed around the world single-handed. As we left we were all presented with little silver butterflies.

There were also invitations to garden parties at the house of Robert Maxwell, which were held each year for the people who worked for him. I was one of those people, since he owned the publishers of my books. I really enjoyed these gatherings, rubbing shoulders with the rich and famous. I remember one garden party in particular, at which all of Robert Maxwell's children came to meet the guests, dressed from nursery rhyme characters.

I also made a lovely friend there called Julia Fitzgerald. She was with the same publishers as me and was hailed as a queen of romance. She was a beautiful young woman (she seemed young to me, for I was in my sixties and she was only in her early forties). She wrote of mystic romance, and had something mystic about her own presence. She had lovely big hazel eyes that looked straight at you, as though looking into your very soul. I remember her looking very artistic in old-fashioned black lace, with long gloves to match, and her chestnut hair falling down to her shoulders.

We knew from the beginning we would be friends and we were to meet again at the Cumberland Hotel at Marble Arch, where we both received a lovely award from American publications. There were a lot of American ladies there, mostly writers, and a film crew moved around us as we all stood discussing our books in the foyer of the plush hotel. To this day the award stands on my mantelpiece, an ornate golden piece with my name inscribed on it, and I look up at it with pleasure and pride.

I also met Claire Rayner, who gave me some good advice, as we often appeared together on radio or TV, and Derek Jameson. He told me his life story: he had started as a newsboy on the *Daily Express* and his boss there saw possibilities in him and sent him to evening classes. Those grass roots of his were much like my own and when I wrote my Cockney novel, *Lizzie*, Derek did much to inspire the character of Charlie.

In *Lizzie* my character was not romantic, or an opportunist like Nelly Kelly – her family came first. She was a born foster mother, brought up a big family but not having any children herself. She was a childless woman who gave love and care to unwanted children, not for gain, because it was before the time of the welfare state, but out of the sheer goodness of her heart. If some of you remember a foster mother who really cared for you and brought you into the adult world, then you would love Lizzie. She had an old-fashioned, mixed-up sense of values, but I can assure you she did exist. She was a real East Ender, who stuck thick and thin to her man, who was a gambler. Lizzie came from the 'Nile', a part of London that has slowly disappeared, and nothing or no one would get her out of the East End.

The days at the theatre, the radio stations, and the TV shows all inspired me to write. While I moved in these circles, it was almost as if writing was my life, and whatever happened around me, and whatever people I met, I wanted to hold close, for I knew it would never come again. So I listened and watched and kept it all in my mind as best I could.

While I was travelling and meeting people I always had my notebooks with me. Often new ideas would come to inspire whatever book I was writing at the time, as I always had one going, if not two, and I would scribble them down.

When I was in America on a promotion tour, I started thinking of my grandparents, who had arrived at Ellis Island from Ireland during the potato famine. In fact, my own father was born in the middle of the Atlantic, and was named Cornelius Erin Kennedy: Cornelius after the Dutch captain, and Erin after the ship. All his life he had duel citizenship of Ireland and America. His father was David Kennedy and there was a story in the family that had been handed down by word of mouth through the generations, that David Kennedy was the first man to bang a nail in the South Pacific railroad, for he had found work on the new railroad after travelling across America in a wagon train.

I thought a lot about David Kennedy and his family while I was in the States and when I came home I did some research and eventually wrote to my cousins in Ireland to ask them if anyone knew the name of the ship David Kennedy had travelled on. I was pleased when the reply came, enabling me to trace his name on the ship's logs, which dated back almost a hundred years.

Here I found the seeds of my novel, 'Eve's Apples'. David Kennedy and his family were to inspire the main characters of that story, which spanned three generations and swept over three continents. I always like to write about strong women and in this novel I took the wives of the three families who walked behind their men in the wagon trains.

On my trips to Australia and New Zealand with my publishers I was inspired once more. Fred and I stayed at the luxurious Town House in Sydney harbour, and I could not help wondering what it was like many years ago when the lands of Australia were first inhabited. I began to think of the times of the gold rush, and this place became in my imagination a brothel and was to be a central site in my novel.

The women of those hard times who pioneered the land of Australia beside their men were the rock of their families. I was going to entitle the book *Petticoat Pioneers*, but on reading Shakespeare's sonnets, as I often did, I found the very title I wanted, as the great man himself wrote of the first temptation. Eve reminded me of my strong heroine, for she was the first lady to take the initiative by handing Adam the apple, so long ago when the world began in the garden of Eden. '*Eve's Apples*' is my first trilogy, and is very special to me.

After Paddington Press went bankrupt I needed a new publisher, and I was taken on by Fuhira. They wanted to put a lot of publicity into *Nelly*, and I was invited to their offices to discuss the promotion. I took Angela with me, and when we arrived a long line of pickets halted us at the door of the building. There was some kind of industrial press dispute going on and we thought it rather funny when a big butch man stood across the entrance to the office and stopped us going in. They handed out leaflets to passers-by and waved banners in our path. The pickets knew all about my books and challenged me, but I just listened to their advice and wished them luck. I find that I am nearly always on both sides in these strikes.

Rosemary, my publisher, was very worried and harassed by all this, and I felt sorry for her. The fact that
she was once the boss's secretary, which the butch man
had joked about, meant little to us. Rosemary wanted
to get out of the office for a while and we went with
her to a little pub for lunch and talked to some of the
old inhabitants. Angela looked so nice – she does not
often look so happy – and we had quite a fuss made of
us. We always have a good time together, Angela and
I. I'd sooner be with her than anyone else, for we have
the same kind of temperament and butterfly minds.

'Well,' I finally said to Rosemary, who was very nice,
'let's hope I have some good news soon – something like
a big cheque from Pocket Books.'

I was growing quite accustomed to being the 'kingpin
of the family', as I ironically called myself. By now
I had a very busy itinerary with the publishers, as
well as trying to cope with all the family problems.
I answered many fan letters from all over the world
and would often be requested to appear to open clubs
and bazaars, as well as appearing for the publishers at
different venues. Wherever I went I made friends and
lapped it all up.

When I appeared on the Pebble Mill television show
I met a lovely artist who was also on the show, and we
afterwards corresponded with each other. I happened
to mention to her that I had always loved the famous
painting by Holbein entitled 'April Love' and I was so
pleased when she sent me a print of it – she must have
gone to some trouble to acquire it.

I often appeared on LBC radio and had got to know
Dan Damon, the broadcaster. He invited Fred and me
to his lovely house in Blackheath for lunch and I was
glad to have made friends with him.

One day I took Angela with me to the BAFTA
awards ceremony in the West End, and it was just

like the academy awards you see on television. We sat in the audience with other famous people to see my bestseller come up on a big screen and I had to get up on the stage and talk about my books. I wasn't at all nervous and talked about my life and books and thoroughly enjoyed it. There were several other authors there, and afterwards we met the journalists in the bar and had a lovely lunch. I was in my element. I loved to be with people and eat and drink and talk my head off – and on the publicity bandwagon I could do just that.

Chapter Four

Good Times and Bad

My career as a writer had really taken off, but things were not going so well in the family. Angela was miserable and lonely at the cottage in Essex, and she and Apples were not getting on at all well. My grandson Georgie was now at a private school as a weekly boarder. It was a posh school, but I had to go to the headmaster and complain because I was so fed up with Georgie's constant phone calls telling me that he was hungry – I found myself wondering if the school was like the one in *Oliver Twist*. Sometimes I felt overwhelmed by these people, worrying if I had done the right thing in sending Georgie to that posh school, worrying if Ali would miss him, worrying if Angela and Apples would lose their cottage – they were in a lot of debt. But then I would find an outlet by scribbling about it all.

I liked to get away from all my problems by spending time with my old friends. I had lots of offers to go out for drinks so I'd go and have a good old chat and forget my worries. Often I called into the library, which I also found therapeutic.

One weekend our friends Sheila and John invited us to go to dinner at Leeds castle. I wanted to go but Fred wasn't keen. However, eventually I cajoled him into going. I wore my new pink dress and we had a good afternoon with John and Sheila and their friends. Lots of food and booze was consumed, and I really let off steam. I didn't stop talking, then suddenly out bounced my false teeth! Fred retrieved them from the floor and I continued drinking and dancing till the morning in my old style. On Sunday it was as if all my worries had left me and I felt like a new woman.

While all these problems were going around in my head, my whizz-kid agent Caradoc rang to tell me some wonderful news. I had been asked to open an exhibition at the Festival Hall, which was a real honour. I was very excited about this and went to have my hair permed. I bumped into my old friend Dolly and we had a drink together. I told her my news, then we swapped family problems; it was great to be able to share my problems and let off steam.

Despite all my worries, I was really looking forward to Christmas that year. I had a bit of extra cash and as Apples was not working (as usual) I thought I'd give the children a nice time. I spent a busy week cleaning and making the front room look really christmassy, with lots of tinsel and balloons and a nice tree.

Keith was going to Guernsey, taking little Horatio and his wife off on a special trip, so I did not expect him back until after Christmas. It solved my problem of the squabble that would otherwise go on as to whom I would eat Christmas dinner with, for my children still did not acknowledge each other.

But Keith dropped in unexpectedly on Christmas Eve with Pat and 'Orri'. I was happy to see them, but a bit confused, not having sorted out the presents yet. I couldn't find the wrapping paper, so I collected the presents up and put them in a bag for them, saying, 'We'll have an extra Christmas Day on Saturday,' but Pat did not want to come. I opened Keith's present, a beautiful wristwatch, but I was worried about him: he was behaving strangely, and seemed distant. 'I'm so glad you came, darling,' I said, 'that was all the Christmas present I wanted.'

I wept after they had left. Fred tried to console me, saying that Keith was not very well, and then I worried even more, thinking he would have a heart attack. I could not believe my loving, hearty, self-assured son was behaving like this.

I tried to put the niggly worries from my mind and get on with the Christmas cooking. Angela and Apples and the kids arrived, full of beans. They brought their dog and cat with them, but they fought with my dogs and cat so we had to keep them apart.

The children were happy with the presents and the Christmas tree, but they all complained they needed baths as there was no hot water at the cottage. I was pleased when Angela washed her golden hair and I brushed it till it shone, then we had a laugh with the kids. Apples had a shave and was full of his usual jokes, but Fred was a bit disgusted, for when he went to shave he found that his razor blades had all gone.

Christmas dinner was a success, and afterwards we went and sat in the front room and played cards and had a good drink. Apples sang some of the old songs, which I really enjoyed, and all in all, I began to cheer up.

On Boxing Day they all went off happily, the old van crowded out with dog, cat and motorbike. They were off to visit their other grandma down the East End. Angela would have preferred to stay, but she didn't want to deprive the boys of their Christmas presents, and Apples' family were very generous and fond of the kids.

I was just dozing off to sleep that night, when there was a knock at the front door. I opened it, and there was Angela with my grandchildren. Georgie was holding the little cat in his arms, looking pale and cold. 'Nanny, let me in,' he called. It turned out there had been a punch-up at the in-laws' and Angela had decided to return, with the children leaving Apples there, so it was a proper Boxing Night after all.

Eventually Angela and Apples sold their cottage, and settled in a lovely house. There was no mortgage – I had seen to that – so she would not have so much to worry about. I had been heartbroken to see my daughter destroyed by poverty.

I had many commitments for new novels, and they were all going round in my head, but my eyes were fading and I was not feeling too well. I visited the doctor, who told me I had a cataract in my eye, and sent me to Moorfields Eye Hospital for an operation to have a lens implant in my eyes.

It's strange how a different atmosphere can change you – in hospital you seem so shut off from the troubled, worrying world outside. I met people who were so grateful to have their sight restored that they felt humble and forgave all past hurts and wounds: there seemed to be an atmosphere of easement within these closed walls.

I made friends with a beautiful young nun on my ward whose name was Sister Winifred Dolan. Her skin was smooth and unblemished; her figure was tall, straight and very graceful; and she had beautiful black short-cropped hair. She had been blind all her life, but it was hoped that her sight could now be restored. After her operation she could see just a little bit with contact lenses. Patiently she sat poking a hand to put them in, refusing to let anyone assist her, but just keeping on till she got it right.

I thought she was so brave and so beautiful; it will be many years before I forget that holy smile. She had many gifts to give the world and taught braille to blind children – so let us not despair about our world, telling ourselves that it has become a horrible, corrupt place.

Being in the eye hospital restored my sense of hope and faith.

While I was there I also met a Jewish man called Mr Herman, who had an operation on his eyes and was able to see for the first time. He was so grateful that he cried. 'My dears,' he said, 'I have been led around by the hand for such a long time that I am afraid to go and visit my family – I've never seen what they look like. There is no way to explain my gratitude to the caring young doctor who gave me back my sight.' He was a very nice man and we had a chat about the old East End of Black Lion Yard, Whitechapel and Petticoat Lane, and Sammy Isaacs, the kosher restaurant.

My little operation was a success and the cataract on my eye was removed so I could once again see clearly. In the bed next to me was faithful Katie. She had a husband whom she had not seen for years, and I was amazed when she told me that he still paid her one pound a week but had never divorced her.

There was a young volunteer who went round the ward and talked to us. She took a real interest in my books and one evening she asked if I could give a little talk about my work to cheer up the patients. I spoke of old London, of the Cockneys who have known the true grit of poverty, and of my heroines who came from different parts of London: the sweet, naive Maggie, Nelly my opportunist and Lizzie, the born foster mother.

They asked me questions about my characters and I told them about how I often got myself in a bit of trouble when I did my research. For example, one time I went to the pub to talk to the old boys there about gee-gees. This was to help me with the character of Bobby in *Lizzie*, as he was a compulsive gambler. One old chap got really haughty: 'Don't pick my brains,' he said, 'I might as well write a bloody book myself.' This little talk went down very well with my fellow-patients, and made them laugh. I told them I hoped my books would go on to tapes for the blind one day.

I would be sorry in a way to leave this sanctuary of peace and love and I would never forget it. I was so thankful to hang on to God's most gracious gift – my eyesight – to see the blue sky and the green grass, the blossom in spring, and the roses in summer.

Chapter Five

Little Green Apples

My publishers would often phone me to go out to publicity venues during the week and I always had to look nice, whatever problems were going on or however I was feeling. I had to drop everything and spruce myself up, to look and act the part.

One day my publishers sent an escort to accompany me to a lunch at the Savoy to meet the press. I chose a plain blue dress with a pleated skirt and a tweed coat. Blue is my colour and the dress was simple but expressive.

I had met my companion before. He was well spoken and well educated, and I was surprised to discover he came from an ordinary background. We talked about 'old London' and had a very good time.

During those years of fame that spanned a decade of my life a lot happened to me and my family. Whether it was for the better or worse I am not sure, for I wonder if my family found the change too much to cope with. I had become the moneyspinner, and I was treated like Lady Docker with limousines pulling up outside the house to take me to all the different functions. To my family I had always been the little woman, waiting on everyone hand and foot, cooking and comforting and listening to all their problems, but when I became a celebrity, a person in my own right, I became a person who was always rushing from radio broadcasts to television stations. The family demanded attention and now I could not always give it. Between all these commitments I had my writing to do.

Sometimes I got very tired of all the pressure around me, and wished I was back in the time when Angela and I would take the kids round the market, with only a few pounds in our pocket, but so pleased when we got a bargain, and I would be creating my stories and holding that little dream inside me that one day I would be famous.

In the years of fame much happened to Angela and Keith and their children; they did not seem to cope with the change as well as Fred and me, who were old soldiers who just marched on regardless.

I had helped Angela and Apples get a nice house back in London, since she felt left out living in the country and wanted to be part of all the celebrity, but they were leading separate lives. They had never really got on and the children had grown up. Georgie became a rebellious teenager and the quiet young Alan graduated into his secondary school, very aware of his parents' conflict. They were very close to me and I supplied motorbikes and modern clothes, and coped with their demands while their parents fought like cat and dog.

My son Keith had done well and came out of the transport business with enough profit to buy a farm where he reared sheep. His young son Horatio worked beside him, running around with a pet black sheep named Charlie. Such joy I had from that boy. But Keith spent much of his time organising my affairs and trips abroad.

I gave many talks for groups of pensioners, rotary clubs, libraries, and literary clubs, and very much enjoyed my involvement with the Jewish Societies where I often gave talks. They told me I was a natural at entertaining whenever I was before an audience, and somehow I know that then I was at my best. It was something that never scared me and was never difficult; I just responded to their needs and affection as though I was talking to my neighbour down the street. Somehow I held their attention and made them laugh, so I guess it was something natural in me like my writing. The people and the places were an inspiration to me and I loved it.

As my publicity manager, Keith would often be called upon to take me up north to a television station or to a dinner with my publishers. Each year the W.H. Smith's dinner was held in a mansion that was once the home of the dancer Isadora Duncan. Her portrait stood in the great hallway, and I would look up at this graceful lady with admiration and sympathy. She had beauty and money, but how she suffered.

Keith also dealt with all my business affairs, promoting my books abroad, collaborating with my agent and keeping the taxman happy. He lived his life to the full, flying his plane at weekends and playing golf. He was trying to hold everything together, but he was having problems in his marriage. I would often go down to the farm where he lived, but there seemed to be a cold atmosphere there, and on the way home I would say to Fred, trying to make light of it, 'I am not going down to "Cold Comfort Farm" again, not until those two are speaking.'

The long list of happenings since I have been published is almost unbelievable even as I reflect on them now: the way my family separated; the behaviour of Fred to me when sometimes he thought I was not going to need him any more; the spite and jealousy of some relations who thought I'd become a millionairess overnight and expected me to throw my money around . . . There was always a stream of callers, folk who had seen me on the television and aquaintances that I had completely forgotten. They would turn up to visit me, then sit around me all day, talking a lot of drivel.

Then there were the women I knew who decided to write a book, the attitude being, well, if that old fool can do it, so can I. They would come with the manuscript for me to read and advise on, already suggesting that I could then help them to publish. It almost drove me mad, for they had no idea what a rat race it was, and how lucky I had been to get in at the back door. So my friends became offended, thinking how selfish I was in not trying to promote them.

The years I have left I will put to good use, not for the money, which seems to have its bad side, but for my grandchildren, so they can have a good start in life. I want my children to remember me, so in this book I have painted a picture of our lives together. So darlings, if I am not with you when it's published, remember that I loved you dearly. I know I was a little over-fond and possessive, but for that you will forgive me.

One terrible day my son Keith had an accident and was rushed to hospital. He was given only a fifty-fifty chance of surviving an operation to try and save his life. I don't know how I lived through that time, wondering whether he would get over it. I expressed my fears to Angela that perhaps he would not have a long life if he lived, for an operation on the brain is very delicate. Little Horatio kept asking about his dad, and I coped as best I could and got him talking about building a little shed for his egg business on the farm. He was just like his father – a real head for business.

During that anxious time, I lay in bed one morning, looking at the apple tree outside the window. I told it: to think that you were only a little baby tree from Woolworth's when I planted you. Yet you have spread your strong branches as if to protect my little shack every year, giving me a harvest of fresh, rosy apples. In the spring your blossom gives out a perfume that pervades my little room and gives peace and beauty, reminding one of that great God and Master who takes care of us all.

The tree was the same as ever, but the apples it bore were green, so plentiful that they were already falling. I could only think of bitter apples – those tiny ones that will fall – for in some ways this had been my bitter summer.

The weather had been unsettled, sometimes bringing long, hot days that I spent in my garden, hoping to recuperate and leave the unhappiness behind me. For that summer my lovely son was fighting to survive. He was my one source of strength. I could not handle the financial side of my writing, things like the taxman, VAT, agents and bank managers – all the kind of people who were a source of anxiety to me, but Keith had always relieved me of the pressure.

Slowly my son recovered and went on to lead a normal life, but the scars remained and I am still doubtful what the future holds for him.

I had another blow that summer: two weeks after Keith's accident Fred suffered a slight stroke. I was lucky in getting him to the hospital in good time, and physically he seemed fine, but after that he found it difficult to talk and struggled with his words.

We went to stay at Cliffe when I got him out of hospital, trying to resurrect some of our past happy days, but, suddenly it seemed, we had both become old. Since I had become rich I had bought Fred a motor mower he could sit on as the lawn was now much bigger than the green patch in front of the shack I had started with in 1958. For some reason, as soon as he arrived home from the hospital he charged out on his motor mower like some knight on a crusade, as if to exorcise his demons; but he crashed into the plum tree, fell off and hurt his chest. I was terrified that he would have another attack and lay awake all that night worrying.

I began to wonder what I had done wrong since I had become the 'Goose that laid the golden egg'. I knew this gift of mine was very precious, and it was not the writing that was difficult, because I knew I could turn out one of the Cockney novels in just a few months; it was all the family problems I had going on around me that seemed to destroy my creative inspiration. I would dream of being alone and left in peace with only my writing to fulfil my needs. I so much needed again that time 'to stand and stare'. To write had been and always will be the one thing that I enjoyed, and somehow it had been my destiny. But I could not desert my family or their demands when they needed me most, because they were part of me.

Not long after Keith's accident Angela moved in to live with us at Wellington Road. She had split up with Apples after he was violent to her and she had to get two injunctions until he finally left her alone.

At the time all this was going on I was on a promotion tour in Canada, where Fred and I were wined and dined and really made a fuss of. I had many signings and we saw the country. I loved talking to different people, but my anxiety about the family back home never left me for long.

I returned to find Angela a quivering wreck. She and Apples had fought, and she had fled her home in fear, and now everyone's life was turned upside down. I felt so sorry for the children. He kept them from us and in all there were six court appearances in one year.

The only place I could find solace was in my beloved garden, where the flowers still bloomed full and rich and where, as I sat in the sunshine, I could watch the wild birds visit my bird bath. At least nothing had changed here – it was still my own little retreat where I could come to revitalise myself and renew my strength.

Shortly after my return from Canada I had a call from Lynne Barber, a journalist on the *Sunday Express*, who said she wanted to come and interview me. On the day of the interview I opened the door to a sweet, smiling woman, who wore large antique earrings in the shape of little dolls, which stood out against her plain, plump face. She sat and talked to us in the front room and seemed more like an old friend of the family than a journalist. I told her all the information she required about my professional life as an author and gave her a signed copy of my latest book, *Susan*, which had just topped the bestseller charts.

The next week we were quite astounded when we saw the article. It was quite flattering to read all about my great talent, but Ms Barber had also divulged all the personal chit-chat that went on that afternoon over tea – so it seemed tea and sympathy was more the article of the day. Angela had done too much talking about her life, playing up to the journalist like a frustrated actress, and the journalist had obviously found this all very interesting for her story. She described Angela as a beautiful Botticelli angel who chainsmoked, and referred to her persecution by my son-in-law. She reported that I had said he was 'a Philistine' and that the house he lived in was mine. Lynne Barber had written her piece, but given it her own interpretation.

She had told us that she would like to do a mother and daughter piece next, but I am glad I didn't take her up on this, because it was not long before we suffered the repercussions of what she wrote.

Fred got very fed up with all the problems and didn't take too kindly to Angela being back at home. He was used to having me to himself, so instead of sitting round the TV on cold winter weekends he insisted that we went down to the woods just to get out of the house.

* ★ * ★ * ★

When the Lynne Barber article came out in the *Sunday Express Magazine*, Georgie was a victim once more. He arrived one evening, an angry, gangly teenager, his father's mouthpiece and messenger, and stood on the doorstep of Wellington Road. I held out my arms to him. 'Come in, darling,' I said, but his little face just stared at us. He looked wild and unkempt; Angela and I had not been allowed near him by his father and the boy had suffered.

He waved the article in front of our faces, shouting that we had made a fool of his father, and we both knew his father had sent him because we could see him sitting outside in his truck.

Soon after this episode I sent Angela off to spend Christmas in the Middle East with a friend of mine, as Fred had got very tired of all the trouble that was going on and wanted a peaceful Christmas. Lately we had been woken up all hours of the night as Apples kept ringing and putting down the phone. Poor old Fred tried to cope – every time he answered the phone he would say, 'It's what's-his-name.' I did not ask him who he meant as he struggled with his words, but I knew only too well who 'what's-his-name' was, and what he meant.

During that Christmas holiday Fred mostly slept in front of the fire with Sandy the dog dozing at his feet. Because I was feeling so fed up myself, I got pen and paper in hand and started to write *Down our Street*. This was to become my eighth bestseller. It was the story of the lives of the hard-up but happy Flannigan family and I was only wishing that my family were the same, but I lost myself in my characters for compensation, while Fred dozed or occasionally woke up and muttered how very peaceful it was without Angela or the boys (or 'what's-his-name') knocking on the door upsetting us all.

I sat the Flannigans round the table for Christmas

dinner and they pulled crackers and filled the room with talk and laughter. I decided to dedicate this book to all my old friends of Witham Street who grew up with me in the slum streets and who inspired this book in me through the letters they now wrote to me as a famous author.

As I wrote that book, I could see in my mind's eye the shop on the corner where I got my first job. It was not far from Dick Whittington's stone, and I remember standing as a young girl and looking at this stone, thinking how I would like to leave my mark like him, and those words 'turn again, Dick Whittington, thrice mayor of London' would go through my head on my way to work. The shop was run by the rosy-cheeked Mrs Appleby and close by was Coren's Fish and Chip Shop in Hyde Road, where we used to have a ha'p'orth of cracklings and pease pudding and faggots. We never went short of food if we had a penny to spend.

So through the gloom of Wellington Road that Christmas I took my mind back to those old days and remembered the little gang of mischievous boys that roamed our street. I especially recall Dinny, who got the George Medal for bravery in the Second World War but then lost it to Long & Dowty's, the pawnbrokers, because he was hearts of oak. So many of this gang were lost in the war but those who survived were strong, fine men who made good lives for themselves. Then there were the girls whom I played endless games of hopscotch and skipped with. We fought and made up, and stayed out till dark in the street, which was the only place left to play as there was no room in our overcrowded houses.

We were all poor, yet our little community survived, until that big bomb razed it to the ground, leaving us just with sad and fond memories.

I decided the Flannigans would live in a typical small backstreet of London's East End. There would be thirteen children, and sunny-natured Amy with blonde curls would be the youngest and the darling of the family. Little Amy would marry an irrepressible Cockney boy, Sparky, who would sweep her off her feet. He would have a mass of red hair and be big and strong, but life would not be good to him and he would end up in hospital in a wheelchair. In the fictitious life of Sparky I put down my own heartache that I felt when my lovely son Keith had his accident. So I kept myself sane creating these characters, and Christmas came and went without a sign of my grandchildren.

I had been very lucky, for I had fought off the cancer that had been inside me for eighteen years, and it had apparently gone into remission.

I was under a terrible strain, for although the courts had granted us access to see young Alan, he was still kept from us and Apples' persecution continued. I did not want to tell Angela about my poor health at this stressful time, but eventually could hide it no longer and told her about the lump that had returned in my breast. It was on the other side from the previous lump all those years ago. Angela's face paled as I told her and she started to cry, but I told her not to worry as I had survived it before and God willing I would have another fifteen years to go. 'Anyway, darling,' I added, 'I have had my three score years and ten, so whatever it is, it will have to be faced.'

'Don't say that, Mum,' she said, getting upset. 'You can't leave me now, I need you so much.'

I went to Whipps Cross hospital to see a specialist, a Dr Thomas, who said straight away, 'That's got to come out.' He insisted on prodding about around the old scar from the operation many years ago. I kept telling him that side was fine now, but he insisted on sticking a needle into the scar so that he could do tests. Afterwards I wondered if he awakened something when he did this, because I began to get a pain in that spot and it does not seem to go away.

That evening I calmed Angela down as she cried and told her, 'I will never leave you, dear. I will always be with you, whatever happens.' Her frightened eyes looked deeply into mine, for she knew how much I loved her. 'Anyway, darling,' I said, trying to cheer us both up, 'I think they will have to bloody well shoot me first.'

Her smile returned and she said, 'You're still the kingpin of the family, darling, and we both have a lot of work to do.'

We poured ourselves a glass of whisky and got back to the books that we were researching.

It was decided that Fred would be told, and I would go to the hospital for an operation within a few weeks. I was not surprised at this serpent that reared its head. I had not felt myself for a while – I had fretted so much over my grandchildren and somehow seemed unable to fight off that heartbreak as well as I used to, and since Keith's accident I worried about him, too.

Something very odd happened one evening as I sat in my little office with Angela. I was reading a book on the sinking of the *Titanic* for my novel, *Eve's Apples*, and Angela and I were discussing this when the phone rang. On the other end of the line was my friend Doris Stokes, the medium. She had not been very well since undergoing an operation and I told her about the lump in my breast. She then gave me a long lecture on how I should look after myself. I didn't mind that, but when she went on to tell me in an uncertain tone that she was very concerned about my health, it put the wind up me straight away. I listened to her words but could not wait to get off the line. Much as I liked to talk to Doris, this made me very nervous, and I joked to Angela, trying to make light of it, 'I think Doris is going to find me up in heaven before I get there.' For a moment Angela and I looked seriously at each other, for there was no mistaking our underlying fear, but we gave way to laughter almost as though it was a release. As our laughter faded I could only add, 'Well, let's hope she's wrong this time.'

Through all the pain, however, we tried to keep our sense of humour. One day the *Sunday Express* phoned to say Apples had been to see them several times, being very angry about the article, and the poor editor spoke to me in a very nervous state. I said to Angela, 'I thought it had been quiet; I suppose he's driving them up the wall now.' In the end the editor, wanting a quiet life, did a retraction in the next edition of the magazine, saying that there had been some kind of misinterpretation and Apples was 'not a Philistine'.

I said to Angela, tongue in cheek, 'I only ever called him "Philistine" but I would like to have called him a lot worse for what he's done to my family.'

Angela asked, 'What is a Philistine exactly?'

I explained how the Philistines destroyed all the beautiful temples that the Israelites had created, 'and did he not try to destroy you, darling? And now he's destroying my grandchildren.'

'Well, Mum,' said Angela, her courage now returning, 'he has not destroyed me yet and while there's breath in my body I will fight for those boys and win them back.'

I had certainly had my fill of 'little green apples'. My mouth was so full of them that even the beauty and peace of my lovely garden could not take away the taste, after all those terrible scenes and troubles. Yet Fred and I tried to make the best of things, and we spent a lot of time tending our garden, particularly my beautiful roses, each of which held a memory of the past.

Pat and Keith had given me a lovely collection of fuchsia which I arranged in pots outside the shack. They looked really beautiful and when I sat behind them they seemed to smile at me. It gives me great comfort when I think of the time my lovely son gave them so proudly; he is still unwell and I pray at night that all will be well with him.

One day, working in the comfort of my garden, a poem came to me:

The Garden of Life

Oh beautiful spirit, come unto me,
The one in my garden forever watching me.
Are you a fairy, gnome or sprite,
Or a deep dark phantom that comes out at night?

Always while I labour, amid this green scene,
I get this strange feeling of something unseen;
Are you a goddess of nature who protects all wild
  things
Or a nymph from the woodland to herald the spring?

Primroses glow golden, violets pale blue;
It's a lovely portrait – is it painted by you?
The huge bumble bee sucking the nectar –
Is he one of your children, or just a reflector?

O Mother Nature so calm and serene,
Such peace and tranquillity you spread on the scene,
Always watching and waiting in the garden of life,
Away from care, trouble and strife.
So quiet, peaceful spirit forever watching me,
Guard my garden, my family, every plant, flower
  and tree.

Chapter Six

Woodland Retreat

After my operation I went to my woodlands, hoping to recuperate, and I prayed I would see another spring, but I wondered whether I would beat the illness a second time. The specialist had told me that 'they had caught it in time' and that I should undergo radiotherapy treatment and all should be fine. So I was hopeful, but I still continued to get a nagging pain in my back that worried me. Nevertheless, I still sat at the same worn table – a wedding present from Fred's brother, which has witnessed so much over the past forty years – doing my scribbling and intermittently watching the birds through the window.

It was at my wits' end with Angela's problems. Her divorce had gone through and I thought it was the end of everything. Georgie came to see me and said he was sorry, but he still went home to his father. I went on clinging to both my grandsons, writing letters and sending pocket money in the hope they would call to see me.

Another source of sadness at this time was the break-up of Pat and Keith. They had not been getting on well for some time, and finally decided to split up. Again, it was my grandchild I felt sorry for – the heartache would never leave me.

★　　★　　★

I was beginning to think I would never have that bungalow of my dreams, when fate took a hand and something wonderful happened to me. It all happened when we popped down to Kent when the weather was not too bad just to see the little shack and get away from the trials and tribulations of family life and London.

I still did not have the house of my dreams and the years were passing, but I had always been one to accept situations and make the best of things, and I told myself it was not the end of the world. I was thinking about this when there was a knock on the door of the shack, and who should be there but Roy, my neighbour who owned the very nice bungalow just next door to my plot, looking sad and cold.

Fred welcomed Roy in and gave him a drink, and he told us that he had been ill all that past year. The doctors had diagnosed that he was suffering from a rare allergy, which was probably caused by gardening. Roy and his wife had made up their minds that the solution to this dilemma was to move to where he would not have a garden to worry about, somewhere near the sea.

My heart missed a beat when he went on, 'I know you like the woods, Lena, and I wondered if you would like to buy my bungalow and save yourselves the bother of building your own place.'

Immediately I was on cloud nine and forgot about my worries. 'Roy,' I said before Fred got a chance to put in a word, 'you can have a cash deal – just name your price.'

So on that Sunday morning Roy and I shook hands and the bargain was clinched.

Early the following spring the purchase of the bungalow went through, and excitedly I prepared to spend my first night in my new house. It was lovely to have central heating and double glazing and all the luxuries I never had before. It was a beautiful spring day: the sun shone all day and melted the frost in the garden, so it was moist and green once more and the blackbirds were singing merrily.

It felt strange that at last I had the bungalow of my dreams. However, even though I had always coveted this bungalow, I did not feel possessive about it in the same way as I have always done about my old shack, with all its cobwebs, dog hairs and the occasional field mouse in the cupboard.

Fred and I walked over to the little old shack. It was quite warm with a big log fire that Fred had made as I did not want to neglect our faithful little shack. I am so fond of it and have made it look nice and welcoming.

I have achieved both of my dreams: to become a famous author and to own a cosy bungalow in my beloved woodlands, which is more than most people can boast. Now all I hope for is that my health does not fail me and I will have time to put the woodlands into a book for future generations to read, so that they can share in the adventures I have experienced.

As I wait for the warm summer days and dream of lying under the oak tree to do my scribbling, I know my health has deteriorated this past year but all I hope for is a few more bright summers sharing in the glory of the roses blooming, the sun setting over the river and the storm clouds riding on the horizon, and inhaling the heavenly scent that fills the garden – sights and smells that have been part of my life for well over thirty years and kept me going when I was ill – and I will be content.

I asked Fred if we could leave London and spend all our time in the woodlands, but he was upset at the idea of leaving the house in London, mainly because he had worked hard all his life to buy it for us. 'Look, Fred darling,' I cajoled him, 'you don't have to give up Wellington Road – we can afford to keep them both.' So in the end we reached a compromise.

Even though we now had a posh bungalow to live in, I still liked to visit my little old shack – no place on earth would ever replace it – and I would go over there in the afternoons to write, closing the door and shutting out the world and its troubles, and recording the story of the woodlands that I love so much, and all my old friends there.

Once upon a time I had dreamed that I would sit back and enjoy my woodland home after my years of hard work, but as we all know too well, life plays some strange tricks on us. I had planned to invite journalists and agents and all the professional people I had made friends with on my travels down for tea at my smart bungalow with a through lounge and smart bathroom, unlike my little shack with its makeshift loo. But now I found I was feeling too tired; I just didn't want to be bothered with anyone.

Friends and family still continued to call and fuss over me, however. Keith had now come to live with us and was having problems seeing Horatio. It made me think what a mad world it was becoming when a child was deprived of his father. Poor Keith was still unwell but trying to cope. He provided me with bowls of jellied eels, knowing they were my favourite food. They were the only thing I fancied, as I was finding it hard to swallow. Angela arrived with specially baked flans to tempt my appetite and always looked very harassed as she was worrying over me. She insisted on staying with me and it was a job to get her back to Wellington Road.

Often we walked around the garden together. One day our walk took us past the fresh graves of my two pet dogs, Sandy and Pudsy, who had been my companions for fifteen years. Sandy had caught a disease, then Pudsy got it too. I sat up night after night caring for them, trying to get them well, but they kept having fits and eventually I could not stand to see them suffering any more.

'It's strange how they died together after all this time,' I remarked, 'but perhaps they would have only pined away without me. Maybe it's all for the best.'

Angela looked upset, but we continued our stroll. The weary look that came from those pale blue eyes could have belonged to a woman of fifty. I knew she had been under a terrible strain from trying to get her children back and from Apples' persecution of her. He even waited outside her place of work at lunchtimes and she would run in terror to get away from him.

As I listened to the story of her latest flight from Apples I started to laugh. Whatever life threw at us we would always insist 'we might be down, but we're never out' and somehow we would always find something to laugh at. We had the same kind of perverse sense of humour, in that we could laugh in the face of despair.

I had been chuckling to myself that morning at an article in a newspaper. Now I showed it to Angela and we shared the joke. 'Look, darling,' I said, 'I always knew I'd make the *News of the World*.' In fact, it was a terrible write-up, quoting pieces of my writing and saying that I spoke of lovers who said, 'Let's do it one more time for luck.' The article was entitled 'Cockney Cheek', and we both laughed and agreed it certainly was a right cheek.

I suppose many of you find it amazing that a woman of my age and ordinary background could produce a novel that reached the top ten on the bestseller lists. It does not amaze me, for I can assure you I worked hard at it.

I would never recommend anyone to jump straight into writing a long novel. When that creative bug strikes you, you might think what an excellent novel it would make if you told the story of your own life, but I suggest you start off with small episodes, the things that you remember most clearly, as it is a well-known human failing that there are huge gaps in our memory of past happenings. Close your eyes and try to recall the house you lived in as a child – the way the furniture was placed and the pictures on the wall – then suddenly the characters will appear. Sit in an armchair by the fire, or dig in the garden, or look at it through the window, and you will be home again in the history of your childhood – *then* write it down. It is better to enjoy your characters like this, as then they will come clearly.

A certain critic once telephoned me about *Autumn Alley*. 'This is not a literary novel,' he said. I was inclined to agree with him. Perhaps I am not a literary woman. I write while doing my housework and caring for my family; I never learned to write on any warm university seat, but you will find my novels very stimulating. It has been said of me that I write only of squalor and poverty, but this is not entirely true. I admit I take my material and my characters from the world I have lived in, and from the period when there was no welfare state, only bleak charity to look forward to, but so many of those families worked hard and achieved respectable lives against all odds. Some, like me, even achieved a rags-to-riches story. I have always had a lot of pleasure from my 'compulsive scribbling', and as long as you enjoy what you do and don't give in, there is no reason why you should not discover the same pleasure.

Chapter Seven

The Final Tribute

The family were behaving strangely – relatives avoided me as if I had the plague, and Angela and Fred were always whispering together. I got a bit worried and thought they had heard bad news about my illness and I must be about to pass over, but I was asking no questions and therefore hearing no lies.

Then one day my publishers sent me on an assignment to Kingston, which I thought rather strange, and I was even more suspicious when I saw such a large crowd waiting for me. Then Eamonn appeared with his big red book and you could have knocked me down with a feather. Yes, I was to appear on *This is Your Life*. I couldn't help saying, 'You're better-looking than you are on TV, Eamonn.' He was taken aback for a moment, then his face beamed in that wide, cheerful smile.

'Why me? I asked. 'I'm not a celebrity.'

'We think you are,' said Eamonn, with such a charming smile that no one could refuse him anything.

Feeling a bit like the Queen Mother, I sat with Eamonn in a big posh car, and we drove to the studio. On arrival I found my best dress hung up in the dressing room, and knew the family had conspired together. From then on it was all go.

The show was wonderful but I was a little apprehensive because of the trouble in my family. When my son arrived, his red beard well trimmed, and looking happy with Pat by his side, I was so pleased. I asked him where the baby was and he told me, 'He's minding the sheep,' but I knew Horatio would not be far away. Sure enough, at the end of the show he was announced and came in carrying his pet lamb Charlie – from then on he stole the show. Auntie Mary, who was eighty-four years old, managed to come along and I am sure she was happy when after the show she was given a little dish of jellied eels.

All the girls I had worked with in the past and lots of friends and neighbours from my old address were there – it was all a great laugh.

Fred was the first to come in and he kissed me – he doesn't do that too often in public – he had known all about the special evening and had kept it all dark. 'Wait till I get you home,' I told him.

After the show there was a grand party and I was able to meet some of the celebrities who had come along. It was good to have a chat with the writer Leslie Thomas, who gave me a hug. We had previously met to judge a short story competition for Pebble Mill TV and he admitted that I had given Bob Langley and himself a really hard time when it came to picking the winner. I introduced him to Angela, who looked lovely in a crocheted green dress that set off her golden hair. I was so very proud of my family.

All the neighbours and friends from Hoxton were there – all those kids who had played in those slum streets with me long ago. Some of them I had not seen for many years and they all hugged me and said they were so proud to have known me. We all danced and talked of old times and I realised how very lucky I was to have achieved this wonderful tribute, and I was very grateful to all those who had worked so hard to give me such pleasure.

After the show Angela and I got together and sat out on the lawn under the branches of the oak and spent a lovely afternoon talking over the events of that evening. I couldn't believe my ears when she told me her tale of woe about how Apples had refused to let the children go on the show, and thought it just as well that I hadn't known about this dilemma at the time. Apparently the researcher had almost camped outside Apples' house as he refused to answer the door and had warned him off, saying that he and the boys wanted nothing to do with their mother or grandmother. By the end the researcher was afraid he'd get a black eye.

'I didn't tell you at the time,' confessed Angela, 'as I was told the show had to be kept secret, and that if you found out it would all be cancelled.'

Eventually Apples had agreed to negotiate with the TV people – provided they supplied him with a guest list. Once this was in his possession he cut out all the people he thought should not go on the show; otherwise he would not let the grandchildren appear. The poor researcher for the show was the go–between for the irate Angela and Apples, and I couldn't help feeling sorry for him as I listened to her tale. Evidently he had informed Angela that she should agree to Apples' demands, otherwise Lena would be very upset if the children were not there. Many names were therefore crossed off the list, all friends and relations who had helped us when he drove Angela from her home, and he hated them. The researcher admitted to Angela he had never been involved in a show like this before.

The funny part of it was that when the night of the show came Apples demanded a place in reception where he could view the guests as they came in. Evidently he was adamant that if they tried to bring in any of the people that he had deleted from the list then he would take the boys away and they would not go on the show.

It seemed he had even insisted on a limousine to pick him and the boys up – he made so many demands and got away with it. I could just imagine him sitting there with his fag and a very superior expression on his face.

By the end of our conversation Angela looked almost sorry that she had told me, but we had always been so close and found it difficult to hide things from each other. However, we were both happy that Georgie had been found. He had gone missing and we had wandered the streets searching for him, but it seemed his father had been hiding him out somewhere. We were glad that the show had brought him out into the open and safely back to his family.

'You'll win the children back in the end,' I told her. 'You've been a good mother.'

I couldn't get over the fact that Apples had actually succeeded in holding Thames Television to ransom. It all seemed hard to believe, and more like something out of a movie than anything that could happen to us. I felt quite sorry for the researcher, who'd had a terrible ordeal, and Angela exclaimed in a mischievous tone, 'I wonder if his nerves will ever be the same again, Mum.'

We both burst into laughter. 'After all,' she said, 'it was a Kennedy show. I don't suppose they'll forget that one in a hurry.'

Chapter Eight

The Way to the Woods

I was 'away to the woods' once more. We had just passed the Black Prince Public House. It looked smaller and kind of desolate now, as the big road swung around it. It used to be very gay there in the summer evenings years ago, with lines of coaches, girls and men in funny hats dancing 'Knees-up, Mother Brown', as this had been a kind of half-way house for the factory outings. I used to like to stay for a beer and a bag of crisps on our way to Cliffe, and the children loved to play in the garden, but now there was no stopping or drinking – not since the new law on drinking and driving. Fred was very strict on the matter of breaking the law; still it was a good thing I must admit. I had seen some nasty accidents on this road after the Black Prince dispersed its customers.

Over Dartford Heath the sun had come out, pale and cold-looking, but the clouds soon dispersed. I liked this part of the journey where Rochester lay ahead in a valley of rolling, undulating farmland, with earthy brown ploughed fields and rows and rows of winter cabbages. We passed the Tollgate – it was getting bigger and more prosperous each time I saw it. I remember it as a cosy inn, with a log fire and oak beams. To my mind it is the gateway to Watling Street, that great road the Romans built on their way to conquer London. We were leaving the motorway now, skirting Gravesend, where there's that nice little thatched farmhouse in a hollow; I am glad no one's tried to modernise it. We went through the village of Chalk that was a village no longer, with new bungalows, schools and shops. This was where Charles Dickens spent his honeymoon and where he came to find peace and beauty.

We passed a solitary gypsy caravan, with washing strewn on the bushes and a dark young lad leading a pony to grass. There used to be a long line of gypsy encampments along the road back past the Tollgate near the old Roman diggings. I liked to watch the varied pattern of colour they gave – some new caravans, some very old, with brass shining in the windows, outside dark children around the camp fire, and untidy women, all busy getting water and burning rubbish. I used to like the look of it all, and wonder if I had the courage to go among them and talk and listen to their strange gypsy patter, but then I would think better not – they liked to be left alone.

Dolly Cottage was ahead; it wouldn't be long till I could spot the green wood. I could see the Thames in the distance, winding to the sea, that wide open mouth of the great river, drawing in the big ships of trade for hundreds of years – barges, four-masted schooners, and now long, slick, grey tankers that left a slime of oil to pollute the shore and kill the wildlife; such is the progress of civilisation. I often wonder what lies ahead for the rivers and the wildlife. I noticed that Mortimer farm cut down the old orchard, which distressed me as my children used to love playing in that orchard, scrumping the apples and pears.

At last we reached Cliffe Woods. There was a huge notice advertising new bungalows for sale in a spot where two old shacks used to be – replaced by eleven bungalows. Oh dear, what would they do to my lovely woodland next?

We drove down the long concrete stretch that used to be a shady lane, but then the sight of my little wooden honeysuckle-covered shack took away my fears.

I was still there, the last of the shack dwellers, the great oak smiles a welcome. I kissed the old rough bark, Hello, darling, I'm back.

The weather was now warm, even after the sudden show of summer rain that brought with it a beautiful rainbow which stretched from the silver strip of river in the valley, across the meadows, giving them a silver sheen. From the damp earth rose a sweet smell, and my roses hung with raindrops. It renewed my strength to see those rich blooms more glorious than ever. As I looked up at the rainbow, I thought of the proverbial pot of gold at the end of it. Well, I certainly got mine, I thought with some irony.

I walked up the path, I thought of my dogs. I missed them. I could smell the honeysuckle as it rose up from the earth like wine. There were lots of little blue forget-me-nots on my lawn; each year they came up and Fred mowed them down to keep the lawn tidy. He became very aggravated when they soon came shooting up again, but I would only smile when I saw them return.

Angela came down to visit, and we sat on a little bench that Fred had made of bricks with an old tree placed across. The birds flew about us and in quiet moments hopped at our feet. I told her how I had received lovely flowers from some of the famous guests on the *This is Your Life* show. I was particularly pleased that Eamonn Andrews had sent me a beautiful bouquet, but I could not help admitting to Angela, 'I really think I must be on my way out if Eamonn sends me flowers.' My humour did not go down too well, and I wished I had never made this remark, for Angela got very upset. I noticed how thin and drawn her face was, and I knew I had to have enough courage for both of us.

'Don't cry for me, darling,' I told her firmly, 'for whatever happens, I have had a good life.'

Angela dried her eyes, for she knew when I meant it. I had achieved my two dreams, as I told her, and felt I had been fortunate.

For a while we were silent as we walked around the garden on that warm summer's day. Now and again we talked of the past as though we were going back down the road of life. We went on to discuss *Eve's Apples* and my mind was once more far away from the trials of life. As always, we talked of the characters as though they were people we knew and Angela could not help nagging me to finish the book. 'It's your best work, Mum,' she said, but that was Angela, always urging me on in my work, almost as if she were trying to keep me alive. I knew she was right, for this was a great story and spanned three continents and three generations.

We sat for a while and I recited some of my latest work to her. She looked amazed and asked how I could remember all the details about the characters whose lives spanned many years and keep them all in my mind, but I had been writing seriously for fifteen years now, and the more I wrote the easier it became. I told Angela I thought she should try and write about her own life – I knew there was definitely a story there – but she just shook her head and said, 'I can't, Mum, it hurts too much.'

But I had learned to love that hurt that comes when you write your true feelings down, in fact I thrived on it. I told her, 'I could do it, darling. I have taken out my heart and stamped on it and one day you will be able to as well.'

We sat under the oak, which spreads out its branches in majesty, with a book of Shakespeare's sonnets. 'You are the April of your mother's prime,' I told her as I read the words aloud.

I felt tired and we went to the little shack to relax for the afternoon. It's cosy and it's mine and it spells home. Each spring the big oak has smiled a warm welcome and the little golden primroses bid me good day. In all weathers – sunshine and showers, and even the storms I am so scared of – I always felt safer in my little shack, which wrapped around me like a warm blanket. It's my cherished possession where I have spent my happiest days, Fred and I digging in the wet moist clay of Kent, making a beautiful garden. And I shall hand it on to my descendants; no one shall cut down my tree or dig up my flowers.

Whenever I take a nostalgic look around my little shack, the memories come floating back to me: the beautiful bouquets of flowers arranged in vases, each one a vivid memory of the person who presented it to me on my last assignment; above my flowers a lovely hand-drawn print of Rochester Castle given to me by a young artist and admirer, and the brass plaque Keith brought home from Devon so long ago when camping with the cubs. The pots and trophies that have been bought at jumble sales and won at fairs, all presented to 'Our mum with love', are scattered about, and among them is a lovely Japanese sugar bowl decorated with swans, which belonged to Nanny Murphy. Next to that is my Wimbledon trophy which Fred presented to me after he found it on the rubbish dump. I only discovered what it was a couple of years ago when I saw a photo in the paper of a similar trophy. I always intended to do some research to try to find out who it belonged to.

On the wall is a little print of Ireland my sister Molly once brought back from holiday. Also there are all the plates that Fred bought me in the good old days and the old sketches he got for me over twenty years ago. There used to be a pair of pictures of forest deer, but I gave one to Henna and Mrs Polish to copy and it was never returned.

I am so proud of my collection of knick-knacks which holds so many fond memories and helps to fill up and brighten my dear little shack.

Outside in the garden the swing still remained on the big oak tree and I could still see my children playing there. The leaves of the oak spread out over us like a beautiful canopy and Angela joined me. I wrapped my arms around that old silver-grey wrinkled bark. Deep vibrations came from the earth and a kind of warmth, as if some large, gentle beast lay sleeping. We both felt those vibrations of nature as if the old oak spoke to us to nourish our very beings. Angela pulled away as if afraid, but I kissed my oak tree and said, 'Goodbye, dear, I won't be long. I'll see you next weekend.' I have done this stupid thing for thirty years and will to the end. We were silent for a while, content and at one with nature. 'Do you wish that we had not done it, that we had not had the success?' I asked after a while. She looked at me thoughtfully and our eyes met in a kind of recognition, as though we were summing up the whole of our lives. Her eyes filled with tears, but she only shrugged and turned away and I wondered if the question was too painful and something that neither of us wanted to delve into too deeply, for we had both lost a lot.

We went to look at the new blooms on the roses, bending to smell the soft petals, remembering each tree in turn and the loved ones I had planted them for. I told her how tired I was but she only recited those words from Kipling that I had often quoted:

'If you can force your heart and nerve and sinew
To serve your turn long after they are gone
And so hold on when there is nothing in you
Except the Will which says to them: "Hold on!"'

I knew she had learned a lot from me – she was so much her mother's daughter.

I told her that the little man inside me had stopped singing. It was a strange presence that had always been in me ever since I was a child and seemed to sing a song. I had never told anybody else – only Angela – for the rest of the world would think me mad. 'He will come back when you're better,' she reassured me, but I wondered and told her that I wanted her to follow me in life. She looked concerned. 'What do you mean, Mum? Do you mean I should write? Because I find that very difficult.' Then I reminded her of a lovely film we once saw together called *I Remember Mama*, about a little Norwegian girl who wrote lots of stories and had one rejection after another. She came from a very poor family and one day her mother said to her, 'Why don't you write about my life, darling?' The girl followed her mother's suggestion and had a great success. Angela smiled dreamily as she listened to my recollection of this story and told me that she remembered it too.

'Well, darling, you must always write about what you know.'

'I will try, Mum,' she said, 'but you're a hard act to follow.'

'But anybody can do anything if they try,' I replied.

We sat in silence and watched the birds come down to drink at the bird-bath that was part of that long lost community of the woods. Here am I, the last of the shackdwellers, and those characters and times pass through me like rays of the sun. I smiled to myself as I looked at the tall pine trees that had been grown from the single pine cone that Fred had brought back from the army camp in Bobbington to the woods and nurtured until it took root. I see also how the Christmas trees that I had brought down from London have grown, tall pines reaching skywards, standing like landmarks of a lifetime.

We sat there till late in the evening, talking about the things we should have done, and Angela mostly talking of the things I still had to do.

The evening sunlight filtered through the trees and I thought I could see the little face of Kitty Daliley smiling at me, that little spirit that had been with me ever since I was a child. Perhaps she was my creative spirit, I am not sure, but she was always within me in quiet, dreamy moments. Her face was clear and her eyes were looking into mine and I was so glad to see her again.

Over the hills, the sun was going down, the whole sky stretched red and yellow in the distance. I watched the golden ball go slowly down, flickering and throwing out a bright light across the sky in its last life force. I thought I would not be afraid to go like the sun behind the clouds, to sleep the night, or eternity, away – whichever is its space in time. As the sunset faded it was taking with it the light from my trees and the warmth from my garden.

We locked up the little shack and I suddenly felt afraid and told Angela to tell the family, relations and friends after my burial that in no way should it be sold or disturbed.

I would leave it to posterity and I hope to be remembered there. I would like a blue plaque put on the door:

> Remembering evermore
> that Lena Kennedy lived
> and worked here

I hated to leave my little shack but the birds had now flown to their nests and darkness had descended on my woodlands. Angela took my arm and helped me back to the new bungalow and my thoughts began to stray to a story of a secret woodland, but then I heard her voice asking me, 'What is your favourite flower of all the flowers in your garden?'

I told her, 'It's the red rosebud, darling, and the morning dew upon it is the tears a mother cries.'

Afterword

1st August 1986

Lena Kennedy died.
The star 'Super Nova'
faded from
the heavens after a million
years.

September 1987

The London Borough of
Waltham Forest named a street
after Lena, Lena Kennedy
Close, in Chingford, E4.
In the street they placed a
plaque and planted a white
cherry tree. The plaque reads
as follows:

*This road is named in memory of the Authoress Lena
Kennedy who lived in the Borough for 50 years until
her death in 1986. She is regarded as one of the finest
contemporary storytellers of her time and her bestselling
novels about East London life describe much of her own
life story.*

Her son Keith made the
opening of the street a great
day for the residents. He put

up a marquee on the site and a street party was held in his mother's memory.

18th August 1989   Lena's great grandson Daniel George was born to George and Tracy.

20th December 1989   Lena's beloved son Keith died suddenly at the age of 41.

16th May 1991   Lena's great granddaughter Jade Lena (Jaylena) was born to George and Tracy.

Don't miss the classic, heart-warming novels of Lena Kennedy:

MAGGIE
From the East End of the twenties, through the London Blitz to the
Australian outback, *Maggie* tells the story of one of Lena Kennedy's most
memorable heroines.

NELLY KELLY
In the turmoil of London's East End between the wars, young Nelly Kelly
soon learns that life may never match her expectations. Fortune may crush
her proud spirit but when faced with a crisis which will test her courage
to the limit, no tragedy can change Nelly Kelly's determination to be her
own woman.

AUTUMN ALLEY
Set at the turn of the century, *Autumn Alley* is the tale of a formidable
Irish-American suffragette, an unhappy wife, a wayward husband and
quick-thinking Arfer who escapes the poverty of London's East End.

LADY PENELOPE
Caught up in the dangerous intrigues of Queen Elizabeth's court and forced
to marry a wealthy but repulsive nobleman, the beautiful, flame-haired Lady
Penelope pours all her passion into her children . . . and her lovers. But through
her heart often rules her head, Penelope survives her loveless marriage and a life
filled with tragedy to emerge triumphant.

LIZZIE
Warm-hearted and totally devoted to her charming rogue of a husband, Lizzie
mothers her brood of nephews and nieces through the perils of the war-torn
capital, making a home for them in the bomb shelters of underground London.
Lizzie is a survivor with the unquenchable optimism and indomitable courage
that sums up the spirit of the East End.

SUSAN
Lena Kennedy tells the story of a sensual woman who rises above her tragic
background as a London slum child and young prostitute, to forge a successful
life for herself.

LILY, MY LOVELY
The story of cockney red-headed Lily and the romantic Dutch seaman
who sweeps in and out of her life throughout the post-war years and the
swinging sixties, filling her life with passion, but leaving Lily sadder and
very much wiser.

DOWN OUR STREET
Sunny-natured Amy is the youngest and dearest of Annie Flanagan's lively
brood of thirteen, and the one who pulls the family together during the
momentous years of the Second World War. But it is Amy who suffers
times of bitter heart-rending when family ties war against the needs of her
feckless husband.

THE DANDELION SEED
An innocent in the decadent, dangerous London of James I, Marcelle de la Strange finds herself with child. Kidnapped by the powerful Howard family, the baby is an innocent pawn in a deadly political game and Marcelle's desperate search for her son threatens her health and her reconciliation with the man she loves . . .

THE INN ON THE MARSH
The Malted Shovel Inn is the home of Beatrice, Dot, their invalid father and their pretty orphaned niece, Lucinda. It is also the focal point of a village community stained with murder, violence and rape. Time alone can ease the sorrows of the village of Hollinbury, when bright dreams banish the old unhappy ghosts.

EVE'S APPLES
Childhood sweethearts, Daisy and Jackie are destined never to marry but their love takes them to the other side of the world and back. Their various children, like Eve's apples, will spread out across the world to create new lives thousands of miles away from their East End roots.

OWEN OLIVER
In the heart of teeming nineteenth-century London, Owen Oliver walks out of his gloomy, unwelcoming lodgings – and he doesn't stop his travels until he reaches Kent. This is the turbulent tale of a young man's growth from innocence to maturity in the harsh world of Victorian England.

KATE OF CLYVE SHORE
When young and poor Kate is chosen to become a maidservant to the beautiful Lady Evelyn, she thinks it is a dream come true. But Kate finds that a life of abundance and riches brings with it blackhearted men, evil in thought and deed.

IVY OF THE ANGEL
A wealth of lively East End characters and true-to-life situations are brought together in this vivid and compelling collection of stories exploring the enduring power of love and the triumph of hope over adversity.

QUEENIE'S CASTLE
When teacher Joe Walowski finds himself lost in the East End in heavy fog his bad fortune soon turns to disaster. An incident ends in murder and Joe is falsely accused and imprisoned. On his release he heads back to the East End to discover the truth about that fateful night but soon becomes entangled in London's underworld and falls under the spell of the enigmatic Queenie, landlady of The Castle pub.